Carbon Neutral

Written by Richard Cutler
Edited by Michael Mattes

D1089216

Briley & Baxter Publications | Plymouth, Massachusetts

ISBN: 978-1-954819-00-9

Book Design: Stacy O'Halloran
Cover Design: Mackenzie Wells
Cover Art: Maddy Moore

This book is dedicated to the scientists and engineers who strive to save our world from ourselves.

Contents

Introduction

Serendipity: the faculty of happening upon fortunate discoveries when not in search of them.

In *Course Correction*, the first in this series of books, Humanity has reached Epsilon Eridani's second planet from the sun, known as EEb, and established a colony called New Hope Island around a wormhole Gate. This was not a simple task. Politicians had pushed this notion because there were more people on Earth than the planet's resources could support. As a distraction, these same people proposed that a Star Ship fleet should build the wormhole Gate through which masses of people could pass to relieve the stresses placed on Earth. Unbeknownst to the astronauts during the voyage, Mother Nature had stepped in with the Death Flu and reduced the Earth-bound human population by 90%.

Survivors had to adapt to a world where high-tech systems couldn't be supported, and governing bodies were mostly military. Clever people were still around, but the greatest intellect was isolated in the Star Ships. The travelers were now almost forgotten, leaving them isolated in ignorance.

From the early beginnings of civilization, a benevolent order not of Earth had provided guidance to individuals and small groups in the hopes of correcting a dangerous course for mankind. It was at this point in time that the members of this order reappeared. They had to find those who would support the Star Ships' mission while at the same time reverse the general apathy of people left on Earth— an apathy that led to the world's continued population decrease as people died of old age and fewer births filled the void.

This benevolent order went to work with loose guidance from a trio of individuals on their home world, collectively referred to as The Boss. As if by plan, members of the Order found that most of the people needed to get things back on course were from one extended family. Some were already on board the Star Ships while others had remained on Earth.

Eventually, the enthusiastic seeds of humanity that had been in the interstellar space fleet were now returning to Earth through the wormhole Gate. They instilled a new sense of wonder that was contagious. In spite of the serious problems that were still on Earth, a new space mission was born. This time it was because the world wanted it, and maybe—just maybe—a solution to the remaining problems on Earth could be discovered. This new enterprise was a mission of discovery, not one of desperation.

There are always people who want to explore where others have never been. And there are always those willing to fund these adventures. While there is usually a goal in mind with these explorations, often the serendipitous discoveries make the biggest contributions. Certainly, Christopher Columbus didn't plan on finding another continent. Could Earth's released excess carbon and continued global warming issues be resolved from an unexpected discovery?

Disclaimer

I have used names of real places in this story. There was no particular reason for this except to make the reader run to the atlas to see where these places might be. Any description by the author of these places is pure whimsy.

The people named and described in this story are pure fantasy. Any similarity to any person living, deceased, or yet to be born is purely coincidental. They are just names!

Acknowledgements

Science fiction is made up of two parts: science and fiction. My wife Gini wonders how my mind works sometimes, but she leaves me alone so my mind can wander off into the realm of non-reality. That's the fiction part. Thank you, Gini.

I believe the science part has to have some truth to it. For decades, I worked at the Marine Biological Laboratory (MBL) in Woods Hole, Massachusetts. I am not a scientist, nor do I play one on TV, but during that period of my life some science knowledge was absorbed through osmosis, though not enough to make me "wicked smart." So while I have knowingly ignored many scientific facts based on what we know to be true on Earth, I couldn't have created a new ecosystem on a faraway planet without a major influence from the MBL's Ecosystems Center, especially the Center's Director Dr. Anne Giblin. Anne is a science fiction fan, so I hope she forgives me for what I have done with oxygen and carbon while she actually works to understand and solve Earth's environmental issues. Any real science that is screwed up is by me, the author.

It would be insincere on my part not to acknowledge influences such as Jules Vern and H.G. Wells. Many things they wrote about were thought to be impossible but ultimately became possible.

There are wonderful books written by people much smarter than me about how our planet Earth and our atmosphere came to be. One of these books is simply named "Oxygen" by Donald E. Canfield. It's an interesting read even if you're not a scientist!

It should be obvious that Star Gate had an influence on me. However, in Star Gate vague "ancients" had built the Star Gates, short-circuiting the need to roam the stars to get them in place, where as my characters build the wormhole Gates. Perhaps well into the future they will be the ancients. There are no shortcuts.

I did not intend to write a second science fiction book after writing *Course Correction*. My goal with that book was to have at least one person read it and make them think. My goal with that book was exceeded, and many that read it kept bugging me to write a sequel. To those people, and you know who you are, thank you. I hope you enjoy this one as well.

Places & Names

Epsilon Eridani (EE): 10.5 Light Years from Earth
EEb: Second planet from the star

Tau Ceti (TC): 11.8 Light Years from Earth; 4.8 Light years from EE
TCe: Fourth planet from the star
Indigenous Population: Tall Ones; Mobile Ones; Stranglers
TCf: Fifth planet from the star, (New Polyarnaya settlement)

Union of Africa Nations (UAN)
Pokola, Congo: UAN Capital
Charm-E-Ine (Princess Charmy): UAN benevolent dictator
Adio Mwanjuma: Senior Advisor to the Princess
Erta Ale: A volcano in N.E. Ethiopia

United Nations Stellar Commission (UNSC)
Dawn (Sylva) Cohen: UNSC Operations Director
Richard Sylva: UNSC Science Director
Rudolf Rottenfusser: UNSC Operations Director (successor)
Mei Ping: UNCS Science Director (successor)

Star Ships
British Commonwealth (Flag Ship)
Neil Dodson: Admiral
Kristie Marshal: Vice Admiral of Operations (VAO)
Shinya Ishikawa: Vice Admiral of Academics & Science (VAAS)
Alan Parks: Captain
Shawn Murphy: Chief Academic and Science Officer (CASO)
Lieutenant Wellington (Shuttlecraft 1)
Lieutenant Christian (Shuttlecraft 2)
Dr. MacFarland: Ship's Doctor
Sharon Hooding: Head Bartender
Zanck: Second People's World Overseer of Curiosity
Raman-I-El: Rescued castaway
Mai Tran: Biologist
Thanos Tzounopoulos: Biologist
Jessica Peterson: Horticulturist
George Miller: Construction Superintendent

China
Ying Yue: Captain
Ling Zhao: CASO

Lieutenant Wang (Shuttlecraft 2)
Lieutenant Lee (Shuttlecraft 3)

Russia
Gigory Kazakov: Captain
Alexander Pushkin: CASO
Natasha Smirnov: Senior Engineer

United States
Carlos Monteiro: Captain (First Crew)
Lillian Westgate: CASO (First Crew)
Katherine Hickey: Captain (Second Crew)
Kendrick Foreman: CASO (Second Crew)
Dakota Bickmeier: Gate Specialist (Second Crew)

Africa
Chiku: Captain (First Crew)
Adeyemi Kanayochukwa: Captain (Second Crew)
Lebechi Gilbert: CASO (Second Crew)

South America
Jose Cabello: Captain
Camila Garacia: CASO

Significant Dates

1100: (BC) Bronze Age
2067: (AD) First Star Ship Fleet leaves for Epsilon Eridani (EE)
2071: Death Flu pandemic
2096: Star Ship Fleet establishes Wormhole Gate on EEb
2102: Pokola, Congo, becomes capital of United African Nations
    Princess Charm-E-Ine is named Benevolent Dictator
2107: Star Ship Fleet leaves EEb for Tau Ceti solar system
2113: Raman-I-El Rescued
2114: Star Ship Africa launched towards Epsilon Eridani from Earth
2120: Star Ship fleet reaches Tau Ceti solar system
2122: Star Ship Russia abandoned
2123: Star Ship United States heads back to EEb
2134: Second Star Ship Fleet leaves Epsilon Eridani for Tau Ceti
2146: Wormhole Gate on TCe opens

Prologue

Raman-I-El had been so excited that he had been initiated into the Order. But even with the years of training and indoctrination, he was still a novice along with four others that would be part of the team. Only Sham-El, the team leader, had any experience.

The Order had been established so far back in history that, to most, it was considered ageless. Of course that wasn't true because few things, if anything, are without a beginning. Still, it certainly was a long time!

In Raman-I-El's world, there was passive contentment, and not much excitement. No one had ambitions to out-perform the next in any worthwhile endeavor, except perhaps in the areas of intellect. There was no violence to speak of, and resources were much more than adequate to meet everyone's needs. No one wanted for anything. Nothing, that is, except a purpose. But if someone needed a purpose, the committee of three, known as The Boss, provided one through the Order.

It was understood that less-intelligent societies on other worlds might need some guidance as they developed. The Order was formed to provide that guidance. There were mistakes, for sure. And there had been unintended consequences when what seemed to be good ideas went too far and created different issues. But for the most part, the Order seemed to provide a positive impact. At least that was the common understanding.

The Order had sent one team to a particular planet many, many centuries ago. Since that time, as the population on that planet increased, other teams had been added. It was now time for yet another team to be sent, and Raman-I-El's team was next up.

The mission was simple in concept. Once on the planet, members of each team would remain in stasis until it appeared something was going out of control. The usual run of disease, environmental changes, or even local armed conflicts were not

1

something any member of the Order would get involved with, up to this point, that is. Issues such as these were to be allowed to run their course. Even when things were getting way out of control, no one in the Order was to do anything more than guide others through enlightenment and to encourage different behavior. This was usually done through selected individuals of the indigenous population. The number of Order members called upon for any event was determined by the size and location of the problem. Once the issue was dealt with, Order members would go back into stasis until called upon in the future and at the same time be rejuvenated back to a base age.

How and why an Order member or team was called upon was a mystery. Only a very few understood this process, and supposedly this was on a need-to-know basis. Raman-I-El didn't understand this concept, and when he asked he was told, "You don't need to know. Trust the system."

Raman-I-El 's team had not gone into stasis yet. His first experience with this extended sleep would come on the long trip to the designated planet. He was told that most Order members returned to age thirty-three. As Raman-I-El was currently thirty-four, he didn't see any relevance to the number. He supposed he might if he was woken up and stayed awake for decades.

The rejuvenation did not mean that team members were immortal. If they were out of stasis for an extended period, they could eventually die of old age. There were stories of an Order member that had simply had enough and consciously decided not to return to stasis. Raman-I-El had a difficult time understanding that thought process. Disasters and accidents were also possible and could quickly end one's life. Raman-I-El didn't want to even consider this possibility. He felt strongly that he didn't want to miss experiencing history!

The target planet was apparently just entering the Bronze Age, where only a few groups understood the technology and were using it to dominate other groups. Raman-I-El's team was told that by the time they reached the planet, a closer balance would be reached thanks to teams already in place. But the planet's population was expanding, and new teams had to be strategically placed for whatever might come next. The trip was very long, but once in stasis it didn't matter.

The ship appeared relatively simple in design considering it allowed for efficient travel to another world while carrying occupants in a state of suspended animation. As a result, it only needed limited power for the systems on board. Travel accommodations for the occupants were only the stasis pods. Someone would be brought out of stasis only in the case of an emergency, though that itself was an agonizing process that took more than a little time.

Only just enough food supplies were stored on board in case of an emergency. Eating, however, was a top priority for all Order members once out of stasis. Their high metabolism required a lot of food. To accommodate this priority, the ship was staffed by a number of drones and robotics. They would be activated as needed, with their primary function being to gather food supplies and prepare meals once at the ship's destination.

As a ship neared the target planet, the ship would identify a suitable place to land. The team leader would be brought out of stasis to potentially override the on-board controls if the landing site wasn't initially identified properly. Most sites had some form of thermal energy to maintain the systems. Dormant volcanoes, geothermal areas, and even undersea thermal vents were possibilities. Once in place, the ship would transform into a habitat for the occupants. It would never fly again.

The team leader would spend a few weeks surveying the situation on the ground and communicating with any other team that might be active. He would then go into stasis with his companions until called upon. In no case, however, was an Order member maintained in stasis for more than 350 cycles around the star of the destination planet. Scientists had determined that long-term stasis affected the brain in unusual ways. Order members were told this, of course, but at the same time weren't told what the side effects might be. When they asked, they were told, "Don't worry about it. It won't happen."

Tomorrow, they would launch. Once well on their way, they would then enter stasis. Each member of the team would undress and then lay down in their stasis pod. A clear cover would encapsulate the pod, making it air-tight, and a mild sedative gas would be introduced to make the prep for actual stasis less egregious. Raman-I-El would then insert tubes into all his body cavities and wait for the stasis process to be completed. Raman-I-El would experience a brief period of discomfort before being rendered unconscious as the stasis fluids filled his body. He thought he was prepared for this, but as the time was getting closer a sense of dread came over him; this was actually going to happen.

If Raman-I-El could have viewed the future, he would have had far more to dread.

Long into the voyage, with everything on board operating as programmed, the ship had an unplanned encounter with a small moon-sized rock. Its speed in relationship to the ship's was slightly faster. It was likely the rock's relatively slow speed that caused the ship's systems to fail to detect the object. Therefore, no evasive action was taken by the ship. The collision happened in slow motion. So, while the ship wasn't crushed, it did sustain serious damage when it became one with the rock.

The ship's occupants never knew what hit them. The team would never reach their destination.

Chapter 1
United Nations Stellar Commission

Following the less than smooth, but eventually successful, establishment of the wormhole Gate on Epsilon Eridani b (EEb) back in 2096, humanity started to reemerge from its lethargic view toward just about everything. Realizing that there was now a colony in another solar system and that travel between EEb and Earth was now instantaneously possible, apathy was being replaced with a sense of wonder. People wanted more. But getting more wouldn't be easy.

When the fleet of six Star Ships had left Earth in 2067, there had been over ten billion people crowding the "third rock from the Sun" exacerbating all the negative impacts of climate change. The world had been ready for some kind of relief, so support was easily obtained for any idea, no matter how far-fetched. Building a wormhole Gate between Earth and another planet, with the hope of moving a large portion of the Earth's population to a "new Earth," seemed like a good idea. Only the most thoughtful people knew this was a "Hail Mary" project.

In spite of the odds of success for this ridiculous mission, it worked! Sort of. Epsilon Eridani b, the second planet in that solar system, was quite suitable for humans, except for one tiny little problem; it was already inhabited, and the inhabitants weren't really ready to turn their planet over to the newcomers. The inhabitants, calling themselves "the Second People," did allow a trading colony to be set up and the wormhole Gate to be erected. It was all so easy, except for those actually doing the work. And for them? Well, not so much.

Before all this was going on in another solar system, Earth's human population had dropped down to less than one billion—ten percent of what it had been before the space fleet had left. As a result, technology and the people trying to support it were now decades behind where it had once been. So, while people were in favor of more missions, it wasn't going to be easy.

As for those heroes associated with the success of the first mission, many moved quietly into retirement. Groups of very large people with strange habits who had made all the difference between failure and success simply disappeared. The two vice admirals, the brother and sister twins of Admiral Ada Sylva, returned to Earth in 2097 to become the head of the now loosely reorganized United Nations Stellar Commission (UNSC) at the tender age of 62.

Richard Sylva and his sister Dawn (Sylva) Cohen took over UNSC, not fully comprehending that they might be rebuilding the organization pretty much from nothing. While Richard's title was Science Director, Dawn's title was Operations Director. In theory, Dawn was Richard's boss, but in actual practice they made every important decision jointly. Both were very intelligent and as dedicated to each other as any brother and sister could be.

Their Uncle Karl and their cousins Don and Len Bickmeier had been primary movers in getting the Earth Gate functioning and ready to be activated when the Gate on EEb came online. Their mother, Ada, retired to Homer, Alaska with her brother Karl's family when she returned to Earth.

Don's son Len Bickmeier stayed behind in South Dakota after he married the Gate Keeper Summer Snow and together they had one child, Dakota. Len and Summer maintained the Gate operations. It was these next generations represented by Dawn, Richard, Len, and Summer, and now Dakota, that would move humanity forward. But forward to what? They had few new resources and no new goal.

Much of this was a reflection of a very different Earth from the one that Richard and Dawn had left behind in 2067. The Death Flu had been the biggest culprit in reducing the Earth's population, but other factors had contributed. As the remaining population continued to age, there were few children being born to replace them. This trend was slowly reversing, but for those that had been away for so long there was no means of comparison.

Consistent with the reduced size of the general population, there were also fewer people with high levels of education in science and math. Advancement in these areas was decades behind where they would have been under normal circumstances. They were certainly far behind what was experienced in the space fleet, where learning was more than just required.

UNSC headquarters itself had been abandoned during the Death Flu pandemic. Office space was once in an expanded UN building in New York City. When Richard and Dawn returned to Earth, they found that the fortified infrastructure around the city, built to hold back rising seawaters, had failed due to a lack of personnel, and quite frankly, lack of interest. The new UN headquarters was built just outside Albany, New York. It was similar to the original, though there were far fewer people residing there. To save travel, many meetings were held via video, when the staff could get it to work and when the remaining operating satellites actually relayed transmissions. The few UNSC staff members that survived the pandemic returned to their posts when Richard and Dawn accepted their new positions, though it wasn't clear what they were supposed to do.

The UNSC fleet of Star Ships was now reduced to four useable ships out of the original six. They were still orbiting EEb. The skeleton crews left on the ships weren't sure what the fate of the ships would be, so they didn't do much more than what was absolutely necessary to keep them functioning. Since the fission/fusion hybrid engines couldn't be shut down, they were maintained in an "idle" mode.

These were the circumstances in which Richard and Dawn found themselves. Instead of being the leaders of a prestigious, well-funded, highly advanced operation, they found themselves in a position where they were leaders of, well, not much.

At one point when entering the office suites, Dawn said to Richard, "Might as well start with a dustpan and brush. Maybe while we're mopping the floor, we can get inspired."

Governments had stopped budgeting for the UNSC when the UNSC shut down, but there remained unspent money, and as Richard and Dawn learned it was more than enough to help get things started again. But determining what to do in order to get started remained the question.

They had backing from the United States government, but a new international space commission had to be established. They had decided to start small, but they would focus on the previously big-player governments to acquire both staff and additional funding. As other governments expressed interest, they would be brought on board as well.

"So," said Dawn, "let's see. We have an office. We have a very small staff right now twiddling their thumbs. We have four useable Star Ships in another solar system. We have some talented people on EEb and here on Earth who we might be able to encourage to join us if we had something to do. I believe we have one useable space shuttle here on Earth, which one of us might be able to fly but no one else. OH! And we have lofty titles."

"Yeah, *great* titles," agreed a sarcastic Richard. "What we don't have is a *real* job. I mean what exactly are we supposed to be doing here?"

This very big question kept repeating itself. What would be next? It seemed a shame to have Star Ships and not use them. But use them for what?

Both Dawn and Richard were firm believers in managing by wandering around. Since they had little else to do, they wandered. Dawn focused on identifying staff members. She wasn't planning on bringing them into the UNSC until there was a mission identified, but she wanted to know who was out there should the day arrive when certain talents were needed. She already had a list of scientists and engineers who had been on the interstellar mission, many of whom were born on the ships and were still available to do something, almost anything, that was interesting. Using whatever transportation was available, Dawn traveled first to the technical schools in the United States that were still functioning. Next, she traveled to the schools that were in the original host countries. This second list was turning out to be disappointing. There were interested individuals, but these people were truly inferior compared to what she had become accustomed to working with.

When Dawn finally arrived in Japan, she was an honored guest at the Tokyo Institute of Technology. She was used to being an honored guest, as she was, after all, a celebrity and hero to many. This visit was a bit over the top, however. She couldn't help but think that something was off. It seemed that every dignitary in the country was in attendance and wanted a piece of her time. Dawn kept insisting that the elaborate dinners and parties weren't necessary. Her visit was intended to identify scientists and engineers at the highest level. So far, after several days at the school, she hadn't interviewed anyone.

"Not a problem," said a highly ranked smiling official from the central government. "We have already found the perfect person for you."

Dawn asked, "How can that be when I haven't told anyone what we might need in the UNSC?"

Without skipping a beat, the official said, "He is Dr. Shinya Ishikawa. His primary interest is biology and botany at the microscopic level. But as this requires a lot of data manipulation, he has developed some impressive math models. He is currently splitting his time between basic research and teaching here at the school."

"Well," said Dawn, "he sounds interesting. I'd certainly like to meet him as well as anyone else you can recommend."

The response from the official was swift, stern, and to the point. "There may be others later," he said. "But you will find a position for Dr. Ishikawa—a very high-level, high-profile position. The government of Japan feels strongly that we did not get proper representation within the UNSC originally, and we don't want that to happen again. We are prepared to support any new effort with

9

significant financial resources, but it is conditional on the acceptance of Dr. Ishikawa."

A stunned Dawn Cohen thought, *Crap, I don't need this.* But she said instead, "I will certainly take this into serious consideration."

Then, looking around the room, she noticed everyone quietly watching as the still-smiling official said, "I'm sure you will." And then much more loudly in Japanese, he said, "A toast to Dr. Dawn Cohen."

Dawn never did get to meet Dr. Ishikawa on that visit. She did review his curriculum vitae, and he certainly looked good on paper. However, there was no indication that the good doctor was at all interested in anything the UNSC might offer. Not exactly shocked, she smiled to herself when she also learned that he was the son of the high-level government official she had been talking to and that father and son had a less-than-happy relationship.

Later she would tell her brother, "I was set up. This might all work out, but we might be forced to do something we'd rather not do."

While Dawn was ferreting out potential staffing candidates, Richard spent time at the various facilities on Earth that fell under the UNSC jurisdiction. The first visit was to the communications facility at Poker Flats, Alaska. With communications now occurring primarily through the wormhole Gate, Poker Flats had only a skeleton crew. Occasionally it was tested, but as it would only be used if there were a catastrophic failure of the Gate, it really had no practical use for the UNSC. Poker Flats was another relic of the past.

Next, he visited Houston with John Carpenter, the last person to work there and the one that sent the message in 2071 telling the fleet, "You're on your own." Houston was now flooded from the rising sea. There was nothing to be salvaged.

Multiple countries had spaceports. Some of these were still useable, but with no space missions in the works only the one in

Colorado was reported to have a functioning space shuttle. Richard's examination confirmed that it was, in fact, functional.

When Richard, Dawn, and their families sat down for a Sunday meal after their surveys were completed, it was a somber occasion. Before-dinner drinks followed by too much wine allowed feelings to fly that were far from being even remotely optimistic.

A catalyst of some kind was needed.

Chapter 2

The New Mission

As it turned out, the efforts that Richard and Dawn put in while "wandering around" had some benefit. Governments anxious for something positive to show their countrymen appointed new commissioners to the UNSC so that by the end of 2098 there were enough commissioners to actually have a meeting.

These new commissioners met with Richard and Dawn in the United Nations Stellar Commission headquarters. They didn't all physically attend, of course, as travel was limited by the inaccessibility of planes and fuel. Still, video conferencing meant that at least their faces and voices were in attendance. The countries that sponsored the remaining Star Ships—the United States, the British Commonwealth, the China, and the Russia—were well represented, as were the sponsors of the ill-fated India and the decommissioned South America.

Not everyone was in agreement as to what the UNSC should do. Some thought they should leave the ships in orbit around EEb and maybe abandon them. Others thought they should return to Earth, though they had no idea what to do with them once they returned. Most agreed that both options were a waste. While the original purpose of the mission—to relieve the over-population crisis on Earth—was moot, people had become inspired by this historic and heroic journey to another solar system and wanted more. Still, some decisions needed to be made, and as was pointed out by Dawn, "Doing nothing is still a decision." After that comment, the conversation went something like this:

"So, we have these five Star Ships circling EEb," said Lord Harold Barrington of Great Britain.

"Actually, we really have four. Star Ship South America isn't really functional," said Richard

"Whatever. So, we have four ships. The question remains: what do we do with them?"

"Do we really need them? We could just leave them there."

"Not really. Remember the engines are fission/fusion hybrids, and once they're started, they can't be shut down. So, they are in idle mode while they are sitting in orbit. Plus, we have a crew on each ship. A small crew to be sure, but still people employed by us."

"Won't the engines wear out or something?" came another voice.

"Probably, but we have no history or data to know when."

"Well, what about the engine compartments, or shells, or whatever is containing the reactions? Won't they eventually give out?"

"Ah! Great question", said Richard. "The reactions are actually being contained in a force field generated by the engines themselves. Basically, there's nothing to wear out—um, we think."

"'You think' doesn't give me a warm, fuzzy feeling," Said Harold.

"They made it to EEb, didn't they?" asked the Argentina Commissioner.

"Not all the ships, and certainly not everyone that had started out."

It was quiet for a minute while that sobering thought reminded everyone that space travel was nothing to be taken for granted.

"Still, we have these ships. We should do something with them."

Dawn and Richard mostly listened, but this last statement looked like an opening. Therefore, Dawn said, "We've been looking at other solar systems. Tau Ceti is only 4.8 light years from Epsilon Eridani. We could send the ships there and establish another wormhole Gate. There are four planets, and two of them look to be habitable. Maybe this time we could find a planet that won't have the restrictions on us that the Second People put on us at EEb. There is always the potential of more resources we could use here on Earth. From remote observations, the two larger planets look promising."

"Only 4.8 light years away? You make it sound like it is right around the corner," said the Russian Commissioner.

"Compared to the distance to Epsilon Eridani," said Dawn, "at almost eleven light years, it *is* just around the corner. We could ship enough parts and supplies for a new Gate through the Earth Gate to the EEb Gate to supplement the redundant material we sent to EEb in the first place. All we need is a crew and supplies."

"Well," added Richard, "to be honest it isn't quite that easy. The ships do need some TLC in the living quarters and a few upgrades here and there, but in the end, it is all doable."

"TLC? What's that?"

"Tender, love, and care. You know, like, someone cared. Just as an example, if we're going to crew these ships, we don't want the new folks sleeping on worn-out bedding, do we?

"If we're thinking about that kind of detail, does that mean we've made a decision?" added the Chinese Commissioner.

Then adding "I move that we authorize Richard Sylva and Dawn Cohen to prepare a comprehensive package outlining what needs to be done and when. Included in the package must be a detailed analysis of the costs and what we on Earth hope to gain from this proposed mission. We will then present to our member nations for approval."

"Second."

"Any further discussion?"

"Well, yeah!" exclaimed the almost shouting South American Commission member jumping to her feet. "Wait a minute, I want to talk about the South America. Why can't we get our Star Ship South America back into the mix? Isn't sending off a fleet of four ships risky? After all, we wanted seven ships in the first mission and ended up with six, and then India blew up getting us down to five. Now we're saying four is enough?"

Richard answered calmly with, "The main issue is the engines. We used a couple of the South America engines for power on New Hope Island, and the other good engines were used as backup engines on the other ships. As for the number of ships, I agree that more would be better. But it is a shorter trip, and we've learned a lot on the first mission, so it should be safer. Four ships are what we have."

More people piped in:

"Maybe we learned a lot, but we have also lost a lot of so-called 'corporate memory' with so many of our scientists and engineers that designed these things in the first place now among the dead."

"Right, so more ships would be better."

"Ok, so what's to keep us from bringing new engines through the Gate to outfit South America?"

Again, Richard answered, "If we can build the components here on Earth, we can get them to EEb Gate at the New Hope station for assembly and then shuttled up to the ship. But, and this is a very big 'but,' we can't ship the fuel through the Gates. The fuel has to be handled very carefully, and we're pretty sure there is significant risk in trying to send it through the wormhole Gates. It wouldn't take much of the fissionable material and/or the fusion components to become unstable and destroy the Gates or disrupt the wormhole. Best case would be we lose the Gates forever. Not good. But, worst-case scenario is we lose the Gates while also spraying radioactive material all over the receiving end, and maybe even the Earth's end as well."

Someone added, "Well that would be rude, wouldn't it?" This brought a few uneasy smiles to the thus far staid assembly.

"OK," said the Commission Chair, "we have a motion and a second. Do we move forward to the next step or not? Is there any further discussion? And I'll remind you that we are only asking for a plan at this stage."

"All in favor?"

"All opposed?"

It was a unanimous decision to move forward with the planning. Richard and Dawn looked at each other and smiled.

Within a month, the UNSC had put together a plan. On the surface, it didn't look too different from the discussions at the Commission meeting. It was still very broad-brushed, but it was enough for support from the member nations. Simply stated, the plan was to send an exploratory mission to another solar system, erect a new Gate, and establish a new colony. The one major caveat, of course, was that since the United States was where the Earth's wormhole Gate was located and since the United States had taken the initiative to rescue the first mission, the United States would be the major supplier of technology and resources.

Team leaders would remain Dawn Cohen as Operations Director and her twin brother Richard Sylva as Science Director. They planned to retire in a few years, giving them ample time to plan for the future. For now, they were the ones that would work out the details because they knew if you take care of the details, then everything else falls into place.

With the fleet down to four ships, it was still enough to carry what they needed to build a functioning Gate and support structures, but it didn't provide much of a margin of error if there was a significant problem. Losing another ship along the way would truly be a disaster, but confidence in the plan was high. One benefit of the smaller fleet was that fewer people were needed to crew the ships. While there were still nearly one billion people on Earth, that was a much smaller labor pool than the over ten billion that the Earth hosted prior to the first mission. Worse was the fact that the technological community of scientists and engineers was disproportionally much smaller, and of those people the level of knowledge was even less. So finding 60,000 qualified people to staff the ships wasn't going to be easy. There were people willing to go, but the key word missing in most cases seemed to be "qualified." The best and the brightest were on the original mission, isolated from what happened on Earth and decades ahead technologically. Some of these people were willing to go on another mission, but the majority had had enough and wanted to do something else or retire. They were tired.

Fortunately, so thought the twins, *the Commission member nations were to make the initial recommendations for the crews. All we have to do is confirm their qualifications.* That would eventually bring about disaster, but for now the problem of selecting the crew wasn't theirs.

The issue of getting what was needed to EEb to stock up for the mission was two-fold. The low-tech material for the construction equipment and spare parts was reasonably easy to obtain; much of it was already at New Hope Island. The rest would come from Earth through the Gates. Most of the food required could still be raised on the ships. Fresh water tanks could be filled from EEb with permission from the Second People of EEb.

The second issue, however, was the high-tech requirements for the new Gate. Pulling the parts together was one thing; having the ability to put it together was quite another. As there were no spare Gates hanging around on Earth to be dismantled and sent to EEb, the UNSC authorized trips to either Earth's moon, Saturn's moon Titan, or Mars to dismantle one of those abandoned Gates. Eventually, Mars was selected, as it was likely the most complete.

At the same time, the UNSC authorized the construction of two new shuttlecrafts. These would be used to service essential satellites for communications. With the UNSC primarily meeting via video conference, it was becoming apparent the neglected system of satellites needed corrective maintenance if communications were to be dependable.

Things were starting to come together. The four commissioned Star Ships were readied at EEb. Supplies were being sent through the Gate to New Hope Island on EEb, the member nations of the UNSC were actively recruiting qualified crewmembers for the new mission, and soon the missing parts for a new Gate on a Tau Ceti planet would be salvaged. The level of excitement wasn't as high as it was for the original mission to Epsilon Eridani, but there was interest and general support. For many, however, general support didn't mean people were volunteering. Some did of course, but most said, "Yeah, I like it here. I'm not going. Get someone else."

Chapter 3
Ships and Crew

For most of the Star Ships' crewmembers, this was the first trip through the Gate, instilling within them a great deal of angst. Standing on Earth one moment and then after a brief psychedelic-like trip suddenly standing in another solar system is hard to grasp. Some didn't stomach it very well.

The agreement with the Second People of Epsilon Eridani b, allowing no more than 70,000 people on the planet, meant there were only a brief few days on New Hope before crew members were ferried up to their ships, usually in groups of twenty. The new arrivals were surprised at how well the local humans looked and acted, apparently pleased that New Hope was the current center of attention for this new mission.

With the five 3,000-foot-long Star Ships in orbit over New Hope tethered together at the bows, the ships looked like a small moon. Upon approaching the ships, nearly everyone was overwhelmed at the sight. The ships were huge; the pictures and simulators on Earth did not do them justice. It was humbling to think that it was a past generation that conceived of and built these things, and at the same time they realized that it probably couldn't be duplicated now. It was like looking at a more modern version of the pyramids. *Would man ever be able to do it again in the future?* was the universal thought but never said.

The ships' engines were the original fission/fusion hybrids but with a few upgraded safety features, with the hopes that there would be fewer operating issues. To say these modification efforts were tricky with the reactions in the engines being maintained would be an understatement. Far too many workers were killed and injured in the process. Many more received a lifetime dose of radiation and were retired from the service. Each accident reminded people why the engine room pods were mounted on rings 500 feet from the main hull. They weren't the safest things to be invented, but until something better came along this is what was available. Having spare engine pods on each ship was the extra safety precaution;

rather than risking the ship and everyone on board if something went wrong, an entire engine pod would be ejected dramatically away from the ship, and a spare pod rotated into place.

Some spaces in the ships were reconfigured to provide a more village-esque atmosphere. Different lighting and environmental controls made some areas a little less institutional, but overall the original layout and plans for each deck didn't change.

The ships original design to hold 18,000 people each didn't change. This time, however, the planned crew for each ship was set at 13,000. The assumption was that if one ship had to be abandoned, the remaining three ships would be able to accommodate the abandoned ship's crew. In the end, even the lower 13,000 number was hard to meet.

Another assumption was that if one ship were abandoned, that ship's Gate components would also be transferred so that the remaining three ships would be able to carry everything needed for a successful mission. It wasn't deemed likely to happen, but it just seemed like a great precaution.

It was more likely that a ship's engine pod would be jettisoned if the fission/fusion reaction went critical. It had happened before. It might happen again. That, of course, was why each ship carried two spare engine pods. If they weren't needed to reach their destination, two would be needed to power up the Gate as well as the community once the Gate was constructed. Some questioned the wisdom of using these engines on the planet, where failure would have long-lasting effects. In the end, however, there wasn't much of a choice given the power demands of the Gates. Burying entire pods deep into the ground with a reinforced containment structure would be the reasonable solution to a potential failure.

For the most part, families were encouraged to join the mission. In spite of this, none of the senior officers, including the captains, were married. Though some correctly made note of the Admiral and Vice Admiral of Operations living arrangements.

One lesson learned from the original mission from Earth to EEb was that those who came from small islands or back-country villages fared better than most. Island-style living meant you had to get along with the rest of the population in close quarters, even if you didn't like them. You would see these people nearly every day and often relied on them when there was a problem. Islanders and isolated populations also often had to make do with what they had at hand. You couldn't just hop over to a store to get something you needed when the nearest store might be days away. The Star Ships mimicked the same island environment, so those that volunteered for this latest space adventure who came from these areas were usually chosen over others that might be similarly qualified.

Living quarters were still the same, but recreational areas were redesigned, and with a smaller crew there was more growing space for fruit and vegetables. Other non-human and Second People members of the crew remained the same as before, with chickens, canaries, a few service dogs, and honeybees joining as well. This time, however, honeybees were to be managed better, with the goal of avoiding bee populations in non-agriculture areas. Also, this time tilapia fish farms were added to help clean the water source and provide additional protein. It was hoped they could be raised well enough to have a satisfactory taste.

Lounge areas were spruced up, but the functions remained the same, with the oversight being provided by the Head Bartenders on each ship. As before, Head Bartenders were also responsible for the brewing of standard and low alcoholic beer and sometimes other alcoholic beverages. Beer-brewing was viewed as important on the first mission because it helped make recycled water palatable and safer to drink. While some thought of this as a little tongue-in-cheek ploy during the early days of the first mission, it became abundantly clear after a few years that beer brewing made with recycled water was essential to everyone's well-being.

Yes, indeed, we have thought of everything, was the smug conclusion.

Everything, that is, except the actual makeup of the crews. Recruiting crews was more difficult than anyone would have thought. The recruiters never got to the stage where someone only needed to simply be breathing and have a pulse to qualify, but some rather marginal individuals were eventually deemed fit.

Admiral Neil Dodson, the two Vice Admirals, four of the ships' Captains, and four of the ships' Chief Academics and Science Officers (CASOs) were the first of the new crew to arrive. They were welcomed on board their respective ships by the skeleton crews who lived on board to keep things working. About half of the skeleton crew would stay on board each ship for the new mission. Evenly split, that meant there were approximately 250 people on each ship who had first-hand experience out of the expected crews of 13,000.

Admiral Neil Dodson and Vice Admiral Operations (VAO) Kristie Marshal were the only two of the eleven officers shuttled to the ships who had been on the ships during the mission to EE. Admiral Dodson's family was originally from New Zealand when they signed onto the Star Ship British Commonwealth in 2067. His dad was an Operating Engineer. His mom was a high school teacher. Neil was three years old when the family joined the mission. Neil excelled in school on board the ship, and while taking college-level classes he worked in engineering. Being tutored by his dad and the other engineers pushed him along rather quickly. Through unfortunate deaths and advances by others, Neil started moving up the chain of command. Eventually, he outranked his dad, a man who was very proud of his son.

Neil was appointed Chief Engineer when the former Chief died in an accident. As Chief Engineer, Neil was one of the first to recognize the ingenious simple solution to the faulty engines that had led to the destruction of the Star Ship India. When the First Officer of the British Commonwealth had a mental breakdown, Neil was asked to temporarily fill in at the age of twenty-five. His quiet determination and his constant self-education regarding the intricacies of his duties eventually earned him the promotion to Captain at the ripe old age of thirty, replacing his terminally ill predecessor. Being in the right place at the right time certainly helped, but there was no question that Neil was a brilliant individual and well suited to be Admiral for this new mission.

You couldn't tell by looking at the Admiral that he was anxious in this new role. He wasn't afraid of the future, but he knew that everyone involved with this new adventure was relying on his leadership, and he didn't want to screw up. He projected calmness and confidence, and deep down inside he knew that he was probably the best candidate for this job. Of all the officers in the fleet, Neil was the one who knew the ships best after having lived through the worst of times on the first mission.

Once the New Hope Island settlement had the wormhole Gate firmly established, many had returned to Earth, leaving only the allowed population of 70,000 on EEb. A few of the ships' crews never left, and some that had gone home to Earth decided that they would rather go back to the ships and join the new mission.

Neil was one those people. He had returned to New Zealand only to find himself a stranger in his own country. While it was good to be back on Earth, he felt a void. He discovered that he missed the unknown challenges of space travel. So, when the UNSC asked him if he would consider returning as Admiral, his response was a simple "yes." And with that simple answer, Admiral Neil Dodson traveled to the Earth Gate in South Dakota, was transported to EEb, and then shuttled to his old ship Star Ship British Commonwealth, where he took command. He was forty-three years old.

At 5'9" and with an average build, he did not command attention with his physical appearance. Instead, he was both respected and feared because of his intelligence and attention to detail. He also had the ability to make just about anyone shrink into a babbling blob with one look. Sometimes, Neil did it for sport, but usually it was in response to something stupid someone said or did. In many respects, Neil was still a bit old-fashioned and was one of the few people who would still wear glasses, which he would use as an intimidation prop. Without saying a word, he could lower his head, purse his lips, look over the top of his glasses at someone with an expressionless face, and the recipient of this look would know that Admiral Dodson was now in a cranky mood and that a better response needed to be delivered.

The Admiral didn't usually drink any heavy alcoholic beverages, but he was never inclined to make others follow his example. This was especially true when it came to his VAO since she certainly enjoyed a regular glass of wine and an occasional beer, often leading to a welcomed romantic mood in the Admiral's quarters.

Kristie Marshal allowed the Admiral to think that he chose her from the pool of engineers who had decided to return to the fleet. It was true that Kristie had proved herself to be more than just a competent engineer, and with her PhD in nuclear engineering she had the theoretical knowledge to help with the upgrades of the engines. Her ability to see and understand multiple issues and solve them with one combined solution—in addition to her dry sense of humor—garnered her a deep respect from her staff. Kristie was a healthy 5'6" brown-haired beauty. While she usually wore her standard-issued uniform, most of the women in the fleet envied the way it looked on her.

Kristie was actually born on Star Ship British Commonwealth when it was two years into the trip to EEb. Her parents were part of the construction battalion, and they encouraged Kristie to take advantage of the training available on the ships. Once she started, she simply sucked up knowledge like a sponge.

She and the Admiral were close. In fact, they shared everything, including the Admiral's quarters. She wasn't about to let Neil go without her. Period! Neil had first noticed Kristie when she was fifteen, and Neil was completely smitten. Neil being five years older knew what he wanted, but he was willing to wait. As they matured, they both realized they were to be a couple for life. The only downside for Neil was Kristie's ability to make him blush, usually at the worst possible time. The downside for Kristie was Neil's unwillingness to get officially hitched in marriage.

Dr. Shinya Ishikawa was named the Vice Admiral of Academics and Science (VAAS). In contrast to the VAO, the Admiral had very little to say about this choice, and in fact when he did say something about his concerns, it was summarily dismissed. Everything Neil and Kristie shared, Shinya lacked. It was true that

24

Shinya had multiple PhDs and had numerous academic awards from his home country of Japan and elsewhere. On paper, he was top-notch, but there was something else that got him the appointment. While Neil never completely understood what that was, he knew that the influence of Ishikawa's family got him the job.

Shinya was thirty-seven years old. He was rail thin and would have been six feet tall if he stood up straight. He did bathe regularly, but he always looked disheveled. His official uniform, which he was required to wear, hung on him like a rag and was never crisp-looking. Not only had he never been in space, but he had only physically left Japan once, preferring to stay at the university where he studied and taught—when he remembered to show up for class, that is. Two officials were required to escort him from the University to the Earth Wormhole Gate and then to the space fleet out of fear he would wander off.

What really concerned the Admiral was Ishikawa's focus. The Admiral found that the VAAS often focused so intently on the smallest detail that he would forget the overall objective. Neil concluded that Ishikawa was in fact the scientist who people had joked about for years. Ishikawa really was the one who knew more and more about less and less until he knew absolutely everything about nothing.

As the VAAS, all scientific and educational activities were his responsibility. It didn't take long, however, before his staff learned to operate without a true leader at the helm. Department heads would meet regularly and make important decisions. While the Admiral knew Shinya was going to be a problem, he knew that he had no real choice, at least initially, and vowed to make the best of it. Orders were orders, but once they were underway and out of sight, Neil hoped to find a real leader and Shinya would be demoted.

For the most part, the EEb indigenous population, known as the Second People, had little desire to leave the planet. There were a few, however, who asked to join the fleet, and they were readily accepted. Zanck, the Second People's World Overseer of Curiosity, and three of his subordinates joined the fleet and were assigned to the Star Ship British Commonwealth. The humans could only tell them apart by the colorful clothing they wore. Of course, the Second People thought all humans looked the same, too, except for their color. Zanck and his subordinates stood between three and four feet tall standing on four legs. Two other upper-body appendages were used as humans use arms. They had a resemblance to large ants except that they were upright from the waist up.

Communications issues between the humans and Second People had eventually been overcome. Initially, only one individual in the space fleet could communicate with the native population when the fleet had first reached EEb, though no one knew how he managed to know the "language," which consisted of using rapid eye movement to communicate. With some effort, very few were able to learn how to communicate, but with the unfortunate side effect of severe headaches. Eventually a variation of human sign language was developed, which the Second People eagerly and readily learned.

Zanck had multiple missions. As his title indicated, he wanted to learn as much as he could from the humans while at the same time teaching them the lessons his people had learned both through their own inquiries and from the First People that had once been the dominant species on his planet. Zanck believed the First People's own success in ruling the planet was eventually its downfall, as the planet couldn't sustain them. They had all died off rapidly, leaving the Second People in their place, who instinctively understand the ecosystem and worked with it rather than continually trying to modify it. And not least of all, Zanck and his subordinates were to assimilate into the crew as much as possible. No one knew what this would mean, but it was widely believed by both species that the Second People would be more adept at "something" than the humans.

Some protocol was modified for this mission. On the first mission, the Admiral would rotate the flag from ship to ship and never had the Admiral and the Vice Admirals all on the same ship in case of an accident. This time, the flagship would remain British Commonwealth. Neil and Kristie would periodically inspect the other three ships, but they would remain together. Shinya would initially be assigned to another ship, but the idea of Shinya being left in charge if something happened to him and Kristie so repulsed Neil that another line of progression was developed.

Captain Alan Parks was chosen for the Star Ship British Commonwealth. At 6'2" and 220 pounds, he presented as a formidable figure. Ramrod straight with thick, curly, blonde hair, he stood out in a crowd. Captain Parks always displayed dry British humor, which sometimes disguised the fact that he could quickly evaluate nearly every problem put in front of him and provide a well-considered solution. When he had any time off duty, he read a lot and as a result displayed an uncanny grasp of the English vocabulary. He was so well-respected that in spite of his age of sixty-two when the mission started, he was the Commonwealth's first choice for the mission.

Captain Parks enjoyed nearly a full crew of 12,450. They were all true volunteers from all around the world, with most of them from the old British Commonwealth countries. To round out the crew, there were few from Western Europe in the mix.

The British Commonwealth's Chief Academics and Science Officer (CASO) was Shawn Murphy. Shawn looked as Irish as his name. At age thirty-one, he had a Doctorate in Astrophysics, a very sexy wife schooled in the arts, and two very rambunctious daughters. Where the Captain provided a moderate appearance, this CASO provided a very animated antidote, especially when he had a pint of beer in front of him.

Ying Yue captained Star Ship China. Captain Yue was an attractive thirty-seven-year-old who, like Kristie Marshal, made her standard uniform look as though it came from a fashion magazine. Her jet-black hair in the latest style enhanced the image. Ying was 5'5" and weighed about 115 pounds. Her poise made her appear taller than she was. Her usually solemn, serious demeanor, combined with a quick no-nonsense response to everything presented to her, made her both respected and feared by her crew. She had no sense of humor and always seemed anxious for a fight. Even the Admiral sometimes seemed nervous around her.

Her CASO was Ling Zhao, who was very much like the Captain, always wound up tight and never accepting anything her staff did as a job well done. She was well-schooled and made sure everyone around her knew it.

Star Ship China enjoyed a full crew of 13,001. The Chinese government wanted to make a point by having exactly 13,000, but one of the couples selected ruined that by having a baby while briefly passing through New Hope Island. The crew was very disciplined and knowledgeable in their respective fields. Unlike the original crew that went to EE, this crew had learned everything by rote, so they had a difficult time coming up with solutions to problems that hadn't been in the textbook. Even the scientists had a difficult time with interdisciplinary solutions to problems. This was all in complete contrast to the general mentality on the other ships, where most could think through a problem and could devise a solution without necessarily have to look in a book.

The Star Ship United States captain was Carlos Monteiro. Captain Monteiro could only be described as a character. He was the product of parents who had immigrated to the United States. His mother was from Cape Verde, and his father was from the Portuguese Azores. He was thirty-eight years old, stood about 5'5" and was a very robust 185 pounds, with a lot of muscle. A very dark complexion thanks to his mother and a somewhat balding, black, curly mess of hair thanks to his father gave him an appearance that didn't say "captain." Like the other captains, however, he had a very sharp mind.

What really set Captain Monteiro apart from the rest of the officers was his constant animation. He couldn't sit still, and when he talked, he was loud with his hands always in a state of motion. Everyone believed that if he sat on his hands, he wouldn't be able to talk. He had an incredible ability to drink anyone under the table and eat huge meals. He was always smiling or laughing and was a favorite at every social gathering. Only his intense daily exercise regimen allowed him to stay ahead of the possible weight gain.

The United States CASO was Lillian Westgate. Contrasting her Captain, she was a petite, 5'1" thirty-eight-year-old, who looked at least ten years younger. In most meetings, she would quietly sit back and listen with her hands folded, looking very unconcerned. When discussions became serious, she would continue to listen until there seemed to be an impasse. She would then sit up and, with a soft voice, summarize everything that had been said before reaching a conclusion. In early meetings, others in the room would continue to talk, but Lillian would say her piece with her soft voice as if she were the only one speaking. Gradually, everyone would shut up as she continued. It didn't take too many meetings with her for everyone in the room to suddenly stop talking when she sat forward and then listen intently. She was always correct. She scared the hell out of everyone. Lillian's only non-passive facial expression was when she at times rolled her eyes when Captain Monteiro was on a role and becoming more animated than usual.

There were 10,543 crewmembers on the United States. There had been far more volunteers for the mission than the number selected. The countries that worked with the United States of America all agreed that quality was better than quantity. While it might become more desirable to have more people during the Gate construction, fewer highly qualified people was deemed a better option.

The Captain on Star Ship Russia was Gigory Kazakov. Gigory was about 5'8" with thick black hair, eyebrows, and a beard. He weighed close to 190 pounds. It would be easy to picture him in full Russian winter clothing looking like a big Russian bear. He was sullen most of the time, preferring vodka to beer and wine. He made certain his Head Bartender knew how to make his favorite drink. He gave the impression he didn't want to be there, reflecting the attitude presented by nearly everyone in his crew.

The Russia CASO was Alexander Pushkin. While he shared the same name as a famous Russian poet, the only thing they had in common was a dislike for authority. The hypocrisy never occurred to him that he himself had always been in a position of authority.

Star Ship Russia had the smallest crew of 9,350. The UNSC directive had been that everyone on the mission was to be a volunteer because the mission was risky. Officially, that was the case, but Richard and Dawn had the distinct impression that the majority of the 9,350 Russia crewmembers had been told they were going and were not volunteers. Adding to the suspicion was the fact that nearly everyone in the crew came from the same town. Richard and Dawn quietly mentioned their suspicions to Admiral Dodson that something was a bit off with this crew. "Wonderful," responded a sarcastic Neil. "Just wonderful."

On the day of departure for Tau Ceti, Admiral Neil Dodson thought to himself, *All is good! Well, mostly all good anyway!*

On January 11, 2107, the UNSC fleet uncoupled from their orbiting position and left EEb for TC. Acceleration was steady, providing 1.5 g inside the ships. As the ships left orbit, they spread out roughly ten miles apart. In approximately thirteen years, they would reach TC. Cautious optimism was high.

Chapter 4
Charm-E-Ine's Choice

Charm-E-Ine had never considered that she might end up like this. She had been one of a team of six from her Order assigned to the northeast sector of Africa. She didn't think the team had been all that successful in their overall mission, but because of established protocols they were limited in how involved they could be with the general development of humanity in Africa. Then, with no warning, she was alone.

"Charmy," as those who met her knew her, was 6'2" and weighed about 180 pounds. Because of her perfect proportions, no one from a distance would guess she was this large unless someone else was standing next to her. Charmy had a very dark and clear complexion—not black exactly but quite dark. Her long raven-black hair was about shoulder length; the same length everyone from her world had, male or female. She was very fit, though with her standard uniform of loose white clothing it wasn't that easy to tell.

When the Alaska team had been brought out of stasis in 2085, her team had been activated to try and rally the general population of Africa toward a more optimistic future. To some extent, they had been successful, and when the Earth Wormhole Gate opened to the newly built wormhole Gate on Epsilon Eridani b, her team started to return to their habitat that was melded into Erta Ale volcano. Most habitats like theirs were established in areas where there was a lot of energy. Energy, in this case in the form of heat, was required to keep the habitat systems running. There was usually enough data available to avoid volcanoes that were at risk of erupting, but just like everything else there was risk. Charmy's team had been using the habitat at Erta Ale for a 1,000 or more years with next to no thought of disaster. But in 2096, it happened.

Everyone was back in the habitat except for Charmy. They were waiting for her return for a final celebratory meal before entering stasis. Charmy was 20 miles away, gliding in with her antigravity pack unfurled, when she saw with horror the mountain explode. Ancient sensors were a constant issue, and apparently the systems that should have provided an alert failed. It wasn't until days later that Charmy finally gave up hope that anyone else might have survived.

Charmy was left with nothing but her antigravity pack and her gold and silver coins. Almost in a daze, she wandered around Africa for longer than she could remember or care. When out on her own away from people, she might stay in an abandoned village or out on the plains, sometimes using the shield that her pack provided for protection while she slept. Food was sometimes a problem, as she had a huge appetite. This would usually only get satisfied when she wandered into a village or settlement. Her natural ability to make people feel comfortable and welcome when she was with them afforded her the opportunity to eat well. She was always careful not to take food that was needed by others and always paid with gold and silver coins.

One day in 2098, she had settled down outside a village and furled her antigravity pack hoping no one noticed. As usual, when she walked into the village the elders warmly greeted her. While everyone of her kind had the ability to make people accept her, Charmy had an ability that was stronger than most. As a result, when she asked for food and a place to stay for a few days, everyone in the village went out of their way to make her comfortable. Charmy was given a small house to use, a hut really, and emerged only for meals. She was past mourning but was still lost. She had concluded that she had been presumed dead by her own people and needed to decide what to do next. She had to get serious about contemplating her future.

There was no real protocol for something like this, but in those rare cases where something like this might happen, it was expected that any survivors would try to contact any activated teams and find a vacated position. No one was supposed to be isolated and left on their own.

But Charmy had been developing different feelings about this. Her team had been her family. In fact, they were her only family. One part of her had wanted to join them for an eternal rest;

another part reminded her of her dedication to the Order's mission of guiding the course of humanity.

At 4:32 AM on the morning of September 12, 2098, Charmy woke with an epiphany. She would not seek assistance from another team. She would not join her team members now, but she would live out her natural life doing what she could for Africa. She would break from protocol and be an active member of the African society by not just guiding leaders but by being a leader if she could. She realized this would probably be an issue with the Boss, and under normal circumstances it could get her into trouble. The Boss might decide to try and stop her, but she'd worry about that later. After all, none of her people knew she was alive. Charmy would create her own mission. She was free to do what she wanted. The more she thought about it, the better she felt.

Details would be worked out as she went along, even though she knew full well that details were what directed everything. She thought, *Take care of the details and all the big things will fall into place.* "Yes," she said out loud to no one, "I will start small and develop the details."

Putting things into perspective, Charmy knew that the world, or most of the world anyway, had embarked on a grand adventure. Six interstellar spaceships had been built and were launched in 2067 towards Epsilon Eridani in the hopes of eventually lessening the burden humanity had placed on Mother Earth. The original plan was for seven ships, with the Middle East and Africa hosting the seventh ship. Politics and war never allowed this seventh ship to get any kind of traction, however.

The Death Flu of 2071 had wiped out ninety percent of the world's population, leaving behind a largely lethargic remnant. Africa was no exception, but with no overall central government and selfish power-seekers left behind, there was still a lot of fighting, even now.

There was also the issue of climate change. The pendulum of climate change was still swinging in the wrong direction. The deserts of the north continued to push south. Other parts of Africa continually experienced severe weather patterns, with long periods of drought followed by severe rain and wind that could go on for weeks. In spite of the many positive efforts to curtail carbon emissions that were blamed for the climate changes, the tipping point had been reached, and there didn't seem to be any signs it would soon reverse. Africa was in the crosshairs of continual disasters. Charmy wasn't sure she could do much about climate change, but she would certainly look for an opportunity. On the other hand, she might be able to do something about unifying the people of Africa into a peaceful coexistence.

Charmy considered this to be a long-term mission, and she would pursue it knowing full well that it would be bold. It would require a lot of work, but she felt energized with this choice. There would be no looking back. As far as details were concerned, she thought, *I'll start first thing in the morning with the village elders and see how it goes.*

Chapter 5

Abel and Megan Fisher

Abel and Megan Fisher had been what some would have called "video-lovers" in the early years before the space fleet had reached the Epsilon Eridani solar system. In those days, neither one of them ventured outdoors or interacted with anyone except through their computer screens. They had thought they were living the life. Abel had accumulated wealth using his neural implant to run his very real "Farm Ville" operation. Drones and robotics of every kind did his bidding as he "wasted" little personal energy. He thought he was happy, but in this case, ignorance really wasn't bliss.

Megan Benoit had lived in France and was noted for two things. First was her uncanny ability to visualize how integrated systems worked. She could literally see how electrons moved in the deepest recesses of any system. She was as pale as anyone could be by never exposing herself to anything that resembled sunlight. She was also extremely thin and could fool anyone into thinking she was a child. The second thing that made her noteworthy were the sex acts performed in front of the video monitor that drove Abel crazy long before they actually met.

Both of them were content until two very large men from some benevolent Order dressed in white literally flew into Abel's life using some kind of antigravity packs. Abel was fascinated with this technology, and these two strangers used this fascination to draw Abel—and eventually Megan—out of their isolation back in 2085 to help get the Earth's interstellar communications array up and running and then the Earth Wormhole Gate. Remarkably, up until then Abel wasn't even sure Megan was real or if she were just a computer simulation. In fact, he hadn't cared. But when these strange people brought them together, Abel and Megan realized that that being together in real life was much better than what they had been doing. Megan, as it turned out, discovered that she had been missing out on a lot by not being in physical contact and nearly killed Abel trying to make up for lost time.

Abel never complained, and as the Earth Gate was being activated in 2096 Megan Benoit became Megan Fisher. They had plenty of money and no desire to return to their old ways. They were disappointed to learn they couldn't have children, but at the same time found a calling of sorts. They realized that what they thought had been living was a sham. They had been awakened by these strangers and felt compelled to try and wake up a lethargic world— a world that was provided with a glimmer of hope with the establishment of an Earth colony on the second planet in the Epsilon Eridani solar system 10.5 light years away.

By 2097, Abel and Megan had made it to Africa and were lecturing others on living life to the fullest. They talked about themselves and what naïve fools they had been until an enlightened team of very large men from an obscure Order had shown them the way. They were enthusiastic crusaders, usually filling the largest of venues. On many occasions, a huge tent was set up in what seemed like the middle of nowhere, but people traveled from all over filling it up to hear these two speak, or "preach" as some would soon call it.

It was at one of these meetings under a tent that Adio Mwanjuma attended out of curiosity. His curiosity led to skepticism and then to interest and finally to enthusiasm. Adio listened with rapt attention to the story of these strange men that dressed in white who towered over people. He was skeptical at first about their apparent ability to fly down from above and how their very presence would make people develop an inner peace. On the lighter side, both Abel and Megan marveled at how much these people could eat and drink as well as how they never seemed to do anything physical but were in incredible physical condition. "One was over seven feet tall and weighed at least 300 pounds but was as gentle as a lamb," said Megan.

"And oh yes," added Abel, "these guys were anything but tightwads, paying for things with gold and silver coins. I mean solid gold and silver. Who does that?"

Adio found all of this quite incredible, and he wasn't sure he believed it all. He was a bit of a cynic after all. However, he did notice that he felt different. He was lifted from the lethargic funk he had been in ever since the death flu struck in 2071. He left the tent thinking, *I have wasted twenty-six years. I have ideas. It is time to do something about it. If I fail, I fail, but doing nothing for fear of failing is failure. I need to find the right tool to do it. Wouldn't it be something if I could find one of these special people?*

He pondered this. He looked at every large man with the hopes that maybe they would be "the one." He looked. He pondered. He plotted. And then one day…

Chapter 6
Princess Charm-E-Ine

Charmy could hear the village slowly coming awake in the morning. She had an epiphany and was now so filled with excitement that she wanted to rush out of her assigned hut and announce her plans. But she would wait until midday when the village elders would gather for a meal and discuss village issues.

The village wasn't especially large; there were about ninety people in total. The village was next to a river and had well-tended fertile fields. The village didn't appear rich, but they certainly seemed better off than many. They had fish from the river, plenty of crops, and an occasional four-legged crop-raider that would be turned into a type of barbecue. The village also had a closely guarded secret. Less than two miles from the village itself, villagers would go to a hill and occasionally find a diamond. The elders would trade these from time to time to provide the village with the essentials they couldn't make themselves. The elders were shrewd in their dealings in order to keep the secret safe.

There weren't many children, which was consistent with the rest of the world. A few women of childbearing age were pregnant, though, probably reflecting the work Charmy and her former teammates had done to get humanity out of its lethargic mindset. Still, it meant the majority of the villagers were well above middle age. It was this group of people to whom she would unveil her plan, but in order for it to work she had to make them believe it was their idea.

At midday, Charmy casually invited herself to join the elders in their meal, once again impressing all of them with the amount of food she could pack away. There was nothing significant on the agenda for the day, so a distraction from a very pretty woman was well-received. Small talk gradually got around to Charmy asking, "Has anyone ever tried to unite the African nations? You know, like the United States of America or the old European Union?"

Senior elder Adio Mwanjuma was about seventy years old. He was a large man, and Charmy guessed that he was quite formidable in his youth before adding girth to his waist. He had a large mouth and equally large teeth that flashed brightly when he smiled. They were even more impressive when he gave out a hearty laugh, which he seemed to do regularly. Adio seemed to contemplate everything and made it a point to study Charmy carefully ever since she arrived. Was this the person he had hoped to find, but by fate or perhaps something else, she had found him?

Adio studied Charmy now while contemplating her question and finally answered with, "Well, yes, there have been many that thought they could do it. In fact, there are some today that think that they can do it. Unfortunately, they have all tried to do it by force, and people resist. That's why there is still fighting in Africa. These idiots think that if they defeat another idiot, the general population will fall in line and do their bidding. It's not going to happen. I believe most people in Africa want to peacefully get along. They simply need someone that has a vision for the future that would invite unification but not try to force it."

Charmy said, "Elder Mwanjuma, you could be that person. You're intelligent and the villagers seem to love you."

Adio appeared startled by this comment and then laughing so hard he could barely get out his words. "Ha! Are you—ha ha— are you kidding? Who would want to follow an old man like me? My only vision is to have a quiet and healthful life for our village. You would be a better candidate!"

"No one knows me," said Charmy, a little too quickly to sound credible.

For the longest time, there was an awkward silence, with all the elders looking at Charmy. Finally, one of the other elders said, "Actually, I think that's a good idea. You seem to know most of the languages spoken in Africa. You certainly make us feel comfortable. You have this quiet self-confidence that would go a very long way. Plus, you have an impressive, almost royal, stature. Have you considered a long-term vision for Africa?"

With the slightest of smiles, Charmy thought to herself, *This is going even better than I could have imagined.* Then she responded, "I am flattered, but I don't think I could unite Africa. Certainly not all by myself."

Adio said, "No, not by yourself. We would help. There are twelve of us, and we would help get the ball rolling, like ambassadors." And as he looked around to the other eleven elders, they were all nodding in the affirmative. "And," he added with some excitement in his voice, "I think I have a long-term vision to help with the unification."

Charmy thought, *Wow! Who is leading whom here?*

One of the other elders with narrowed eyes said to Adio, "What have you got up your sleeve?"

"Well," said Adio, "Do you remember when the United Nations originally proposed the Interstellar Space Fleet?"

"Yessss," was a quiet reply. "So what?"

Adio continued, "Remember they wanted to have seven ships. The seventh ship was to be the responsibility of the Arabian and African nations. We could never stop fighting long enough to get our act together, so only six ships were built. I felt we had relegated ourselves to second-class citizens of Earth by not getting with the program. It was a very disappointing time for me."

With much curiosity another elder asked, "And what's your point?"

"We should build one," said Adio.

To say Charmy was extremely surprised by this would have been an understatement, but she remained quiet. Then one of the elders that had also been quiet up to this point said, "Just like that, huh? Why didn't I think of that? Adio, you're crazy. Even if we could get the Arab nations to join in, what would we do with it?"

40

"Wouldn't it make a great place for a party?" said a smiling Adio. "Look, I'm not saying we should start building one tomorrow. In the first place, we would need the Stellar Commission for just about everything to build one. Plus, I don't think we have many astronauts hanging around here looking for work. But wouldn't it be a wonderful source of pride if there were a new star ship with Africa written on the hull? I don't think that should be a focal point right now but hold that vision for the future."

Adio leaned towards Charmy and staring straight at her said. "I'd be willing to bet this is close to something you had in mind right along, wasn't it?"

Charmy was actually stunned with the way this took off. Her mind was racing. *What have I started? A star ship was definitely not part of my thinking. I really have lost control. Correction, it appears I never had control. I'm the one being manipulated. I didn't give this Adio enough credit. He sees right through me.* But she said honestly, "Not exactly."

Adio gave a hearty laugh and said, "Maybe not exactly, but I'm pretty close. You don't need to respond." Taking charge, he added, "Tomorrow we start. We will each go to a neighboring village and invite their leaders to come for a feast of celebration. Let's see, a celebration of the survival. Yes, that's it. A celebration of the twenty-fifth anniversary of the last Death Flu victim."

An elder asked, "Do you even know when that was?"

"Nope," said Adio, "and it doesn't matter. It's close enough. Charmy and I will be heading west to invite as many village leaders as we can to the celebration. The rest of you are to cover the other points of the compass. Once people are here, we will introduce them to our Charmy. Our goal should be to get these people excited about an African future and send them off to even more villages even further out. It's a pyramid scheme, and at the top we will be placing Charmy." Then Adio added, "And I think we need a title for Charmy, something other than President or Grand Magnificent Ruler or any other foolish title some of these crackpot leaders have

41

assumed. I propose Princess Charm-E-Ine. It has a mysterious tone in origin yet seems fitting to someone of Charmy's physical stature and the way she carries herself."

Charmy thoughts swirled. *My God. I never had control over this at all. Adio must have been thinking about it for some time. He is in control and is about to set me up as a puppet.*

As Adio dismissed the group, he asked Charmy to stay behind. When no one was within earshot, he pulled up close to Charmy and with a broad grin looked squarely in her eyes and quietly said the most chilling thing Charmy had heard in a very long time. "I know who you are. Or more correctly, I know what you are. I knew it the minute you walked into the village, or perhaps more correctly when you flew into the village. I saw you. I know what kind of powers you have over people and they don't affect me. I wasn't sure your kind really existed, but here you are. You are what I've been looking for. With you, I can finally bring peace and harmony to Africa. We will be partners, but you will be the face of our new Africa. You have nothing to fear because my goal is the same as yours, and," he added with a chuckle, "we won't need any of your gold and silver coins."

Adio got up, threw his head back, and laughed so loud that everyone within a mile must have heard him. He then strolled off, still laughing and leaving Charmy sitting alone.

Charmy was stunned, having never been a situation like this. Her thoughts went wild. *I don't know what just happened, but I have been played. This Adio is obviously a lot more powerful than I could have ever imagined. Who is he? He says our goals are the same. Are they? Does he really know my goals? Does he really know who I am? How would he know that?*

Quietly she said to herself, "Princess Charm-E-Ine of the Union of African Nations." Smiling, she added, "That does have nice ring to it." But as these thoughts and more kept repeating in her head, she suddenly found herself exhausted.

Chapter 7
Union of African Nations

The village elders had shared their plan with the rest of the village. They all agreed it was a noble cause and enthusiastically pledged support. With that pledge, Adio asked for a change in thinking. New efforts were to be put forth by the village to get things started. Volunteers were recruited to mine more diamonds to help pay for the celebration, travel, and possible recruitment. With that, others needed to put more effort to provide the food, lodging, and entertainment for the many guests that would be coming to the village in the near term.

With the village now part of the plan, it was on to the real test. True to his word, Adio and his village elders did spread out and invited neighboring village elders to celebrate the anniversary of the end of the Death Flu. With the promise of a celebration, nearly all that had been invited to this first of many gatherings came.

Adio strategically organized the seating so that each of the newcomers would be close to Charmy. He knew that her very presence would have a calming effect thus allowing each guest to be receptive to his proposal. Food, drink, dancing, and singing went on for hours before Adio stood up as the sun was setting.

Adio's speech started with the Death Flu and what it had meant to those that had survived. He managed to reach further back in time to lament the fact that Africa, as a continent, did not participate in the historic undertaking that eventually allowed mankind to travel to the stars. "What a memorial it would be to those many millions that died to finally rebuild an Africa united in peace and to take our place among the rest of the world's nations that have moved forward and toward the stars without us. While we here are from different villages and have different beliefs, we are all Africans. We should be proud of that fact and unite—not under some dictatorship but under a benevolent leadership with representatives from all African nations who truly represent our goals of peace and prosperity.

"We are blessed to have someone that can lead us to the path we seek. Princess Charm-E-Ine is the kind of person we want to lead us. She is intelligent. She has a peaceful, loving heart and soul. She believes in a representative government that represents all people. She will work with representatives from all of our nations to make decisions based on what is best for all.

"Princess Charm-E-Ine is the last of her village and therefore holds no ties to any group. She came to our village seeking refuge. She asked for nothing more. But from the time she entered our village, we knew she came from royalty, of the ancient Nubian Empire, and could be the leader we have all been seeking for so many generations.

"Our vision is to spread the word from individual to individual within each nation. Each nation will then determine what is best for them, but it is our belief that most will want to join our new Union of African Nations.

"Now, I know many, if not all, are wondering how do we deal with the dictators and strongmen that want to hold power and have armies willing to do their bidding. Princess Charm-E-Ine is not a mere figurehead to our cause. A derivative of her name means harmony. It is not just a name. Her very presence brings harmony. You feel it today, don't you? The Princess will meet with each and every one of these tyrants and bring them to our way of thinking. If not, I am more than confident their followers will abandon them. Trust me when I say that Princes Charm-E-Ine has that power."

The speech went on for an hour. Whether it was Charmy's presence or the impact of Adio Mwanjuma's speech, Charmy wasn't sure, but at the end of the speech everyone present pledged allegiance to this new and wonderful cause. Obvious to Charmy was only a suggestion of a future Star Ship Africa.

The eleven new delegates and the original twelve elders from the host village slept soundly that night, likely helped along with the abundant consumption of alcoholic beverages. The next day after a grand breakfast, all but Adio and Charmy went off to their villages and beyond to recruit more into the cause.

44

Once they had departed, Adio said to Charmy, "We are going to the one village that did not send an elder. I am not surprised by this one. That village, actually a reasonably good-sized town, has a strong man that intimidates all the other elders and villagers in the area. Turning him will be a good test of our theory that you can make a change."

Charmy, still not comfortable with this so-called partnership said, "You mean *your* theory, don't you? I never said I could change people."

Adio, taken aback by this comment, said, "Well, I guess you are right about that. In fact, you haven't said much of anything since this mission started. You are on board with all this, aren't you?" Then, in an almost pleading voice, he added, "You have to be on board. I am seventy-one years old. Only God knows how long I will be on the top of the sod and not beneath looking up at the roots, so if I seem to be in a rush to see this vision of peace and unity coming to fruition, I guess it is because I am in fact worried I might not."

Charmy thought about this for few minutes, which seemed like an eternity to Adio. Finally, she said, "Yes, I am on board. But I think it is time to set some parameters. I have no issue with you leading the charge. In fact, it is probably good that I am not promoting myself. However, when I signal that you are to let me take the lead, you need to step back."

Relieved, Adio said, "You had me scared for a minute. No problem. By the way, I've been thinking about a new capital for the new Union of African Nations."

Charmy simply stared at him.

Getting the message, Adio said defensively, "I was just thinking! I mean we need to think about this."

"Actually," said Charmy, "I have thought about this. While it is a bit early, I first considered the geographic center of Africa itself."

"Wow! That's great," said Adio. "I like the thought of starting from scratch in the middle."

"Not really that great," said Charmy. "It happens to be in the middle of the Congo, and the conditions there are less than wonderful. There is a town called Pokola that is close, however. It is still in the Congo, but I'm thinking there may be enough infrastructure for us to have a starting point. But I think we should just keep that between us for now. The people of Pokola may have other thoughts."

Contrary to Adio's usual wordy response, he only said, "OK."

"All right," said Charmy, "let's go meet this mini dictator-in-the-making and see what we can do."

Two days later, Princess Charmy and Adio Mwanjuma entered the town run by Mugabi. The first thing they noticed was the look of suspicion they received. Adio couldn't help but notice this look eventually changed to one of relief, and there were smiles as he and Charmy passed by. The same was noticed as they entered the administration building. When they asked to see Mugabi, there was reluctance after they said they had no appointment. After looking at Charmy, the clerk said she would check, and soon after they entered Mugabi's office. It was large and looked like something you might expect to see in a major capital city. Mugabi, dressed in the fashion of a self-appointed dictator, said as they entered, "I am most busy. What do you want?"

Charmy, responding in Mugabi's own dialect, said without wasting any words, "We are here to recruit you into the cause to establish the Union of African Nations."

"Ah, that is my goal as well," said Mugabi. "I welcome your help to make me President."

"No, no!" said Adio as he burst into a hearty laugh. "Not you, you idiot. It will be under Princess Charm-E-Ine standing before you."

During this brief exchange of words, Charmy had moved to the front Mugabi's desk and sat down while simply staring at Mugabi. Mugabi was taken completely off guard and started looking for the right words to counter. But before he could utter a word, Charmy simply put her finger to her lips and held it there until Mugabi sat back in his chair. He was obviously upset. After a few minutes of eternity for Mugabi, Charmy said, "I can see your soul. You are not a good man. You lead by fear. Those days are over for Africa. It is our mission to lead Africa to peace and unity using compassion for all. You can join us following the new direction or move on."

Adio was shocked at how direct Charmy was with this man. Adio was under the impression that Charmy would move much slower, using her special abilities to change others' thinking. There was absolutely nothing subtle about this confrontation.

Just as suddenly as they had entered the office, Charmy stood up and looking down at Mugabi said, "We will wait outside for you answer." Then smiling at Adio said, "Let's go."

The exchanges had occurred with the office door open, and as they left the room, a stunned clerk with her mouth wide open watched the two pass by and take seats saying nothing. The clerk was still standing as the office door slowly closed. Minutes passed before there was a gun shot.

Charmy looked at Adio and said, "He was an evil man. I could see it. He had no redeeming qualities worth wasting our time for, but it was his choice to take the coward's way out."

A now shaking Adio, having never suspected Charmy had this power, said, "You can make people do that?"

"No," said Charmy. "I can only show peace and tranquility. If someone is not receptive, well, I guess it is too much for them to handle." Then, turning to a shocked clerk said, "Do you have the means to call a general meeting of the town's citizens?"

"Ummmm, I, I mean, yes," stammered the clerk.

"Good. Call a meeting for tomorrow at noon. Tell everyone that Mugabi has resigned and that Princess Charm-E-Ine will be speaking to them of a new order. Oh, and have someone clean up that mess in the office. And in the meantime, tell Mugabi's lieutenants that they need to come here for a meeting of great importance. Give them one hour from now."

A wide-eyed Adio sat staring at a new Princess Charm-E-Ine that he felt he had unleashed on the world. His confidence was shaken.

That night after meeting with Mugabi's lieutenants and getting educated with the new order, Charmy said to Adio, "I know that's not what you expected. Actually, neither did I until we met Mugabi. Something inside me said there was little reason to waste time on him. It is done, and we shall move on. Tomorrow, you will introduce me as Princess Charm-E-Ine. Use the same mantra we have been using about peace and unity. I will explain that we are establishing the Union of African Nations. I will then tell them they have an opportunity for free elections to select a new local leader, probably a mayor and a representative to the new Union. I will tell them that you, a most trusted advisor, will remain behind until the election process is complete."

"What will you do?" asked Adio.

"I will be paying visits to more petty dictators identified by the other elders. The elders will accompany me as you did, and, well, we'll see how it goes." Charmy then looked at Adio and smiled.

Two years later, the Union of African Nations was firmly established, with the new capital being built in Pokola. With a nearly unanimous vote, Princess Charm-E-Ine was elected as the new union's sovereign leader. Using Great Britain as a model, Parliament ran the government, but with Princess Charm-E-Ine's ability to influence, she provided far more power than the King or Queen might over British Parliament. The year was 2102.

Chapter 8
African Space Exploration

In 2108, Princess Charm-E-Ine and the Union of African Nations Parliament were ready for an undertaking that would bring new stature to the Union. The entire continent—always with some exceptions, of course—was at peace. With the peace came optimism and prosperity. Mindful that the population was but ten percent of what it been before the Death Flu of 2071, it seemed everyone wanted to make the world, or at least *their* part of the world, a better place. Where populations were small, people were encouraged to move to more densely populated areas. Many tribal boundaries no longer seemed important with the new sense of unity. Abandoned towns and cities were stripped of everything that was useful, and the land was restored to as natural of a state as possible. Through genetic engineering, animals once thought lost forever were being reintroduced into the new wild.

Resources, once in the hands of corporations long ago, were now being managed by the new government headed by Princess Charm-E-Ine, affectionately referred to as Charmy in all but the most formal occasions. The new union had a surplus of funds that were used for prudent investments in the future such as research and infrastructure that would have the least impact on the environment. This was unthinkable only a few years earlier.

Charmy was placed in power partly because of who she was and partly because she was manipulated by Adio, who knew who she was. However, she wasn't naïve and wanted to make certain that the good works in place would remain that way. To that end, she surrounded herself with advisors who had both the ability to see the world as it should be and who would let her know when she might be going astray.

Adio was one of those advisors, and one piece of advice he gave was to recruit the same couple that had made him look for someone like Charm-E-Ine. Abel and Megan Fisher were still in Africa lecturing, now more than ever preaching, on what living should be. They weren't hard to find and were invited to meet with the Princess. They, of course, accepted.

They were not what the Princess expected. On the other hand, the Princess was exactly what they expected.

"Princess Charm-E-Ine," started Abel, "it is a pleasure to finally meet you. We had thought all of your kind had disappeared when the Earth Gate had been opened to EEb."

"In fact," added Megan, "we weren't aware that there were more of you than the six that had been involved with the Gate project. It is obvious to us now that the Order to which you belong is much larger than we understood."

Charmy thought, *Who were these people?* But instead, she asked, "What do you know about the Order?"

"Not a whole lot," responded Megan. "The people we met were all very large and handsome as you are. They said their mission was to help mankind through counseling, but they weren't allowed to physically assist. They all seemed to have the ability to make people see things differently and want to make things better. What they did for Abel and me was so profound there aren't words to express the impact. The leader of the group we worked with, Gabe-Re-El, was a very formidable individual and had a great vision for mankind."

Abel added, "And the technology these guys had was amazing, being able to fly around effortlessly the way they did. But we don't have to tell you about that being one with the Order."

"Well," said Charmy, "it isn't all as it might seem. I have left the Order. I am still a firm believer in the goals of the Order, but I have decided to take a more hands-on approach. As a result, and with a lot of manipulation by my friend here, Adio Mwanjuma, I am obviously in more than an advisory position."

"What do you mean manipulated?" asked Adio, who up until now had remained quiet.

51

Charmy simply turned her head and looked at him with the slightest of grins.

"Well maybe a little," stated Adio, "but it was all to…" Charmy suddenly held up her hand and turned back to her quests.

Abel and Megan exchanged glances and wondered what that was about, but they said nothing.

Getting back on topic, Charmy said, "Look, the UAN is considering a bold initiative. Actually, I suppose the initiative was started long before the UAN was ever conceived back in the 2050's, when the United Nations Stellar Commission was formed to build and send the Star Ship Fleet off to Epsilon Eridani to build a Gate. Africa and the Middle East were asked to participate with its own Star Ship. That, of course, never happened. With our new African union, we see things differently. The Union wants to take its place as a world leader. In fact, many believe we are now the world leader, but are being ignored.

"We want to take our place at the table, so to speak, and have our own Star Ship. We want our people to reach for the stars just as the rest of the world did so many decades ago. The two of you are the most knowledgeable in all of Africa about the Gates and the Star Ships. I would like you to be the official government advisors to me on this project. Your shared title would be Secretaries of African Space Exploration. What do you say?"

Abel nearly shouted, "Good grief! You don't mess around. We're not even African."

Megan added, "You know that's a lot to take in. Can we think about and get back to you?"

"Oh, sure," said Charmy. "Go next door where you'll be alone and get back to me in, oh, let's say maybe an hour?"

Adio laughed. "Ha ha! You won't need an hour." And somehow both Abel and Megan knew Princess Charm-E-Ine had already worked the mind game her kind had inflicted upon them before.

When they left the room and were by themselves, Abel and Megan embraced and whispered simultaneously into each other's ear, "What the hell? Why not?"

Exactly fifty-nine minutes from the time they left the room, Abel and Megan returned to the main room where the Princess and Adio remained, and announced, "OK. We're in." Neither Abel nor Megan let it be known they had made up their minds as soon as they went next door. For the remaining fifty-eight minutes, they sat in the room smiling at each other making the Princess and Adio wait.

Chapter 9
Star Ship Africa

Princess Charm-E-Ine of the Union of African Nations was pleased but far more sedated than her two Secretaries of African Space Exploration. Abel and Megan were nearly giddy as the three of them entered the United Nations Stellar Commission headquarters. Years ago, Abel and Megan had met the twins Richard Sylva and Dawn Cohen when they returned to Earth via the Gates established between EEb and Earth. Richard and Dawn had been Vice Admiral of Academics and Science (VAAS) and Vice Admiral of Operations (VAO) in the space fleet, respectively, under their mother, the Admiral Ada Sylva.

Today was something of a class reunion. When Abel and Megan entered the small conference room, Richard and Dawn stood up and greeted their guests with sincere hugs and kisses—even though they had met and celebrated just that one time when the twins came back to Earth through the Gate. Charmy was moved.

After pleasantries and introducing Princess Charm-E-Ine to Richard and Dawn, Abel and Megan filled them in on what they had been doing since 2097, when they left the Earth Wormhole Gate complex. This led up to their recruitment by the UAN to head up the Department of African Space Exploration.

Richard asked, "So we have heard a little about this African space idea, but it isn't clear exactly what it is. You don't have rockets or anything else space-related that we're aware of, do you?"

"No, we don't," said Charmy. "What we have is a desire to make up for lost time. The continent of Africa, now united in the Union, regrets not being involved with the mission that sent the six Star Ships out to possibly save mankind from itself. We want to fix that by building our own Star Ship for exploration and have a crew made up of mostly Africans."

Both Richard and Dawn were a bit taken aback by this, but not wanting to completely dampen expectations probed a bit.

"Who will pay for this enterprise?"

"The UAN has the financial resources now to fund this."

"Who will actually build this ship?"

"The ship would be built under the authority of the United Nations Stellar Commission."

"Where do you think it will go?"

"Right now, we don't know. We suppose that under the Commission, a joint decision might be made."

"Is it safe to assume you're aware that our fleet of ships is already out in space? Also, the Commission has never considered sending one ship on a mission alone."

"Yes, but we also believe that after all this time the technology has improved. Therefore, teaming up ships may not always be necessary."

Dawn then stated, "This, of course, is a bit of a surprise to us and many, many things would have to be worked out, but here are a few things you might not have considered. First of all, much of the knowledge to build the Star Ships was lost when the Death Flu struck. The shuttle fleet that we had when building the fleet is down to one, though we are building a couple more. We do have limited research capabilities around the country and the globe that have theorized changes to a new class of Star Ships, but they are just theories at the moment. Believe it or not, most of the advanced thinking in this area was done within the space fleet itself because the bulk of the scientists that worked on this here on Earth were wiped out with the Death Flu. The work being done now is a result of those ship-bound scientists returning to Earth and starting research programs over from scratch. Basically, the Commission as it stands today is just a shell of what it once was, only supporting the existing ships and everything else that is already in place."

Everyone starred at Princess-Charm-E-Ine in disbelief, wondering if she had heard anything Dawn and Richard had said. She responded with, "OK. When and where do we start?"

Richard said, "I don't think you were listening. The world is currently not as technologically advanced as it once was. A lot of what we had learned has been lost. We don't have the technological sophistication that went into the ships in the original design."

It was Abel's turn to respond with, "I think I understood that there is a new design for the fission/fusion engines. It is a slightly simpler design as far as controls are concerned and deemed much safer. Is that correct?"

"Yes," said Dawn. "It is somewhat safer, but it still can go critical quickly if it goes out of equilibrium and the overall system controls are still complex. Also, it is just a design."

Megan asked, "Do the systems have to be so complicated? What if we dumbed them down?"

"Well, we could, I suppose," said Dawn, "but that would mean more labor to keep things running properly."

Charmy knew exactly where this was going and, smiling to herself, knew that bringing the Fishers into the fold was a stroke of genius. On the other hand, she had to consider, *Was this really her idea?* But she said nothing and chose to let this scenario unfold.

Megan said, "Seems to me with thousands of people on board, labor isn't the problem. The problem might be a high level of sophistication, with many bells and whistles creating issues and potential problems. I have spent most of my life analyzing systems from the inside out, and while I marvel at what people could design, I also questioned why? I love technology, but not for the sake of technology itself. In this case, keeping it simple might be the way to go. Can that be done? Can we build a rock-solid Star Ship, making sure to build in the technology needed with redundancy but only what is actually needed? Can we train people to not just operate but to make repairs? And if repairs can be duct tape and bailing wire, so much the better."

The twins looked at each and asked to be excused, leaving the African delegation without a word. Lunch was sent in with apparent awareness of the Princess' ability to eat, as there was enough sandwich material to feed a small village. Exactly two hours and thirty-seven minutes later, Richard and Dawn reentered the conference room and sat down.

Richard said, "Look, we're not 100 percent convinced this is a good idea, but you seem to be very determined. Let's start and see how it goes. If the UAN is willing to fund this with the understanding that this might be nothing more than a boondoggle, the UNSC should be in. We'll start with the plans to build the ship. While building the ship, the UAN and UNSC will work together to build a trained crew. Somewhere along the line, we'll figure out what to do with the ship. Agreed?"

Princess Charm-E-Ine, in her most regal manner, stood up, shook the hands of the twins, and said, "On behalf of the Union of African Nations, I accept your offer and will return to my people and announce the good news. Thank you."

On June 1, 2110, the construction of the Star Ship Africa started. Where there had been nothing but space, the ship started to take shape in orbit around Earth. Not only did it boost the pride of the African Union, the pride spilled over the rest of the world, as many saw this as another advancement for mankind.

Chapter 10
Castaway

It didn't take too many months before routines were well-established on the Star Ships as they flew towards Tau Ceti. Very little occurred that wasn't expected. The ships had just finished a deceleration cycle, which provided the 0.5 g that allowed them to swing around and start to accelerate. The plan was similar to one used to get to Eridani Epsilon, alternating between deceleration with the ships' sterns facing the target and acceleration with the bows facing the target, providing the alternating 0.5 g and the 1.5 g inside the ship on each cycle.

Originally, the size of the planets indicated that humans wouldn't be able to survive because of calculated high gravity. As a result, plans were being made to potentially settle on one of the moons. Science, however, always brings about new discoveries and the original theories don't always prove to be correct. Careful studies of the TC planets from Earth and EEb tossed the theoretical gravity pull out the window. The overall planet's size was correct, but the density startled the scientific community because it indicated gravity lower than originally theorized, but it was still greater than that of Earth's. New studies showed that gravity on the two larger planets was slightly more than the 1.5 g being experienced on the Star Ships. Slightly increasing the acceleration cycle of the fleet during the trip would better acclimate the crews. This combined with strategic use of exoskeleton suits on the selected planet meant humans should be able to do more than just survive. With that settled and everything seeming to be working as it should, people started looking for new things to think about. It wasn't boring exactly, but it was just not very exciting.

This all changed when a weak but clear signal was unexpectedly picked up by the communications arrays. Word traveled through the fleet that it wasn't coming from New Hope Island on EEb, and it wasn't from Mother Earth. It was nothing anyone in the Admiral's staff could identify, but it was clearly a repetitive signal of some kind. Excited curiosity grew in the fleet.

The four ships used their antennae arrays to triangulate the signal and determined that it was coming from somewhere off of the starboard stern and at a fifteen-degree angle below the artificial horizon. It was also overtaking the fleet at a relatively good pace.

The scientists and research engineers on board were naturally more than just curious about this discovery, and they soon determined from astronomical observations that the signal was coming from a small moon-sized rock. Or was it a rock? Rocks, no matter the size, don't emit a constant signal. In any case, a collision would not be in the best interest of the fleet.

The Admiral ordered the brain trust to determine what the likelihood of a collision might be. He bypassed the usual protocol of notifying Shinya Ishikawa, the VAAS, and went directly to his staff for fear that the meaning of his order would be lost. The rock was moving at a constant speed, but the fleet in its acceleration mode was continually picking up speed. The fleet could maneuver within certain parameters by slowing the rate of acceleration or turning, but nothing more.

As the rock got closer, the signal got stronger, and as it got stronger, the curiosity about the rock and its signal got stronger. Could the fleet simply ignore this? The answer was "no."

Finally, with a great deal of trepidation, Admiral Dodson allowed himself to be convinced that an investigation was necessary in the name of scientific inquiry. The scientists had determined that in five days, the rock and the fleet would be in visual contact with each other. At which point, the fleet could reduce acceleration long enough to launch two shuttlecrafts to survey the rock and discover the source of the signal. The shuttlecrafts' crew would then have eighteen hours to complete this task before the fleet was out of the shuttlecrafts' flight range. Shuttlecraft 1, from British Commonwealth, and Shuttlecraft 3, from China, with crews of five each would do the survey.

On May 4, 2113, the fleet's acceleration was slowed to 0.3 g and the shuttlecrafts were launched. As they left, Captain Alan Parks couldn't help himself when he conjured up the old Star Wars movie reference, which he butchered, as a farewell to his shuttle crew, "May the 4th be with you." He laughed, but he was also the only one that got it.

The British Commonwealth Shuttlecraft 1 circled counter-clockwise, and the China Shuttlecraft 3 circled clockwise with the goal of meeting up where the signal was the strongest. Shuttlecraft 1 was first on the scene and radioed back, "Admiral, this is Lieutenant Wellington. Ummm. The signal seems to be coming from a ship of some kind that is on the rock. The ship appears to be damaged, like it had a rough landing. In fact, it looks like the ship is partially in the rock."

The bridge crew became so animated with this news that the Admiral had to say, "Hey, everyone, quiet down. I can't hear the lieutenant! Lieutenant, move in as close as you can safely and give details."

"Yes, sir."

To the assembled staff on the bridge, the Admiral asked, "Does anyone have any thoughts? I mean, other than that this is absolutely incredible."

From the assembled staff, the response above the din was, "We better leave it alone. We need to look inside. We have no idea what might be in it. We could take precautions. We can't leave without knowing what it is. Maybe someone is in it. Or maybe *something* is in it. Maybe the beacon was to warn us to stay away. I think it is a distress beacon." And on and on it went for the next fifteen or so minutes.

Finally, an overwhelming curiosity along with the excitement of something new took over, and the Admiral was convinced to look inside.

"Lieutenant," said the Admiral. "What are you seeing?"

"Well, sir, we see something that looks like a hatch, but it is nothing like anything we could dock with. I'm not so sure we want to go in there anyway."

"Admiral, this is Lieutenant Lee on the China shuttlecraft. We have discussed this, and the five of us are willing to take a look inside. We're pretty sure we can jam our airlock door against the side of the ship and cut an opening. Once we leave, however, the seal would be broken and any atmosphere that might be inside would escape."

The Admiral asked both lieutenants, "Have you seen anything that might indicate any life on board?"

"No, sir," was the response.

The Admiral took a few minutes to consider the options. Finally, he said, "We don't have all the time in the world here to figure out what might be the right thing to do. So I guess we'll do something, even if it is wrong. Lieutenant Lee, I accept your offer, but first things first. Do land or whatever you plan to do and jam your airlock against the ship. I want everyone in your crew to put on their suits. Only two of you are to enter the airlock and bore a small hole only large enough to extend a probe to see if there is any atmosphere inside and what it might be. Be aware that if anything goes wrong, the two in the airlock may be sacrificed. Are you still willing?"

"Yes, sir," was the response.

Over the next two hours, the China shuttlecraft maneuvered into place and did as the Admiral advised. When done, Lieutenant Lee said, "Sir, it appears there is very little atmosphere on board. What is here indicates that it is, or was, very much like our atmosphere, but it is impossible to know how thin it might have been. I have inserted a fiber-optic camera and am looking around. There is no indication of any life on board."

After a few minutes, the lieutenant continued with, "I see some kind of glass-covered chambers and will try to get the camera angled for a better look." Then, after another pause, "I see six chambers. One has a slight glow. Oh God! There are people inside! Five appear to be emaciated. One looks like he—I think it is a he—is sleeping with a bunch of tubes stuck in him. He looks human! There is a purple flashing light on what looks like a control panel. Sir, what do you want us to do?"

Back on the British Commonwealth bridge, there was stunned silence. Finally, Shinya Ishikawa said, "I don't know what anyone thought we would find, and I'm not sure what we did find. As you said, Admiral, we don't have lot of time to determine the best course of action, so let me make a proposal. It appears there is the possibility that one being may be alive. I would say that if that is the case, it might not survive if we leave it. It may not survive if we bring it on board, but it seems to me that it would stand a better chance. However, we have no idea of what this being might be. If we can remove the chamber with the being inside, we should do so and bring it here. We can decontaminate the exterior and place it in a sealed isolation room. Once it's on board and we're under way, we'll have more time to consider our next move. I think an opportunity to interact with another species is worth the risk, and as I said I suspect the being stands the best chance of survival with us."

The Admiral looked at Shinya in disbelief. This was the most articulate the VAAS had been on anything up to this point. Neil did note to himself that this curiosity they had discovered was just the kind of thing Shinya would want to study and ignore any possible consequence. Didn't the good doctor once say, "Anything for science?"

"Well, ladies and gentlemen," said the Admiral, "we have a proposal. What do you think? Is it worth the risk?"

There were some murmurs against bringing the being on board, but the strong appeals to do so ruled the day. The one caveat that everyone agreed upon was to use extreme caution.

"Lieutenant Lee," said the Admiral, "if you can remove the chamber with the being inside without damaging it, please proceed. Use extreme caution. I don't want anyone hurt."

"Yes, sir," was the response. And four hours later, both shuttlecrafts were heading for the British Commonwealth.

As they were about to land in the shuttlecraft bay, Lieutenant Lee reported, "Admiral, we had to disconnect some of the cables, hoses, and tubes to get the chamber out of the being's ship. I think we started something. We're seeing some movement inside the chamber. Not much, but something is happening. The outside of the chamber has been sanitized, as you commanded, and we've sealed it with a wrapping. But if that thing opens up, I don't know what is going to happen."

The Admiral answered, "The deck is cleared as well as the passage to the sealed isolation room. When you land, move as quickly as you can."

"Yes, sir."

And as the door to the isolation room was closed, the inside of the chamber cover became foggy.

Chapter 11
Where Am I?

Raman-I-El was jolted with a shock, a kind of defibrillation. Except this wasn't anything like what he'd been told to expect. He understood that this was his first time coming out of stasis, but still his foggy thoughts were, *The training staff could have been a bit more honest about what to expect. Did they think I wouldn't go if they told me everything?* He waited for the purging to start next, not that he had a choice. He was only barely conscious and was not able to move. But nothing happened. *Oh wait,* he thought. *Something is happening. The stasis chamber seems to be moving. That's odd. In fact it is moving quite a bit and there are a lot of strange sounds. Like something or some things are being cut and ripped.*

He couldn't tell how long exactly, but after a period of time the movement stopped. That was good, he thought, but why isn't the stasis fluid purging? *Something isn't right.* After another undetermined period of time, he was able to move, if only slightly, but the stasis fluids and tubes were still in place. Systems were not working. Raman-I-El was now beginning to get concerned, bordering on panicking, and was trying to think about what he might have to do to take control. *This is not going to be pleasant,* he thought, and as that thought concluded, his body started to rebel.

He realized that the chamber was in fact filled with oxygen to help his body recover, so at least that was on track. But that wouldn't make much of a difference if the stasis fluids couldn't be purged. Raman-I-El's still fuzzy brain was racing now as he tried to piece together what the next move might be. Trying to be rational, he thought, *Somehow, I have to get the cover off the chamber and pull these tubes out and maybe, just maybe, I can get my lungs clear.*

And with significant effort, his weak body forced the chamber cover off. The tube going down his throat was pulled out, and Raman-I-El turned his head and started throwing up. At the same time, he could feel his lungs trying to purge as his body convulsed again and again. The pain all over his body was unbearable, but bearable it had to be. There was pain in his lungs and stomach as he started purging fluids gradually being replaced with air. The pain was intense as he gasped for breath, but with each breath there was a slightly greater sense of relief. Halfway through the process, he pulled the other tubes out his most private body parts and everything seemed to release at once. Instead of the fluids being syphoned off as they were supposed to, he found himself lying in a bed of putrid, thick green liquid. He visualized his situation and thought, *God help me, I am going to die!*

After more hours of retching and painful discharges, he thought that maybe he wouldn't die. A passing thought of, *If I do die, at least I wouldn't be in agony,* started to give way to curiosity as the pain started to subside.

He couldn't comprehend how many hours he laid in his putrid chamber completely exhausted. But he was slowly becoming more alert. Finally, he took note of his surroundings. What he was seeing added a new level of confusion and fear. A brown floor, green walls, and white ceiling replaced the familiar gray walls, floor, and ceiling that were there when he entered stasis. There was nothing else in the space, including the chambers of his companions or even his own chamber control panel. He and his chamber were alone in a rather large room devoid of anything else. A hundred unfocused thoughts went through his mind all at once. But they were all overridden with, *Where am I?*

Even more hours would pass before he could swing his legs over the side of the chamber, as the stasis fluids kept dripping onto the brown floor. The space was uncomfortably cold. The chamber seemed be on some kind of table, and it was much higher off the deck than he remembered. Looking around the space, he noted an unfamiliar door and some windows. Fear was replaced by an even greater fear when he saw several strange faces looking through the windows no further than ten feet away. They were all looking at him. Their appearance was similar to his to some degree, but they appeared to be somewhat smaller. They appeared to be talking among themselves about him. *Don't panic,* he thought. *And don't do anything that might get them upset.*

As Raman-I-El's body and mind started to clear further, he realized he must be a sight to whoever these beings might be. He had no clothing. He was covered with the stasis fluid. He had a scruffy beard, tangled hair, and long nails. In other words, he was disgusting looking and smelled even worse than he realized. And not that anyone could see, but he was also extremely hungry and thirsty.

After pondering the situation for a while and not seeing anything happening on the other side of the window, Raman-I-El looked straight at the beings and waved. All the heads looked at each other and became animated.

After a few minutes, as he started to think, *I hope they do something soon,* the door opened and one of the faces started to enter the room. This being obviously had on some kind of suit covering him from head to toe. The being moved slowly towards Raman-I-El, and when it was halfway between him and the door it started to speak slowly saying, "I'm Admiral Neil Dodson." And while the Admiral was talking, he made gestures toward himself. The Admiral hoped this would start some kind of communication.

Just like everyone else in the Order, Raman-I-El knew many languages. Actually, that wasn't correct; he didn't actually know languages. What he did was pick up a language simply by listening to a few words, and through a type of empathic understanding was able to communicate using the other being's language. Raman-I-El had the basics of this means of communication, but as he would learn later he didn't always get it right. Right now, however, he knew exactly what this being was saying and understood it. He didn't know, but he learned later that it was English with a hint of an accent. But while he was pleased to understand the greeting, the being wasn't prepared at all for the response.

Admiral Dodson stepped back in obvious shock when Raman-I-El answered with "Where am I?" Everyone that was watching from behind the windows looked at each other in complete disbelief. Was this creature human? Except for his size, he looked human. And as one female scientist soon regretted saying out loud, "And he certainly is male. Wow!" She then turned bright red.

For hours, the spectators had watched Raman-I-El purge himself of the stasis fluid. They knew he was in pain and felt helpless to assist him. Everyone was aware that they pulled this person—if that is what he was—from a wreck and that they might have killed him in doing so. It had been a decision that had been made in haste, with those involved believing there was no choice. They had felt certain he would eventually die if left where he was. As a group they thought, *We'll give him a fighting chance,* hoping it was the correct and compassionate choice.

That compassion seemed to be paying off, but now what? Still stunned by the question, Neil tried to explain saying, "You are on the Star Ship British Commonwealth. We would like to help you. What would you like?"

Raman-I-El didn't understand any of the Star Ship babble. How could a star be a ship? There was no context. He did understand the last question, though. As his list was getting longer by the moment, he put aside his concerns about where he was and said, "It is cold in here, and I'd like some clothes. I would like water to clean up. I would like food and drink."

Still not believing he was having this conversation, Neil asked, "What do you drink and eat?"

Raman-I-El talked at length, but it made no sense to Neil. Finally, Neil said, "I don't know what you mean. We will bring you some of what we have and maybe there is something there you can eat. Is that OK with you?"

Raman-I-El answered with, "I don't know what 'OK' is, but I'll taste it."

As the Admiral thought, *I suppose OK is somewhat meaningless,* he turned to the observation window and through his helmet radio ordered, "Anything that's in the kitchen."

A privacy screen was set up so the stranger could clean and dress himself. When he emerged, it was obvious the clothes weren't fitting very well. Neil guessed the stranger was about seven feet tall. His hair was straight blond. It was impossible to tell what his normal weight was, but later he had filled out to 292 pounds.

Food was brought out and placed on a table. The stranger stood as he tested, then ate chicken, potatoes, carrots, beets, and a variety of breads. He drank some water, but really lit into the beer; both the near beer and the full-strength variety. He ate and ate and drank and drank. Eventually, he got a little tipsy and sat down on the floor.

Neil said, "I'm sure you have many questions, as do we. I'll try to answer as best I can and hope you will as well. Do you have a name?"

"My name is Raman-I-El. Most call me Raman." And then Raman asked, "Where are my friends?"

Neil explained how they had found him and the fate of his companions. Raman was visibly upset and asked if he could be left alone for a while. He needed to rest. Blankets and a mattress were brought to the isolation room. Raman slept a natural sleep for sixteen hours, after which he once again consumed enough food and drink for four people.

Receiving permission, Neil ordered a physical to be done on Raman. The ship's doctor, Dr. MacFarlane, found a number of physical attributes about Raman that proved conclusively that he was not human. Inexplicably, however, the good doctor reported after some apparent debate with himself, "He appears to be a healthy, human specimen. I suggest a two-week quarantine, just to be safe, and then he can join the rest of us." Later on, Dr. MacFarlane only vaguely remembered doing the physical, even though it lasted for hours.

During the two-week quarantine, the Admiral neglected all other duties and talked with Raman. Some questions would take a long time to answer. Where was Raman going? The answer was meaningless. Where was he from? Again, the answer was meaningless. How long had he been in stasis? Raman had no idea.

Raman had just as many questions. Who were these beings, and how did they get stars to be ships to carry them around? Where did they come from? Having no context, it would take time for Raman to understand.

However the one question Raman and the humans had in common was how long had he been in stasis? To get that answer, Shinya Ishikawa, in one of his more tuned-in moments, suggested carbon-dating the stasis chamber. The results were shocking if they were to be believed.

Chapter 12

Voices

Princess Charm-E-Ine was feeling good and rather proud about what she had accomplished in a relatively short period of time. She wondered what the Boss, which she once reported to, might think of her if they knew what she were doing and liked to think that they would approve. Yes, she had gone rogue in deciding to live out her life trying to do something that she felt needed to be done, but she couldn't help believing that the Boss would approve. They may not have liked the way she went about it, but sometimes the ends do justify the means. In any case, Charmy knew she was determined to follow through.

The traditional uniform she wore as part of the Order had been replaced. The all-white, loose-fitting pants and blouse had been replaced by colorful red, yellow, and green robes with a matching headdress. Charmy took a little guilty pleasure with her appearance but was still naïve enough to not realize how stunning she appeared. Very few could look away when she gave a speech, as her towering size and perfect body proportions combined with a firm but reassuring voice often mesmerized them. The peace-loving people of Africa adored her, and the rest cowered in her presence. Even over the airwaves she could calm the most irritable personality.

Today's weekly meeting with her senior staff members had nothing particularly exciting on the agenda. Princess Charmy listened to status reports from each department and expressed the most interest regarding the nearly eradicated pooching of Africa's most vulnerable wildlife. The atmosphere of the room was casual. People would get up, fill their coffee cups or teacups, and sample a pastry with no pause in the conversation.

Without any indication of any problem, Charmy got a searing pain in her head and heard an internal voice say, "God, help me. I am going to die." Charmy, holding her head, then jumped to her feet. She did not recognize the voice, and looked around the room asking, "Who said that?"

Everyone else in the room froze and stared at the Princess. "Who's in trouble?" she asked.

"Excuse me, Princess Charm-E-Ine," said one cautious staff member, "what are you talking about?"

"Didn't you hear it? How could you not hear it? Someone said they were going to die."

A few tense seconds went by, with everyone in the room looking at each other and with Charmy standing with a look of panic on her face. "I didn't hear anything," said one member with everyone else muttering in agreement.

A few more seconds went by with stunned silence. Suddenly, Charmy left the room, leaving behind a confused and concerned audience full of men and women. Charmy went down the hall without another word, went into her office, and closed the door. Leaning against the door, she tried to gather her wits. *What just happened? I clearly heard a cry for help. It had to be from in the room. Is my staff messing with me for some reason? OK. Let's calm down and think this through.* And with that, Charmy moved from the door to a couch and lay down.

It wasn't long before the confused and concerned Princes Charmy was interrupted in her thoughts by a quick knock on the door. It was then that, without an invitation, Adio Mwanjuma entered. He closed the door and sat down across from Charmy saying, "What's going on?"

"I don't know. I don't believe you and rest of the staff are playing a game of some sort. Are you?"

"No! Of course not, but we are concerned. We've never seen you upset like that before."

"Adio, I heard 'God, help me. I am going to die,' as clear as if you were standing next to me and saying those words."

"Has anything like this happened before?"

"No."

"Forgive me for asking this and remember I'm not a doctor." Trying to add a little levity, Adio continued, "And I don't play one on T.V., but is there a history of mental illness in your family? Some humans suffer from something called schizophrenia, where they hear and see things that aren't there. For us, that usually develops at an earlier age. Not that you are old, by the way! Are your people susceptible to anything like that?"

Adio was one of the very few people to know that Charmy wasn't human, so she felt comfortable talking to him about things that were much more personal than she would discuss with others. "The simple answer is yes, but for those of us selected to be in the Order we have to go through a myriad of testing and anyone with the slightest chance of having a mental illness is rejected. I don't know what happened. I think I'll let it go as something weird and forget it. Let me stay here alone for a while to regain my wits and let everyone know that I'm OK. Thanks for checking on me."

Adio left. But try as she might, the incident wouldn't leave Charmy's mind. She kept mulling it over from every angle. Something that Adio said about mental illness triggered a vague memory of what the qualification exam for the Order had revealed. *What was it?* Whatever it was, there was something right there in some mental filing cabinet just waiting for the drawer to be opened. The drawer would not open, however, and she dozed off.

Hours later, Charmy was jolted awake by someone in the room saying, "Where am I?" It was the same voice she had heard before, but as she bolted upright to confront this person she saw she was still alone. Fear re-entered her mind. *This can't be happening. Someone is talking to me, and I can't see them.* And as that very thought came to her, the mental filing cabinet opened up and she remembered what the examination's doctors had told her so many years ago. "Apparently, you have an extremely rare condition, a unique configuration of your DNA, which gives you the ability to communicate over unknown distances with someone else with the same DNA. Documentation of this condition indicates that it is so

72

rare that you'll never be able to use it, so don't worry about it. You are perfectly fine."

What was that very human expression, she thought. *Ahh, yes. "Never say never."* Maybe "never" just happened. Charmy latched onto this thought, because if this was true then she wasn't nuts. She was "hearing" words from another of her people. But as this seemed to settle her down in one way, another concern rose up. Who was transmitting those thoughts? From where? Here on Earth? Someplace else? And what kind of trouble is this person having? One thing was certain—well, maybe two things. One thing she was certain about is that she would keep this to herself at least for now and not let others know she was hearing things if it happened again. And two, she would try to figure out how to make these communications attempts a two-way street.

For months after she reached this epiphany, Charmy would receive snippets of what she deduced were conversations that this unknown person was having with others. Each time, there seemed to be a sense of urgency or danger, which added to the mystery. Charmy soon believed that the feeling of urgency had been passed on to her. It was up to her to figure it all out.

Chapter 13
Lost Time

When the Admiral reviewed the carbon-dating results, he pursed his lips and looked over the top of his glasses at the VAAS. After a long pause, Neil asked, "Are you sure about this?"

Shinya, wringing his hands and shifting his eyes around the room, said, "Ummm, yes. We took multiple tests, and they are all within five percent of each other. Not much deviation."

Neil slowly looked from Shinya to the report and only said, "Wow," as he got up and headed to the quarantine area holding Raman.

Raman was looking far better than he had when he was first rescued; his hair and nails had been cut and his body was filling out. Neil was impressed—and jealous—with the muscle tone being developed, especially since Raman had been doing nothing except eating, drinking, and sleeping. Wearing his protective suit, Neil sat down across from the table where Raman was devouring even more food and washing it down with a large glass of beer.

Raman said, "This beverage you call beer is quite delicious. We don't have anything like this where I come from."

"That's a great segue to my question," said Neil. "Where are you from?"

"I could tell you," said Raman. He then added with a laugh, "But, as you might say, 'I'd have to kill you.' Seriously, I could tell you the name of our planet and solar system, but honestly it would be meaningless to you. I couldn't even point it out on a chart."

Giving Raman his patented look, Neil said, "Alright then, where were you going?"

Raman stopped eating to consider this and said, "Well, I'm not sure exactly. This was my first assignment, and I was the least senior in our group of six. Also, parts of my memory seem to be a bit foggy. Stasis isn't supposed to do that, but I guess it did this time. It might have something to do with our ship rudely meeting up with the asteroid. Anyway, I'm part of a benevolent order that tries to help civilizations make good decisions that can affect their future. We were heading to a planet that is in what I think you call the Bronze Age. I understand that it is a very violent place. Their idea of culture and their social systems, including government, are in a constant state of disruption. Obviously, they aren't as advanced as your society."

Neil thought about this. He had met and talked with a Head Bartender when the fleet was heading towards EEb. Later, this fellow fell into the good graces of Admiral Sylva and was made an advisor. He was a very big man, like this guy Raman, and it was rumored that others like him had helped get the Earth Wormhole Gate functioning. They never said anything about not being of Earth, but they did make reference to being members of a benevolent order. These thoughts were giving Neil a headache, but he continued his questions: "Do you have any idea how long you were in stasis?"

"No," said Raman, "though we were told when we left that it wasn't good to be in stasis for more than 350 of what I understand to be your year cycles, so it must be less than that. I guess weird things can happen to the brain with long stays in stasis. Apparently, that wouldn't be a problem on this planet we were going to. There was always something that needed attention, so no one would be in stasis that long."

"I see," said Neil. And then he asked, "Was your group the only group going to this planet?"

"Well, at this particular time, yes, but other teams had gone on before," said Raman, "The head of our Order would add teams as a planet's population increased."

The more questions Neil asked, the more he became fascinated, while at the same time feeling himself get angry. He thought, *These people interfere with civilizations and apparently think this is acceptable behavior. Worse, they think it is their duty.*

"Soooo," said Neil, "does the planet Earth mean anything to you?"

"Ummmm, I don't think so," said Raman. "I may know it by another name, but you know names are names, and they can change. Sometimes a name is meaningless, like the name of my planet."

"Yes, I suppose so," said Neil. "So how do you identify where you are going?"

"That's pre-programmed," said Raman. "I do know the planet we were going to is part of an interesting solar system. We were heading for the third planet from their star."

Neil was being jolted by every word Raman was saying, as Neil believed he was piecing things together. "Raman," said Neil. "Our planet is called Earth. Earth is the third planet from our sun. In about 1200 BC, our civilization was at the end of the Bronze Age."

Not catching on yet, Raman said, "That's quite a coincidence." Then he asked, "what does BC mean?"

Wow! thought Neil. But after a second of disbelief, he explained that BC stood for "Before Christ." "Without getting into the religious significance," he said, "our current calendar, or marking of days, started all over with Jesus Christ's birth. That was about 2,000 years ago, making our Bronze Age about 3,000 years ago."

"That was a long time ago," said Raman.

"Yes, it was," said Neil. "But there is more. We did some tests on your chamber using what we call carbon-dating. Guess what? As far we can tell, you were in that chamber for about 3,000 years."

A stunned Raman bolted to his feet, weaved back and forth and then collapsed. As he headed for the deck, his mind couldn't seem to comprehend that he had lost that much time. The irony that escaped him for the moment was that the descendants of the people he was initially sent to help were the very same ones who rescued him.

Chapter 14
Sharon and Raman

The Head Bartender on each ship did more than tend bar. Water used on each ship, no matter what for, was never considered "wastewater," as it would be used again and again. The main water holding tanks provided only makeup water. Used water was recycled with nutrients extracted for use on the horticulture decks. While the recycled water was safe to drink, it didn't always provide the best-tasting water. This was expected from the initial design concepts of the Star Ships. To compensate, the designers went back into the history books to learn what people did long before clean water was always readily available. To make the water safe, it was brewed into beer. Strong beer is what most people consider to be beer, but a low alcohol brew was also made for safe drinking, which everyone consumed. Even the Pilgrims that settled in the United States in the 1600s were more concerned about finding a water source to brew beer than they were about food. (This is ignoring the fact they stole the Native Americans' seed corn to eat, but that's another story.)

The Star Ship British Commonwealth was lucky to have Sharon Hooding as the Head Bartender. In her role, she oversaw the making of some fantastic strong beers and a very drinkable near beer. In addition, using the honey from the on-board beehives, she made excellent mead. Her domain, the Lounge, was a popular place on the ship, both because of Sharon's brews and because of her ability to listen attentively to everyone's woes.

When Raman was released from quarantine, the Admiral told him that he would have to find something to do. Until then, he was to continue to recover from having been in stasis for so long. For an unexplained reason, Raman's aura made the Admiral feel that Raman could be trusted, so he was allowed to have free range of the ship—except for the most sensitive areas, only out of concern that Raman might accidently touch something he shouldn't.

The first foods Raman tasted on the ship were accompanied by beer. It made the food taste better, and even by itself it was good.

Raman ate more than any two people could eat, and he consumed beer accordingly, but it never seemed to damage any brain cells or his psyche. Once he filled out, he presented a formidable figure, and no matter what he ate or drank this never changed. It never occurred to him that he should work out. Instead, he found the Lounge and Sharon Hooding more to his liking.

Kristie was the one that noticed this first and mentioned it to the Admiral, who in turn took Sharon aside and asked her to keep a close watch on Raman.

"How close?"

"I'll leave that up to you Sharon."

Sharon smiled and said, "Oh, it will be my pleasure."

Neil pursed his lips, squinted, looked over the top of glasses at her, shook his head, and left.

Sharon was an attractive lady and from all appearances was about the same age as Raman, if you didn't count the 3,000 or so years he was in stasis. Over the next two months, Raman spent more and more time in the Lounge, especially when Sharon was on duty. Sharon started to show Raman how to brew beer, and in short order he was brewing some very fine variations of his own.

Neil decided not to fight it and assigned Raman to Sharon's department. Raman tried to be a good listener, but as he often misunderstood what the person talking meant, the nuances of the meaning often escaped him. Once when one of the scientists was at the bar, he commented to Raman, "See those guys over there? The big heavy guy is going to drink the other two right under the table."

Raman watched fascinated, but when they all got up and left, Raman said to the scientist, "I didn't see anyone get under the table."

"Huh? No, Raman, they don't actually go under the table, they just...," and the scientist stopped, as he realized Raman wasn't tuned in at all.

Sharon, watching this, smiled and said, "I'll explain later." This is something she would say a lot.

As time went on, Raman and Sharon didn't always go their separate ways after working hours. Much to the disappointment of other women—and to the relief of some men—Raman and Sharon had become an item.

Because they had become close, Sharon was the first to witness an increasing frequency of what could only be called "seeing the future." Initially, Raman's visions themselves were nothing of great consequence, but it was what happened to Raman right after a premonition that was becoming a problem. Raman would occasionally say something about someone or something that hadn't happened yet and then black out for few minutes. If this occurred while he was standing, a crash to the floor would result. When she heard him make premonitions, she'd try to get him to sit immediately.

Raman might see someone, maybe from across a room, and say something like, "He's going to get hurt." Raman would black out, and later that person would be rushed to the sickbay after an accident. As time went on, the "predictions," as they had come to be known, were further out in time and often of an increasingly serious nature. Instead of making a premonition while conscious, he would go into a trance. During one of his trances, and before blacking out, he said, "United States will lose an engine." Sharon reported this to the Admiral. The Admiral then had Kristie check with Captain Monteiro, but everything was confirmed to be within typical operating parameters. Twenty-seven hours later, the Star Ship United States had a critical overload in Engine Number Three, and the engine pod was jettisoned. When it was a safe distance from the ship, it blew up.

Not surprisingly, this really got the Admiral's attention. "From now on," he told Raman and Sharon, "you are to tell either the Vice Admiral or me of any predictions. I mean immediately, no matter what."

The Admiral was more than a little spooked over this development, but it had a bigger impact on Raman. He had never heard anything about this ability happening to anyone of his people before. The warning about avoiding being in stasis for long periods of time due to the unknown effects was sounding more and more ominous to him. *What has happened to me?* he thought. A bigger question was whether or not these predictions were inevitable or whether steps could be taken to avoid something serious.

It took a while, but with Sharon spending so much time with Raman she eventually started to notice something else. It was subtle, but with each predictive episode there was a very slight change in his demeanor. Sharon noticed that Raman was becoming more detached. It didn't seem to matter when they went to bed at night and did what people do when they're attracted to each other, but at other times Raman could be, well, "off" a bit.

In a future not predicted by Raman, these subtle changes would develop into a major disappointment to Sharon that she would have to learn to live with.

Chapter 15
Tau Ceti e

There are four planets around Tau Ceti. The two closest to the sun are relatively small while the two furthest from the sun are larger and from remote sensing looked to be Earth-like. The atmospheric makeup of the larger planets was different than Earth's, but it was still suitable for humans. In fact, it may have even been better than Earth's.

Throughout the mission, scientists monitored the planets constantly to determine which one of them had the best chance of being habitable. As the fleet got closer, the outcome looked better and better. At least, that is what Shinya kept telling the Admiral.

With a great deal of skepticism, Admiral Dodson listened to the recommendation of Shinya and set the fleet in orbit around Tau Ceti e, the fourth planet from the star. Unknown to Shinya, the Admiral next went directly to the scientists under him to make certain he had the full story. Nearly all scientific reports were positive. The Admiral had to admit that the planet did look promising, though it wasn't everything he could hope for. As the fleet approached the planet, it was confirmed that there was a nearly continuous cloud cover, so they couldn't actually see much of the planet's surface. However, the remote sensing systems provided a reasonably clear picture of what was on the surface.

With propulsion shut down and the ships in orbit, it used to mean that everyone and everything on board the ships would have to adapt to zero gravity. But with the bows of the ships tethered together at the forward antennae arrays, the ships were gently rotated on their axis, providing 1.0 g at the middle of the ships. The four ships were maneuvered ever so carefully so that the communications arrays were connected with each ship ninety degrees in a single plane from each other. Once connected, thruster rockets set the ships in a circular motion so from a distance the ships looked like giant rotating spokes of a wheel. It wasn't perfect, of course. The closer you got to the ships' bows the less centrifugal force there was, and the closer you got to the sterns the force was much greater. But it was a lot better than simply floating around with everything else that wasn't fastened down.

As far as gravity on TCe was concerned, it was more than Earth's but about the same as the forces the fleet had experienced while under the 1.5 g acceleration. There were poles covered with ice and snow. Between the forty-five-degree latitudes, temperatures seemed to average about twenty degrees Celsius. It was difficult to determine what the temperature variations throughout the TCe year might be, but nothing indicated wide climate swings. There was a fresh-water sea covering more than half of the planet. There was one very large continent stretching from pole to pole with massive ice and snow depths stretching towards the equator. This was similar to what was likely seen during the ice ages of Earth.

High mountain areas seemed bare of vegetation. Where there was vegetation, it was massive. What appeared to be trees were many hundreds of feet tall creating a densely packed green canopy. Curiously, there were semicircular patches next to the seashore that were up to several miles across where everything was dead. On the edge of these rings was a different type of vegetation that was difficult to define. If there had been any sort of civilization evident, then these patches could be explained, but Shinya said he didn't notice any. The fact that he had his staff focused only on the trees never entered the conversation.

Neil looked at him, trying to read Shinya's foggy-eyed expression, and he wasn't one hundred percent convinced. But with no indication that Shinya would offer anything more, Neil said to no one in particular, "Well, even a stopped clock tells the correct time twice a day." And he thought, *Shinya is the Vice Admiral, and he does have staff supporting him, so, we'll assume there are no intelligent life forms.* The Admiral, at times, went with his gut feeling about things. He would come to regret that he didn't this time, when his gut told him Shinya was missing something important.

The atmosphere on the planet was extremely rich in oxygen. Where the atmosphere on Earth remained relatively balanced at about twenty-one percent, TCe had oxygen levels well over thirty.

Nitrogen, argon, and helium made up an interesting mix for the rest of the atmosphere. Carbon dioxide levels on TCe were nearly zero, making many in the scientific community ponder how the vegetation was able to grow so lush. It was also the reason why they were concentrating their attention on the trees. It was collectively assumed that if the trees—if that was what they really were—were to catch on fire, the oxygen in the atmosphere would make for a rather intense forest fire. It was further assumed that the obviously very humid environment, with constant cloud cover and rain, helped prevent this from happening.

With only a limited amount of data able to be collected from orbit, the next phase was to have shuttlecrafts fly increasingly closer to the planet's surface and gather more details over the next few weeks. The eventual goal would be to find the best place to set up shop and construct the Gate. With any luck, they would find a location with decent soil conditions so they wouldn't have to do a lot of heavy blasting. Unlike on EEb, where there was no useable vegetation for construction, the cleared forest would be used to build the town necessary to support the Gate's construction crews and to prepare for the influx of new arrivals from Earth and EEb. With this oxygen-rich atmosphere, many would love it here in spite of the fact that the gravity was more than they were used to and that the helium in the atmosphere would make everyone sound like a cross between Donald Duck and Mickey Mouse. With no intelligent life forms, this planet was for humanity's exclusive use. The fleet crews were excited and ready to go—not just for the big picture but simply to get off the ships.

So, on June 29, 2120—thirteen years after leaving EEb—Admiral Dodson had a strategy meeting with Lieutenant Christian, VAAS Shinya Ishikawa, and VAO Kristie Marshal in the Admiral's conference room. Linked in were the Captains, CASOs and the other shuttlecraft lieutenants. The plan as laid out was simple. The four shuttlecrafts—one from each star ship—would fly with a small research crew from Shinya's staff at high altitudes over assigned sectors. Assuming the results were favorable, the shuttlecrafts would return, and over a period of a couple weeks they would gradually fly lower over the landscape. Eventually, the shuttlecrafts would land at some potential locations for the Gate and do a ground-level survey of the area. Since Gates require a significant amount of real estate and a lot of construction activity, it was important to get it right the first time before all of their resources were exhausted.

An old Earth saying when using sarcasm was, "Why is it you don't have time to do it right the first time, but you do have time to do it over?" The Admiral was determined to take his time and get it right the first time, because while there might be enough time, there weren't enough resources to do it over. With four Star Ships instead of the six that were sent to EEb, he didn't have the same redundancy and backup for major contingencies.

Chapter 16
The Swarm

Just like on EEb, the Admiral reasoned, the four Star Ships circling the planet could hardly be ignored if there was any intelligent life on the surface, even with the constant cloud cover. Willing to reluctantly trust Shinya's declaration that there was no intelligent life on the planet, the Admiral made the decision to proceed with the surveys. Neil had insulted his VAAS numerous times in the past by asking Zanck for his opinion and often siding with Zanck when there was a conflict. For some reason, Neil didn't ask for Zanck's opinion this time. He reminded himself that his gut had told him he shouldn't just trust Shinya. However, being human, Neil really wanted to believe this was the place, so Zanck wasn't consulted.

Raman and Zanck had struck up a kind of friendship. It might have been because they were both non-human, or more likely it was because Raman could communicate with Zanck using the eye-movement language of the Second People. Combined with Raman's now extremely close relationship with Sharon, the three of them together made for a fascinating and humorous little group. When the ships went into orbit, the threesome was standing in front of the observation windows with the many others that were curious about the planet below, even though there was little to be seen. While others were talking casually about what lay ahead, Raman went rigid and started an intense stare. Quietly, he said to no one in particular, "There is intelligent life on this planet. We are going to have trouble." He then passed out and would have hit the floor, but the people packing the area broke his fall.

Shinya's reports of the scanning data for the past two weeks had indicated only trees on the planet's surface. With monitoring resources focused on the trees, his staff was left reviewing incomplete data and thus incomplete information was compiled. Why he failed to recognize the obvious was likely due to his very narrow focus. If there had been a closer look, Raman's prediction might have been prevented. Shinya literally could not see the forest for the trees.

Shinya's staff did pick up some sort of activity close to the surface of the planet, but it seemed to be limited to a variety of what could be described as insects, some as large as perhaps six or eight inches in length. The biologists in the fleet weren't sure what to make of these creatures, and when their boss was asked for more sensor array time, Shinya dismissed the request as unimportant and the Admiral was left in the dark.

Even with this recipe for potential disaster, Admiral Dodson had the four shuttlecrafts launched. Following the discussed protocol, they flew increasingly closer to the planet's surface in order to be certain there would be no interest from below. The shuttlecrafts had already spent nearly two weeks flying over the planet at high altitudes. Visual observations of the landscape, with its thick forests, were still only occasional. Thick cloud-cover and intense rainstorms meant heavy reliance on sensors. The sea was deep with water, which appeared surprisingly clear, showing in some locations what appeared to be aquatic plants at a very high density, much like the trees did on land. While the shuttlecrafts encountered rain almost constantly, severe weather patterns with high winds and lightning were never observed.

With the first phase of surveying completed, Admiral Dodson ordered the other shuttlecrafts to move in closer with the Shuttlecraft 2 from Star Ship China, which was descending first. All was calm for the first few hours, until they reached an altitude of 35,000 feet. Then the trouble started.

Within minutes of reaching 35,000 feet, the Shuttlecraft 2 pilot, Lieutenant Wang, reported being attacked by hundreds of the "insects" coming up out of the clouds. At first, he and his small crew were confused. The insects, or whatever they were, weren't being splattered all over the front of the shuttle. They were surprising agile, rapidly moving out of the way of the shuttlecrafts, and even more surprising was that they seemed to be moving even faster than the shuttle. They were also spitting or shooting something, something that seemed to be a thick yellowish-green liquid. Lieutenant Wang maintained the same altitude and continued a running dialogue of what he was seeing.

"Admiral," Wang reported, "these insect things are moving out of the way as fast as we approach. To me, they resemble our honeybees, only larger, much larger—some over six inches or more in length. They have wings like bees, and these bugs are amazingly fast. Every minute it seems the swarm increases in size and they are all shooting this yellowish-green substance at us. I'm not sure what to make of it."

"Lieutenant," responded the Admiral, "continue flying at this altitude, but try evasive measures to see what this swarm will do. No one on the bridge has any idea what is happening, so we're hoping you can gather some data." And with the rest of the shuttlecrafts listening, the Admiral added, "All other shuttlecrafts are to remain above the 35,000-foot altitude until we have a better idea of what we are dealing with."

Vice Admiral Marshal, pointing out the obvious to no one in particular, said, "This is a surprise. If these insect creatures are attacking the shuttlecraft, I can't image they would welcome our company. We'd need some pretty big fly-swatters!"

"Admiral," said Lieutenant Wang with a sudden alarm in his voice, "this stuff the swarm is flinging at us is eating holes in the hull!"

The Admiral nearly yelling at the lieutenant, "Disengage. Get out of there and return to your ship. Everyone else, return to your ships now!"

"Umm, Admiral," said Wang, "the only direction we're going to go is down. I have no more lift. I will attempt a controlled crash landing. I will stay in contact as long as I can. Please tell my family…" And just like that contact was lost as the shuttlecraft dropped down deep into the cloud cover.

The bridge of the Star Ship United States went silent as they watched on the sensor screen the slow descent of the China Shuttlecraft 2 until it disappeared. Scanners could only detect the shuttle on the ground. No one wanted to say it, but everyone knew that the crew was either dead or soon would be if the swarm attacked them.

This was a rapid and stunning turn of events. With everyone's attention now focused toward an equally stunned Admiral, he managed to gain some composure. Via video, Neil said to Captain Yue, "I cannot explain yet what we just experienced. Please stand by."

Captain Yue, however, said, "I'll not be standing by for very long. I want my crew back."

The Admiral ignored this and ordered, "All senior staff, please move to the conference room. Kristie, get Raman, Sharon, and Zanck in here."

"What about Shinya?"

With what was a characteristically agonizing look, Neil said as sarcastically as possible, "Yes, I suppose our all-knowing Shinya, too."

As they entered the conference room, Admiral Dodson pulled out a bottle of single-malt scotch and some shot glasses. Without saying a word, he indicated that anyone who wanted a shot should have one. But though he thought some might need a little bracer, he skipped it. Most accepted the invitation.

"OK," said the Admiral, "I'm not sure what just happened, but it is obvious we need to figure it out. We need to assume that the shuttle crew is still alive. It isn't fair to anyone to think otherwise until it is proven to the contrary. We need a rescue plan."

"Admiral," said the excited ship's CASO, Shawn Murphy, "you're not suggesting we send another ship down there, are you?"

"Of course not!" snapped the Admiral. "Not yet anyway. Not until we have a better idea of what we're dealing with. We need to capture one of those bugs and determine some sort of counter measure. I think it is safe to assume that if we send another shuttle down, this or another swarm will meet it. The trick is to grab one of these little bastards before they start attacking."

As the Admiral finished this retort, Neil turned his attention to Vice Admiral Ishikawa.

"Shinya," said Neil, "You didn't mention anything about these bugs. How did we miss this? You said there were just trees down there."

Shinya said, "I didn't say there was nothing else down there. Some of my staff said they saw something, but I didn't think it was important, so I didn't bother you with it."

Neil stood up and in what was far from his usual casual demeanor, turned red in the face, and slammed his fist on the table causing even the largest person in the room to shrink. "You knew about this?" he asked Shinya. "You said nothing? You were tasked to provide a full report on what we might expect. Any kind of life form is something we should know about. What were you thinking?"

Seemingly unfazed, Shinya said, "I was looking for various species of tree. I found that fascinating. You know how it looks like the trees are all the same? Fascinating!"

Quietly, but obviously angry, Neil said with tight lips, "I'll tell you what is fascinating, you incompetent fool. It is how I allowed myself to listen to you. When did you learn about these bugs?"

Still seemingly unfazed, Shinya said, "Oh, Zanck mentioned it."

Through sign language, Neil asked Zanck, "You saw these bugs?"

"Yes," signed Zanck. "I fully expected Vice Admiral Ishikawa would relay the information. Also, something new developed just as the shuttlecraft were leaving the ships; I was at the observation deck with Raman and Sharon, and as the shuttlecraft were descending Raman had one of his spells."

"Yes," said Sharon, "I was there when Raman passed out. Before going down, he said, 'There is intelligent life on this planet. We are going to have trouble.' I signed with Zanck, but we couldn't get to you in time."

Neil's head was spinning. He stayed quiet for a moment, took a glass and poured himself a drink, coughed, and looked down at the table. After another moment, he looked back up at the silent assembly and then at Shinya. With quiet anger in his voice, he said, "Shinya, I'm tempted to send you down to the planet's surface as a one-man rescue mission. What do you think about that?"

"Oooohhh," sighed Shinya. "I don't know how to fly a shuttle."

"Really? That's your only concern? Get out of my sight. Leave right now before I throw you in the brig!"

Seemingly unfazed, Shinya stood up and left mumbling something about being rude.

Mouthing the words as Neil used sign language, he asked Zanck for more detail on the bugs.

Zanck signed back that he had noticed something with sensor sweeps, but he couldn't get enough authorized sensor time to study them. The bugs were about six inches in length, maybe a little bigger, and all of them were perhaps four inches across. They appeared to be egg-shaped. They could fly at great speed using fast-beating wings. Zanck thought that perhaps they had two pairs of wings, but they moved so fast it was hard to tell. He repeated that he had only partial observational information, but it appeared that they moved methodically from tree to tree as individuals. He was surprised that they swarmed when the shuttlecraft descended. He had no idea what they were shooting at the shuttlecraft but guessed it must be some kind of powerful acid.

"And you told Shinya about these bugs?" signed Neil.

"Oh yes," signed Zanck. "I obviously assumed incorrectly that he told you, but you know how single minded he can be. As I said, I was with Raman and Sharon when Raman went into one of his trances. Now I think it is safe to say he was talking about the bugs."

Neil said to Raman, "Ok, Raman, what did you see? What was your vision?"

Raman answered, "I don't know. I don't remember anything. I was just looking out the window hoping, like everyone else, that I might be able to see something. And then the next thing I knew, I was being helped up off the floor."

Neil sat fuming. After several very long moments of silence, everyone in the conference room looked at each other thinking but not saying, *Now what?* Neil looked over the top of his glasses at Zanck and said while signing, "I want you to assemble a team and come up with a plan to capture one of these bugs alive. We need to know what we're dealing with. I'm not sure what I'm going to do with that idiot Shinya, but I'm not leaving him in charge of anything. Is that clear?"

Zanck responded with, "I'm honored, but are you sure that's a good idea? I'm not sure how the human staff will respond to a Second People as their leader."

"So noted. They'll get over it," said Neil. "I'm only asking you to lead this task force. You're a good project manager. I don't want to take anything away from this assignment, but after all these years under Shinya I think everyone will welcome just about anybody else. That said, you have consistently shown that you understand the big picture with no bias. Pick the best we have for your team. Kristie, notify the fleet of Zanck's assignment and ask for full cooperation. They are to ignore any direction from Shinya on this. Not that he would offer anything worthwhile anyway."

With varying degrees, the rest of those assembled nodded their heads in agreement. Everyone knew Shinya's modus operandi, and many wondered why the Admiral tolerated it up until now.

Then, turning his attention from Zanck to the rest of the people in the conference room, Neil said, "I think it is safe to say we weren't expecting this turn of events. I don't think we can just sit around waiting to find out what this bug swarm is all about. We need contingency plans. We need a plan to rescue our people, assuming they survived. We need a plan on what we are going to do next if we can't set up shop here. And thirdly, we need a plan to capture one of these bugs and figure out a countermeasure. This third plan is of immediate importance and is assigned to Zanck. I want you to take these other contingencies back to your staffs and brainstorm. We'll reconvene here in 24 hours."

"But, Admiral," said the CASO Murphy. "You're asking a lot."

With a stern look Admiral Dodson said, "Look, if these tasks were easy I'd do them myself right now, and I wouldn't need you. Get moving. You're wasting time. And oh, we want a live specimen. Got it?"

Turning once again to Zanck, Neil signed, "I really want to get this moving. Get the other ships' CASOs up to speed and see if they have some thoughts. The number one priority is to capture a bug or two. That's your mission."

"I agree," signed Zanck.

With everyone dismissed, Admiral Neil Dobson was now alone with his thoughts. *Of all the things that have happened and could have happened, this is not anywhere close to anything I expected. We were being far too cocky. We're not even close to being as competent or prepared as the first assembled space fleet crew. I pray that isn't going to end up destroying us.*

And with that thought he realized he hadn't actually talked with Raman in detail for some time, so he headed for the Lounge.

93

He wanted a near beer; no, he wanted a real beer to help decompress and talk to Sharon and Raman. Neil thought, *This Raman is turning into an interesting character. I need to pay more attention to these premonitions of his and learn to interpret them before the fact, not after.*

Chapter 17
Capture

It was far from sophisticated, but it worked. Zanck and his hastily assembled team of engineers, biologists, and shuttle crews examined every possible way to catch a bug. They concluded that the thick yellowish-green goop that the insects were shooting was in fact some kind of acid. That meant whatever they used to capture and contain the little bastards had to be acid-resistant. They concluded that a container of glass would probably work as a holding pen, but trying to simply scoop up one of these things out of the sky with a glass bottle while dodging shots was a lot easier said than done. Actually, it didn't even sound easy at all! They were realists after all.

Everything they considered for the capture was rejected until Lieutenant Christian, who would be piloting the designated shuttlecraft for the capture, somewhat absentmindedly said, "Look, you guys have come up with some interesting thoughts, but I think we're being too narrow in our thinking. We need to cast our net further out to see what other ideas we're missing."

"That's it!" yelled one of the biologists. Then remembering Zanck, he signed the response.

"What's it?" signed Zanck.

"Can we cast a net, or drag a net long enough to get at least one of these critters caught? I'm sure we could make a net out of a glass fiber. It wouldn't have to be super durable. It only has to last long enough to get the bug on board and into a glass enclosure."

Lieutenant Christian said, "I guess we can release a net from the shuttle stern hatch and drag it through the air. Fins on the sides of the net to keep it open will slow the craft down a bit, but not much. I suppose a quick turn when the swarm attacks might snare one or two. I think I can do it, but the tricky part will be getting the little bastard—or bastards—reeled into the container before any damage can be done."

And so it was settled, and the task force immediately went to work to implement the plan. The net was made. A glass containment vessel used to make beer was put into service, and a pair of biologists was assigned to the task of securing the specimen. They would use mechanical arms to remove the specimen or specimens from the net and transfer it to the enclosure. Other members of the team were assigned the task of washing anything down that might come in contact with the yellowish-green goop. Everything would depend on speed. The team had to snatch the specimen and escape before the swarm could bring down another shuttlecraft. Trying to be cute, Lieutenant Christian called the mission "Project Castanet." While he laughed at his own joke, others shook their head and Zanck was left not understanding.

The Admiral thought the plan, not the name, had merit and was worth a try. Fourteen hours later, the very tired task force members got the mission underway. Just as before, a few insects came to meet the shuttle at first but were then followed by a swarm of perhaps a hundred insects. The shuttle slowed, lowered the net, and using some small fins to open the mouth of the net, the shuttle made a quick turn and captured three insects. The shuttle climbed to a higher altitude and the biologists pulled in the net. Two of the insects managed to shoot out their goop and made large enough holes to escape, but one couldn't get out and that's all they needed. It was placed in the glass container, and Lieutenant Christian brought the shuttle back to British Commonwealth.

The two biologists, Mai Tran and Thanos Tzounopoulos, expected the captured critter to be agitated and flying around in the container. Instead, it just landed on the bottom of the container and didn't move. They hoped it was just stunned and not killed during the capture. Besides the simple fact that the Admiral had said he wanted one that was "alive," the biologists also knew they could get a lot more data observing a live specimen. They could kill it later for dissection. For now, they just wanted to catch a short break before serious analysis would start.

Thanos was busy securing the equipment while Mai moved closer to the container. Suddenly stopping dead in her tracks, Mai said, "Umm, Thanos, you better take a look at this."

Curious, Thanos stopped what he was doing and moved next to Mai. He stopped breathing as he said ever so quietly, "Are you kidding me?"

Mai and Thanos stared at the glass container and watched what they would later describe—along with many expletives—as "unbelievable!"

Chapter 18
Indigenous Species

Everyone who had been given assignments previously had now returned to the Admiral's Conference Room, with the addition of the two biologists Mai Tran and Thanos Tzounopoulos. Thanos was pacing with his head down and was wringing his hands. His hair was a mess and his face was clearly a mixture of dread, confusion, and exhaustion.

"Well," said the Admiral, obviously wanting to get down to business, "we know you captured one of the insects. Have you learned anything yet?"

"Yes, sir," responded Thanos.

With annoyance in his voice, the Admiral said, "Would you care to share with us what you have learned?"

Mai said, "It isn't an insect. It appears to be an aircraft."

Nearly everyone that was sitting jumped to their feet and said, "What?"

Kristie Marshal asked, "You mean, like a drone?"

"No," said Mai. "It is manned, though I guess 'man' might not be the right term. When we got the thing into the container, we expected it to be agitated and try to get out. Instead, it settled right down, landing right side up in the container. We thought maybe we killed it. I wasn't certain of course, so I went closer for a look. 'Shocked' probably isn't a strong enough term to describe my reaction when I saw a door, or hatch or whatever, open on the side allowing three small creatures to emerge, each probably a little less than an inch tall. They seemed to be wearing clothing, like a flight suit, I'd guess."

The room was stunned into rapt silence. After a short pause, the Admiral said while looking at the biologists, "And?"

Thanos responded, "And nothing! We think we need Raman and maybe Zanck to try and communicate with these creatures. In the meantime, we have left a couple of the shuttlecrafts' crew to watch and make notes of any changes. I also had guards posted outside the lab, though these creatures don't seem to be hostile. Well, at least these don't seem to be at the moment."

"Yeah," said Kristie, "I sure wouldn't assume they believe we are friendly, lovable aliens based on recent events."

Displaying a somewhat moderate tone, Admiral Dodson said, "OK, you can all relax a little, but stay alert. It appears you have this under control, at least for now. Though I agree with Kristie; we shouldn't forget these creatures shot down one of our shuttlecrafts. Probably in their eyes, assuming they have some, we're a threat to be dealt with. Raman and Zanck, please see if we can establish communication with this crew. I'll meet you in the lab." Looking around the room, the Admiral added, "You know those other plans I asked you to develop? Well, go back to your teams and think some more. I'm not sure what to make of this information, but it does have the makings of a real game-changer. Oh, Kristie, you better get engineering to recalibrate the sensor array. It appears we do have an intelligent indigenous species living on the planet. Now that we have been somewhat enlightened, we better start acting a bit smarter. Dismissed."

Ten minutes later, the Admiral was in the lab looking into the glass containment vessel. He asked Thanos, "Are they going to be alright in there?"

"I think so," said Thanos. "At least for a little while, they should be. The container isn't tiny, but we should probably come up with an alternative in an hour or so."

"And," said the Admiral a bit too loudly while looking over the top of his glasses.

"And Mai has engineering working on something. In the meantime, we're setting up a recording system that will allow us to enlarge everything on screen."

"Excellent," said the Admiral, and as his attention went back to the enclosure he asked Zanck and Raman what they thought. Appearing not to be surprised by what he saw, Raman smiled at everyone and walked up the container. He remained standing there while saying nothing. He was feeling a little smug, realizing he was correct when he said he was seeing danger, even if he didn't actually remember the event. But he did have a faint memory of something.

While Raman was looking at the container, Neil put his hands on his hips and said, "You knew about this, didn't you?"

"Well, not exactly," said Raman. "I seem to recall a vague image of one of our shuttlecraft as if I was on the outside, maybe even from the perspective of one of these little flying machines. I could sense intense curiosity and fear—something beyond simple, primal emotions. It's just a vague memory with no time frame at all."

"Even so, you made it very clear to everyone around you that you saw danger."

"Apparently, but in the past my premonitions were a bit vaguer, and you doubted their validity. That, in turn, made me wonder if I was actually seeing things or if it were perhaps some kind of alternate reality. You know, like a dream."

"But things are changing?"

"Oh. Well, yes. I don't know. It seems that each vision is more detailed. That's what Sharon is telling me. It's actually pretty scary."

"I'm sure it is," said Neil.

Then, returning their attention to the container, one of the tiny figures held up something so small that it was difficult to see except on the recording monitor. It appeared to be some kind of mechanical or electronic device. After a few minutes of waving it around the enclosure, the same being made a motion towards a second being, who then proceeded to remove what was now obviously a helmet. With the helmet removed, the flight suit was then removed, revealing a strange sight.

There were soft mutterings as the small group saw a being that was a little less than an inch tall. The body looked like a broad, smooth-surfaced piece of tree branch. On the bottom was what appeared to be moving roots that slowly propelled the creature like legs. About halfway up the body were six branches evenly spaced around the being's circumference. These were about a half-inch in length and appeared to be very flexible, like vines. At the ends of these were three even smaller appendages, which were also quite flexible and seemed to act like hands. There were no obvious eyes, ears, or mouths anywhere to be seen. At the very top of the creature, there appeared to be very short "branches," with what looked like a green-leaf-like foliage resembling hair.

After a few more minutes, the creature made some movement that resulted in something sounding a lot like creaking wood through the monitor. It was somewhat muffled because of the glass container. Raman asked for a stethoscope, and within minutes one appeared. Raman put it up to the glass container, and the creature made the same sounds. Raman made similar sounds and before long, there was a constant exchange of sounds between the creature and Raman.

The Admiral finally asked, "OK, Raman, what's going on? Do you understand this creature?"

Raman said, "I don't have a complete understanding yet. It will take a bit more communication before I have good comprehension. But, yes, I'm getting the gist of what it is saying."

"I'm not even going to bother asking how you can possibly figure out what is being said," said a somewhat perplexed Admiral, "but what's going on?"

"The creature that is before us is what we would consider to be the pilot of the flying craft," said Raman. "These creatures, beings, or whatever they are, have names or designations that I don't understand. Not yet anyway. The one doing the communicating with me is the pilot. The other two are, I guess, what we would call the flight engineer and weapons officer."

"I think I'll call the leader Branch and the other two Stick and Woody," said Kristie with a twinkle in her eye.

"Really?" said Neil while looking over the top of his glasses at Kristie. "This could be serious, and you're making a joke? We'll stick with Pilot, Engineer, and Fire Control." And as he said it, he cringed knowing what would come next.

Kristie didn't disappoint. She just chuckled as everyone else rolled their eyes and said, "So it's OK for you to say 'stick?' Nice."

Raman, not understanding the back and forth between Kristie and Neil, shrugged and said, "The pilot wants to know why we captured them and what we're going to do with them?"

Turning back to Raman, Neil asked, "Maybe we want to know why they attacked our shuttlecraft? Ask them that."

With Raman doing some more imitations of creaking wood, he turned back to the enclosure. For the next ten minutes, the back and forth of the creaking was non-stop. Finally, Raman turned back to the Admiral and said, "I'm not sure I'm getting this right. Apparently, they considered our shuttlecraft a threat. Besides being quite large by their standards, its thrust exhaust sometimes has some flames. They were afraid the flames might ignite a forest fire, though I'm the one using the word 'forest.' They call it 'the Tall Ones' or something like that. They are deathly afraid of fire and Pilot's species are the protectors. He refers to themselves as the Mobile Ones. When they attacked the shuttlecraft, they were trying to avoid any flames. The yellowish-green stuff they shoot out is apparently an effective fire suppressant as well as a weapon against something they call the Stranglers, or something like that."

"Still," said the Admiral, somewhat irritated, "they shot down one of our craft with people on board with no warning. Why did they wait until we got close before showing themselves? We sent out numerous messages before we went down."

Kristie chimed in trying to calm the Admiral with some logic, "How would they have any idea what we were saying?"

Everyone watched the Admiral as he considered this for a few very long minutes before saying, "OK, let's start over. Though I'm not forgetting we lost a shuttlecraft and crew, tell them we didn't know that there was intelligent life on the planet and we certainly mean no harm. Oh, and are they OK right now? Do they need anything?"

Raman went back to the containment vessel and after some long creaking turned back to the Admiral saying, "I'm not sure I have this right. I think the pilot said they like the air in the chamber. It is refreshing. They can tell it isn't polluted with oxygen. They will be fine provided we let them go and they return to ground. Maybe he meant the surface. The context is very confusing."

Through Raman, Neil told Pilot, "I will consider letting you go later. Before that can happen, I'd like to recover our shuttlecraft, if it isn't too damaged, and the bodies of the crew."

Once that was said, Raman told Neil, "They will talk to their leader." And with that, the tiny crew of the flying bug ship went back on board.

When the pilot reemerged, creaking commenced once again with Raman.

When they were done, Raman said to Neil, "Apparently, the shuttlecraft was damaged but landed safely. The crew is unharmed, but they remain in their ship under heavy guard." Everyone in the room gave a gasp of relief with this news, even though it was clear that the shuttlecraft's crew wouldn't be going anywhere soon.

Neil thought about this, but it was Kristie who said, "They have food and water on board for a few days. I'm guessing their communications were destroyed or they would have said something by now. But assuming we can come to some arrangement with the locals, we still have the issue of potentially igniting a forest fire in any rescue attempt."

"That seems to sum up the immediate problem," said the Admiral, "but thinking down the line a bit, I'm not sure we can ever set up a base and build the Gate. We have a lot of work to do. Kristie, I want you and Zanck to link up all the fleet's top officers and scientists and brainstorm. Tomorrow, set up the link in the Admiral's briefing room so I can hear for myself what the thinking might be. Mai and Thanos, I want you take care of our guests. You can have Raman back in a little while; in the meantime, I want Raman and Sharon to come with me. Everyone, dismissed."

Chapter 19
Raman's New Position

When Neil was alone with Raman and Sharon, Neil tried his best to understand what was going on with Raman. He asked, "Can you help me understand this ability you seem to have to see trouble? Is this something new or do all your people have this?"

Raman struggled with an answer. "I don't know what's going on. Remember I said that staying in stasis for more than 350 of your years was not something we liked to do. The effects of a longer stay in stasis are supposed to be detrimental, but it was never completely understood what that meant. I guess it affects each one of us differently. I know I get confused and no longer seem to understand the meaning of everything that is said, in spite of the fact I understand the words. When you rescued me, I was depressed and felt lost. Sharon pulled me out of that funk, and your beverage beer seemed to help," he added with a smile. "But I do find myself blacking out from time to time after I receive a premonition, fortunately not resulting in broken bones. Not yet anyway. The blackouts seem to have become less frequent, but the premonitions seem to be related to bigger events and are more detailed according to Sharon. I don't usually remember many of the details. Sometimes it relates to a person, or it can be an event. This last one before the Chinese shuttlecraft went down was interesting in that I have a memory of the event but not of having the premonition. I remember seeing the shuttlecraft from the aircraft that shot it down but no time frame. I don't seem to have any control over whatever is happening to me. Quite honestly, Admiral, I'm scared. Even with Sharon and Zanck being as close as they have become to me, I feel increasingly alone and lost. I wish I could go home and start over."

"Raman, of course you were lost, but now you have been found. That said, I can't help you with your inner torment. I guess you need to open up more to your friends and probably to one of our shrinks. However, I think I can help with your lack of purpose. We, that is to say everyone in the fleet and I guess now the locals, need this new ability of yours." Looking to Sharon, Neil continued, "Whenever he has one of these episodes, report to me, the Vice

Admiral, or Zanck right away. I said this before, but I now think this is more important than ever, so you should assume 24-hour attention is needed. Understand?"

"So if I see something, you want me to tell Vice Admiral Ishikawa?"

"No, not him, Vice Admiral Marshal!"

"Oh."

"Raman, do you think you could train your mind to see more and avoid blackouts?"

"This is all new to me. I suppose I could try what you call meditation," and then adding with a little smile, "and more beer!"

Neil said, "Yeah, well, I don't know about the beer part, but work on the rest. Oh, and let's keep this between the five of us." Neil smiled. "You know Sharon is on the list because these days I actually consider her as part of you. By the way, I'm officially naming you Ambassador of Foreign Affairs. That's an obscure enough title. Even without your ability to see into the future, I think the future of foreign affairs could be intense."

Raman, obviously confused said, "So, you want me to have some kind of an affair away from here in some tents? How do I do that?"

Staring at Raman and then shaking his head, Neil said, "What?"

Sharon almost hurt herself from laughing, "I'll explain later."

When it was explained to him, Raman took his new position seriously. He did need something to work on, and he would do his best. Over time, a program of meditation did enhance Raman's ability to see into the future. Eventually, something else came from these meditation sessions that were completely unrelated but perhaps even more extraordinary.

Raman always understood that his people, especially the teams sent out to other worlds, had certain skills. Some of these skills were learned through training, and some of it was genetic. One of these skills, or abilities, was enhanced with a certain piece of equipment that was used for communication. No matter the distance, two people could wear this mind-enhancing apparatus to communicate using thought over any distance. This equipment proved critical to the rescue of the first Star Ship mission to EEb. Raman, of course, knew about this apparatus, but he was neither trained in its use or even had access to the item itself, so it was a moot point.

He did wonder, though, *If my brain is now screwed up, how far could this go? Maybe I could concentrate with a message, but who would receive it? And what use would it be if someone did receive my thoughts?* Raman was getting a headache just thinking about it. Then he laughed. *So now I know I'm getting a headache thinking about thoughts. Wonderful!*

What he didn't know, however, was that he had already been sending thought messages and they were being received nearly twelve light years away by someone anxious to learn who was sending the messages. Raman's DNA was severely altered while in prolonged stasis, and he was now a match with one of his own people. The chances of this happening were so extraordinary that the odds could never be calculated.

Chapter 20
Tau Ceti e Eco System

When Raman returned to the lab and containment vessel, the conversation between the space fleet crew via Raman and Pilot continued for hours. When the crew of the little flying craft was asked if they needed or wanted anything, Pilot said with no hesitation that he wanted to be released and be allowed to fly home. The response was "maybe later." With that obvious request dismissed, Pilot asked if there might be some soil rich in organic matter available. If so, he asked if they could have some. The biologists Mai and Thanos shrugged, but they headed off to the horticulture decks returning later with a bucket of soil. Some soil was placed in the containment and the tiny flying bug crew quickly spread it around and then settled on top. As their root/feet burrowed into the soil they became less animated, though it was difficult to tell, as they hadn't really moved that much since leaving their flying craft.

In time, as the Star Ship's crew and little bug ship's crew became more relaxed, an understanding of what seemed to be a bizarre ecosystem unfolded. While Zanck and Raman seemed to readily accept what was being told to them, the humans were having a lot more difficulty.

There were three basic forms of indigenous species on the planet. They weren't exactly animal, and they weren't exactly vegetable. There was a great deal of debate on the subject of trying to determine what they were exactly, with no agreement.

What appeared to be the very tall trees was another indigenous species that had a symbiotic relationship with the small species. As near as Raman could translate, the tall species were in fact referred to as "the Tall Ones," where the species currently on board the star ship were referred to as "the Mobile Ones."

The Tall Ones never left the spot in the ground from which they grew unless they were willingly transplanted, usually when they were small. They were an intellectual species, content to

108

meditate and think as one unit. They comprehended all matter of science and provided the Mobile Ones with solutions to problems. They were the ones that had designed the flying craft. The Tall Ones communicated with the Mobile Ones in two ways. One was through the same creaking language by shifting and bending. The second way was through what could be described as a root connection, where the Mobile Ones would settle on the "root system" of the Tall Ones and transfer information. Apparently, this was reserved for the most complex of information transfer. The Tall Ones communicated among themselves through interconnected root systems. As Raman tried to explain, "It is like a neural network."

This system worked well from a technical standpoint, but the planet's history was sketchy at best. As far as Raman could determine, the Tall Ones lived for the present and the future with little thought of the past. This resulted in little understanding of the geological changes on the planet or how life evolved on TCe. To them, it didn't seem to matter. The way things were in the present while contemplating new ideas was what was important.

Both species lived for centuries, and when mature each produced something like a seed for reproduction. The Tall Ones relied heavily on Pilot's species for protection and for sowing seeds in a healthy environment where they would grow.

While the Tall Ones provided the high-level intellect, the Mobile Ones weren't just pawns. The Mobile Ones had built the flying machines and had created communities for themselves among the Tall Ones. The Mobile Ones had shops to manufacture and build what they needed, but they had no need for living quarters.

In addition to spreading seeds for the Tall Ones, the Mobile Ones provided protection. This came in two basic forms. One was from a third species that had developed in the sea. This species was more like a vine, with a rebel subspecies referred to as "the Stranglers" having evolved and moved to the land. It wasn't until later in the conversations that it was said why they had been given the nickname. These Stranglers spread out from the sea to the land, and as the leading edges of these vines moved forward the trailing edge died off. As branches spread off from the main vine, they would eventually break off on their own to spread out further as the trailing ends died off, thus separating them from their "parents." Just like the Tall Ones and Mobile Ones, it wasn't clear what these vine things were—plant, animal, or something else.

But whatever they were, they weren't passive. They systematically attacked the Tall Ones to survive and reproduce. Uncontrolled, they could eventually eradicate the Tall Ones, and likely the Mobile Ones, too.

Raman couldn't really translate much more after that, as it was becoming far too technical. Reluctantly, Neil brought Shinya back into the conversation, but not Shinya alone. Neil wanted anything said by Shinya to be backed by people he trusted, particularly Zanck, who could understand concepts beyond what humans had come to accept as the only truths. Neil correctly assumed that since Shinya had spent so many resources studying the Tall Ones, he must have some idea—or at least an intelligent guess— about the kind of ecosystem that was on the planet.

Shinya, almost in a trance and in a whisper said, "Ahhhh! Many believe Earth's plants have a level of intelligence and that soft sounds are enjoyed by the plants, thus helping them grow." And just as everyone thought he was done, he continued, "And plants convert carbon dioxide into oxygen by absorbing the carbon." And again after a pause where everyone thought he was done, Shinya continued with "I suppose if there was only plant life, eventually there would be so much oxygen that it could become a problem. Yessss. I see. That's why our little guests don't care for oxygen. They like the air we breathe; it isn't heavily polluted with oxygen. Hmmm."

Thanos interjected, "It seems the type of organic matter that make up the Tall Ones, Mobile Ones, and, I guess, these vine creatures is incredibly resistant to decay, so microbes, such as those found on Earth, never developed. When the end of their life cycle is reached, the breakdown of the organic matter in the absence of microbes is apparently done by sunlight. This decomposition, in turn, provides a correspondingly small source of carbon dioxide and nitrogen for the next generation to utilize."

Mai added, "It seems some of these vines, or Stranglers or whatever, started leaving the sea and evolved as the sea increasingly became devoid of the nutrients necessary for their survival. The carbon dioxide and nitrogen levels had dropped so significantly that the seas became intolerable. As they moved from the sea and started spreading out over the landmasses, they wound their way around the Tall Ones, feeding off of the carbon the Tall Ones hold thus killing them in the process, earning them the name 'Stranglers.' When they attack the Tall Ones, or perhaps a Mobile One that got too close, it appears the Stranglers slowly vaporize their victims with powerful enzymes to get CO_2."

Raman picked it up from there with what he learned from Pilot. "Now this is starting to make sense. It is the Stranglers who are forming the cleared semicircles that the Star Ship sensors were picking up. To counter this, the acid weapons used against fires is also used to kill the Stranglers in an attempt to keep them at bay. The Stranglers are voracious and tough, however, so it is a constant battle trying to keep the vines away. So while the Tall Ones and the Mobile Ones have a symbiotic relationship, more and more vines were becoming aggressively parasitic. All species, however, have created the problem common to them all: oxygen."

Shinya, only half-listening to what others were saying, obviously had more that he wanted, or needed, to say before he forgot his train of thought. He was excited now. "It seems clear to me that over the past millennium, the three species converted carbon dioxide into carbon and oxygen. While carbon was good, the oxygen was not. On Earth, the human species had managed to create an undesirable environment, increasing CO_2 and nitrogen levels and somewhat reducing oxygen concentrations. Fires killing the Tall Ones would release carbon, but the Mobile Ones put out the fires as quickly as they could to protect the Tall Ones. While electrical storms, volcanoes, and any other forms of fire ignition are rare on the planet, they do occur. And when they do, the high concentration of oxygen in the atmosphere creates a massive fire. These have to be put out as fast as possible to protect the Tall Ones, causing oxygen levels to continue to build, thus exacerbating the problem."

"So," said Mai, "When Pilot, Engineer, and Fire Control were captured, the relative increase in CO_2 levels in the glass containment were to them a breath of fresh air."

Shinya was getting even more excited and ignoring Mai as he continued with, "They must rely on the organic matter in the soils, which is created with shed foliage and decomposition when they die off. Mobile Ones settle down on their feet, or roots, and feed. Both the Tall Ones and the Mobile Ones extract nitrogen from the atmosphere as a food source. They also need carbon in any form but seem to favor it the form of carbon dioxide. In contrast to humans and other animals, which breathe in oxygen and expel carbon dioxide, the three species on this planet take in carbon dioxide and expel oxygen. But unlike plants on Earth, whose respiration uses nearly as much oxygen during the night as it produces during the day, these creatures mimicked animals where oxygen was expelled all the time." Shinya finished with an enthusiastic, "Fascinating!"

Shinya once again had a rare moment of being thoughtful and logical. Neil thought, *Maybe his focus isn't all bad. I wish I really understood the man.* Instead, Neil turned to Zanck and asked, "Does that make sense to you?"

Zanck signed, "Yes, it makes sense, but there may be other factors about the ecosystem we will come to learn later that might counter some or all of this."

Behind the scenes, Neil later learned that many of Shinya's scientific staff was having a very difficult time with all of this. They fought and argued against accepting these theories as well as everything else they learned about TCe. There were few, if any, microbes or bacteria in the ecosystem. The chemistry they knew was completely counter to all logic.

Zanck had to step in when the arguments were going nowhere. Signing the whole time, he said, "When your people came to my planet, it was difficult for them to understand us and the ways of our planet. The thought that the First People, who looked very much like you, disappeared so quickly because of what they had done to the planet was something that wasn't accepted right away. Eventually you, as a species, did come to understand that, even though you didn't like it. Now you are showing your arrogance once again by believing everything has to follow the rules of chemistry and biology of Earth. It should be obvious that TCe does not have the same dynamics experienced on your planet Earth. My people find the diversity that Earth has enjoyed is exceptional, and frankly we find it hard to believe. We sincerely hope you, as a species, don't ruin a good thing, because unlike my planet, you don't have a Second People to take over where you might leave off. My point is that TCe has an ecosystem that is not like Earth's, or even like that of my planet for that matter. You must put aside all preconceived notions of how things work and accept the facts. For this one time at least, listen to Dr. Ishikawa."

To some degree this reprimand from Zanck was begrudgingly accepted. The scientists didn't like being told they were pig-headed by a non-human. On the other hand, they were determined to study what was before them with their preconceived notions if not ignored then at least set to one side. As one, they agreed to look more closely at what was before them and maybe, just maybe, prove Zanck wrong.

Chapter 21
Options

Admiral Dodson, Vice Admiral Marshal, Vice Admiral Ishikawa, Captain Parks, CASO Murphy, Zanck, and Raman were all in the Admiral's briefing room on the Star Ship British Commonwealth. Linked in from the Star Ships Russia, China, and United States were each of the ships' Captains and CASOs. This was expected to be a long meeting, so the Admiral made sure there was a breakfast buffet and plenty of beverages of all kinds. Behind the food buffet and there to serve beverages was the ship's Head Bartender, Sharon Hooding, partially to watch Raman. Raman was especially thankful for enough food to even make his appetite satisfied. To help wash it down, he had to a large, very spicy Bloody Mary, prepared especially for him with a very knowing smile from Sharon.

The purpose of the meeting was to go over options. It was becoming increasingly clear that establishing a wormhole Gate on TCe was going to be a challenge. In order to set up the Gate, shuttlecrafts would be required to move personnel and supplies down to the surface. The flame in the shuttlecraft exhaust had the potential to ignite fires that would be devastating to the indigenous population.

The planet itself had North and South poles covered with thousands of feet of ice and snow. The poles meant that if the humans could find a location at the favorable 45-degree latitude, which wasn't inhabited by the Tall Ones, they could build the wormhole Gate and maybe a colony. Determining how to do that was going to be problem. The fire threat meant they couldn't use the full power of the shuttlecrafts needed to ferry people and supplies to the surface.

Once on the surface, there were few locations that would be marginally acceptable. There were plateaus that were high enough in elevation, that the indigenous population avoided them. One plateau in particular was ideally suited in latitude to gain the best results from the plant's magnetic field. Installation, however, would not be easy because much of the plateau indicated a granite subsurface. This would require a significant amount of coring or blasting. Combined with hot exhausts from the heavy construction equipment and support facilities, the chance of igniting a fire appeared real. It also meant that the first assumption that the "forest" would provide building material was assuredly off the table.

The Admiral started off with, "If there is anyone here that doesn't understand the problems we're facing, now is the time to say so. If not, where do we start?"

Shinya raised his hand as if he were in a classroom waiting to be called upon and said, "Can't we just stay here in orbit and study the planet?"

The Admiral looked over the top of glasses towards Shinya and was about to say something, but he quickly changed his mind. Instead, he quietly stated, "Dr. Ishikawa, I sometimes wonder what planet you might be from." Then, raising his voice and standing he said, "No, we are not just going to sit here in orbit so you can study the planet. What is wrong with you? No, don't say another word!" Once again Neil thought, *I truly wish I could understand that man.*

Kristie asked, "Have we really considered one tiny little obstacle? There seems to be little likelihood that the Star Ship crews would be welcome or even allowed on the surface."

Raman whispered to Sharon, "That doesn't seem like a little obstacle to me."

"I'll explain later," was the whispered reply.

"No." said Neil. "That is certainly an issue."

Captain Ying Yue said with annoyance, "I'd like us all not to forget my shuttlecraft and crew is still under guard and immobile on the planet's surface."

"No, we haven't forgotten about that either."

115

Much to the Admiral's surprise, it was Captain Gigory Kazakov of Star Ship Russia who piped in seemingly out of the blue and said, "Admiral, we have only looked closely at the TCe. There are four other planets in this system, and the next one out, TCf, looks promising. Would it be out of the question to take a look at it more closely? We could send one ship off to make some reconnaissance runs, and if it looked good the other ships could follow."

"If someone didn't suggest that, I would have. Thank you, Gigory," said Neil.

Captain Yue, still focused on her crew, responded, "I suppose blasting our way down and taking over what we need is out of the question. I'd be willing to do so, especially since it is the Chinese Shuttlecraft they have down there."

Captain Carlos Monteiro of Star Ship United States stood up and with his hands moving as fast as he talked said, "That's your answer for everything; just fight it out. If you weren't a woman, I'd give you a fight!"

"Go for it, if you're man enough," responded a now pissed off Ying Yue.

"Enough!" said the Admiral. "Pretend I'm in charge and you will be civil. All suggestions are welcome, even if they make no sense. In each suggestion, we might glean something from it. As for blasting our way in, we have only a few marines on each ship with light weapons. Our little friends in the bug ships would take care of us in short order."

Shinya said in all seriousness, "Admiral, if we're pretending you're in charge, who is really in charge? Maybe that person should be here."

Kristie could see that the long fuse the Admiral was famous for had just become extremely short. She grimaced, looked across the table at Shinya, and put a finger to her lips hoping he'd shut up.

Raman turned to Sharon and quietly said, "I thought that was a logical question."

Sharon said in a whisper and smiling, "I'll explain later." She then indicated that he be quiet and sit while handing him another Bloody Mary and another plate of food.

After a pause and as silence filled the room, one of the CASOs said, "We could go back to EEb, couldn't we?"

"Yes," said the Admiral, "we could, but do we want to?" To which there was no response. "Come on people," continued Neil, "somebody must be able to display a stroke of genius."

"Can we modify the shuttlecrafts so there is no risk of fire?" was one suggestion.

Signing, Zanck said, "If we could figure out a way to exchange some of Earth's CO_2 for some of their oxygen, we'd all be happy. It would be the carbon neutral solution your people have been searching for."

Neil came back with, "Now that's thinking outside the box. Might be too big, but who knows? It would at least be a carrot we could offer the Tall and Mobile Ones."

Raman looked at Sharon and mouthed, "Box? Carrots?"

Sharon rolled her eyes and put her finger to her lips.

Captain Parks said, "You know, if we built a dome we could work under it and contain any potential environmental issues inside. The equipment would run great with all that oxygen-rich air."

Neil said, "That's a mighty big dome you're talking about. I don't think we have anything to make something that big. Do we? Let's look into that."

But Kristie said, "Yes, it would be big if we were to cover the entire site at once. But we don't have to. We could build a portable dome and move it with the construction activity. Also, we don't know if the locals might have something we could use."

"Great," said Neil. "Keep it coming. We do need to consider what happens when all the work is done. Remember, the Gate network will ignite anything combustible on the ground surface when it is transmitting. That could certainly become exciting, but not in a good way. Anybody have anything else? There must be more options we haven't considered."

The meeting was quiet while everyone waited for someone else to say something. From behind the buffet table, Sharon was thinking, but somehow it managed to come out in whisper, "I wonder if the Mobile Ones could shuttle for us."

Everyone looked at Sharon, who said, "Did I just say that out loud? I'm sorry."

"Don't be sorry," said Neil. "Finish that thought."

"Ummm. Well, those little bug ships aren't very big, but I understand they are very maneuverable. What if a bunch of them were to gang together to move stuff back and forth? I don't know how you'd get them to do it. I was just thinking that's all."

Kristie said, "I can just picture a thousand of those bug ships carrying a shuttlecraft to the surface. What a sight that would be! It would sure keep Raman busy translating instructions."

"Huh?!" said Raman, who had his full attention on his food and drink until he heard his name. "What am I doing?"

"Nothing," said Neil. "Not now anyway. Go back to doing what you do best."

"What's that?" asked Raman.

Looking over his glasses at Raman, he simply said, "Well, eating of course." Then he added for everyone else, "We didn't get a lot of ideas today. Think about options and get back to me if you have something. Remember there are no bad ideas, only bad decisions."

Captain Yue, who was still in a fighting mode, added, "What if we help with fighting back the vine creatures. What are they called? The Stranglers? Aren't some of those areas already cleared by them big enough for our Gate?"

"Wow, you are itching for some kind of aggression, aren't you?" said Captain Monteiro.

"Hold on, that might not be a bad idea. Maybe we have enough ideas here to put something together for our plant friends to consider. It seems way out there, but that CO_2 for O_2 exchange is interesting. Maybe Shinya could work on how to do that. Where'd he go?"

"Umm, he wandered off when you blew a gasket and told him to be quiet," said Kristie.

Sharon instinctively knew Raman was about to say something about the word gasket when he looked her way, so she just held up a hand and shook her head before he could say anything.

"Yeah, well, get him working on it. Also, Zanck, I'd like you to put together another team to work independently on the same problem, OK?"

Zanck signed, "OK."

"Anything else for now?" asked Neil. Hearing no new thoughts, Neil concluded, "Thanks everyone. Let's flush out some details."

Raman muttered to himself, "Flush?"

Chapter 22
Divide and Conquer

While small task groups were developing detailed plans regarding some of the suggestions for dealing with the issues associated with TCe, the Admiral wanted to consider Gigory Kazakov's notion of looking at another planet in the system.

Gigory was correct that not much consideration was given to the other planets, because, the fourth planet from Tau Ceti, TCe, looked to be the best option. However, The fifth planet was also about the same size, and though it hadn't looked as promising as TCe it was worth considering. Neil reluctantly concluded that he had certainly agreed with Shinya that the data certainly pointed to TCe as the logical choice. Neil now felt he may have made a mistake and that another planet should at least be surveyed.

Gigory had made the suggestion, and later he volunteered Star Ship Russia to make the survey. Neil thought Gigory was acting very much out of character. Gigory and just about everyone else on that ship complained about everything and always acted as though everything asked of them was an unfair hardship, though they always did what was required of them. Neil thought hard trying to figure out Gigory's angle, as he was sure there must be one, but not finding it he decided to send the Star Ship Russia to TCf to see first-hand if that might be a better place to set up the Gate and colony. The other two planets closest to the sun were too close for comfort; literally, as the temperatures on those planets would certainly bake anything on the surface in short order.

With Russia off exploring another planet, the other three ships would stay in orbit and try to open a dialogue with the locals of TCe to see if something could be worked out which could be of benefit to all involved. Neil thought his Head Bartender's suggestion had some merit. It was certainly worth exploring, and he would start with the suggestion of getting food and a radio down to the shuttlecraft crew still on the planet's surface. If that was successful, then maybe a rescue plan could be developed. Then it would be on to bigger and better things.

The next day, Star Ship Russia was released from the other three ships and headed off to TCf. The Russian crew was quite jubilant, adding to Neil's apprehension about this little venture. He couldn't help thinking, *What are they up to?*

Back in their shared quarters, Neil and Kristie considered the dome idea. Neil thought the dome idea also had some merit, but it was true that there certainly wasn't anything in the fleet that could build a dome big enough. Maybe they could build a small one, but even that would be difficult.

Kristie reminded him, "I know you want to build the Gate, but aren't you getting a bit ahead of yourself? We still have to get the locals to agree to allow us to set up shop. And then, assuming they allow it, we have to figure out how we can get it built and operate it without burning the whole place down. I'm pretty sure the Tall and Mobile Ones would consider anything along those lines to be very rude."

"I know, I know," said Neil. "But if we don't set the goal, we'll never get there."

"Has any report of our situation been sent back to the UNSC on Earth?" asked Kristie.

"Oh, you know I send a report back every day," said Neil, "but by the time we get a response, it will be very late in the game. We need to try and figure this out on our own. I kind of like Sharon's idea."

"You mean a bunch of bug ships carrying our supplies?" asked Kristie.

"Yeah," said Neil. "Do you think it would work? Assuming, of course, we convince them to even try."

"Nothing ventured, nothing gained," chirped Kristie.

"Wow. That was original," said a sarcastic Neil. "I'd like you to see what you can do towards that end. Besides Raman for translation, include Zanck in your little group. He might provide some first-hand experience about how we humans try to work with a planet's indigenous population for a mutually beneficial partnership."

"Yes, sir, Admiral, sir. First thing in the morning, sir. But right now I have a more urgent mission. Sometimes, we need to divide and conquer, but sometimes it is better to simply join forces," Kristie said slyly while looking at the Admiral and slowly removing her uniform in a most provocative manner.

"OK," said a now smiling Neil. "I guess it can wait till morning."

Chapter 23
Negotiations Round 1

One thing was certain after the Admiral had his meeting to discuss options; the local population of TCe couldn't be ignored. The best way to negotiate was to tell the opposing party exactly what was wanted. Sometimes, all the posturing done in negotiations only made things worse. Often, the desired end result was easy to reach if all parties were honest. With that in mind, Neil decided he would try a more friendly approach with the bug airship crew.

Kristie, Raman, and Zanck entered the holding room where the bug ship and its crew were being held. Mai and Thanos had worked with engineering and built a larger containment. Mai and Thanos were rather pleased with the enclosure and said that Pilot, Engineer, and Fire Control seemed somewhat at ease, though without Raman they had no way of knowing for sure.

Raman, using the creaking wood sounds, told Pilot that the Admiral would like to release them, but that they needed to communicate with their leaders. "Did they understand?" he asked them.

"Yes," was the response, though it was made known they weren't happy about it. They had been in contact with their leaders, but the distance was not something their systems were designed for, so it was difficult. That being said, the leaders wanted to know what these aliens wanted. Why were they invading?

Raman introduced Zanck to the crew, though "introduced" was probably not very accurate between the creaking sounds, the human words, and Zanck's inability to talk, which resulted in sign language that Pilot certainly could not understand. But Raman tried to help. In doing so, Pilot was told that Zanck was from another solar system and that the humans had gone to Zanck's planet with the hopes of setting up a wormhole Gate to the human's home planet called Earth. A peaceful relationship between Zanck's people and the humans had been established. The humans now wanted to set up wormhole Gates in other solar systems and to potentially set up colonies.

What Raman got back was that Pilot and his companions were completely overwhelmed with this information and had no idea what a wormhole was, let alone some kind of "gate." They certainly knew what a hole was, but what was a worm? Trying to get an understanding of something Pilot didn't comprehend translated to Pilot's leaders was complete folly. They did ask if Raman was human. Raman kept this inquiry to himself.

Kristie suggested a different tact. She said to Raman, "Ask them if we can send food down to our people. We would drop it from above 35,000 feet if Pilot's people could bring it to the shuttlecraft. We would only send down food that would not take hold, and any leftovers would be destroyed to avoid any contamination."

Raman tried, but the concept of human food took a long time to explain. Finally, there was a breakthrough and Pilot's leaders agreed, and they offered to help. If they dropped the food in small parcels, the 'bug ships' will latch on and deliver it to the humans.

This was a relief to Kristie and the others. Within the next two hours, the delivery was made. A radio was also delivered, allowing Lieutenant Wang to communicate with the fleet. From this, it was confirmed that the shuttlecraft's crew was fine, but they were still not allowed to leave the immediate vicinity of the ship. The lieutenant also reported that the atmosphere was very invigorating, confirming the rich oxygen content. This somewhat made up for the gravity. The communication, however, was a bit humorous, as the helium levels in the atmosphere gave the lieutenant a less than serious presentation.

These talks were brief but exhausting for Raman. He took a break and went to the Lounge where Sharon laid out a light snack of two vegetarian sub sandwiches and a couple of pints of beer. She also made a basket of onion rings. Something Raman had discovered soon after being rescued and liked immediately.

Returning to the lab, Raman continued to translate, trying to use Pilot's language to express what the humans wanted to convey. The next inquiry was how to get the shuttlecraft and its crew back up to the Star Ship. The suggestion of multiple bug ships latching on and bringing to the ship to a high altitude was suggested. Pilot said the Tall Ones would have to consider this.

Kristie considered that it was probably early in the process, but on the other hand she wanted Pilot's people to know what the humans were thinking about. So she brought up the idea of a settlement on the planet to establish a Gate. A location had been identified that might be suitable for a Gate. Also the Mobile Ones and the Tall Ones did not inhabit it. The response to this was nearly instantaneous. Apparently, without actually knowing what this Gate thing did, the locals decided it must be important, otherwise why were these strange beings here? The Tall Ones rightfully had concerns about this Gate thing and its construction but decided that it could wait until later. Instead, they got right to the point and asked, "What's in it for us?" Raman wasn't sure but he thought some very rude, colorful, metaphors were imbedded in the question.

"Well, I suppose that's a fair question. Any ideas?" Kristie asked the few people in the room.

After some time, Zanck repeated the question he had posed previously with the Admiral: "Would it be possible to set up an air exchange program with Earth?"

"Huh?" said Thanos, not really asking a question.

"Well, I don't know how it would work," said Zanck, "but the locals have an atmospheric balance problem with too much oxygen and not enough carbon dioxide. I understand Earth has too much CO_2. Could an exchange program of some kind be set up? Could we at least suggest that to the locals?"

Kristie said, "You suggested that before, and I'm not sure that it was taken seriously. I don't know how we could do this on a large-enough scale to make much of a dent. But what the hell? Ask the little guy if it is something they might consider."

"I'll put it out there," said Raman, "but I need a break. All this translation is giving me a headache."

"You just had a break!" exclaimed Kristie while Mai and Thanos looked at each other and smiled.

Raman asked the question and headed for the Lounge. Sharon saw him come through the door and set out a pint of beer and ordered up some bar food. She knew Raman was hungry. He was always hungry. How he packed away so much food and still looked like a body-builder without working out was mind-boggling.

The air exchange idea was something the bug ship crew understood in concept. They had enjoyed what they considered fresh air, comparatively rich in CO_2 and low in oxygen, when they were brought on board the star ship. Pilot apparently spent considerable time relaying his experience back to his leaders and waited for the response, not that he or his companions had any choice in the matter.

When Raman returned, all Pilot had to say was, "The Tall Ones will consider. They will have an answer in a one-day cycle." That was understood to be slightly less than three Earth days.

With that and making sure Pilot, Engineer, and Fire Control had what they needed, most everyone left the room, leaving Thanos behind to monitor the little guys.

Three Earth days later, the group reconvened. Apparently, the Tall Ones completely understood that the devil was in the details, so they wanted to know more. They were the ones, after all, who were the intellectual equivalent of all of the humans' best minds combined. Raman had difficulty translating the specifics of the Tall One's inquiry, but it was clear that they were very interested in the concept of an air exchange.

Besides the flying bug ships, the Mobile Ones did have other machines that could be considered earth-movers, though it was clear they were much smaller than the bulldozers, excavators, backhoes, and tunneling equipment that was on board the Star Ships. In order

126

to explain the construction of the Gate, the Tall Ones would have to understand the scale of the work. Kristie, for once was unsure of herself, and asked Neil, "Should we show them?"

"Hmmm," said Neil. "I guess they'd find out eventually. It's probably better we show them ahead of the actual construction, so they'd be better prepared. Bring the bug ship crew down to the equipment deck so they can see the earth-movers. Then show them the videos of the machines at work we use for training. I don't think this is going to go well, but I'd rather be up front with this. Well, up front with most of it anyway. You know we also have the training clips showing the Gate in use. Show them that as well."

The bug ship crew was more than willing to go on an excursion and felt a little better about being trusted out of confinement, something they seriously resented. Engineer, through extremely difficult translations, helped design an equivalent to what they used for seating on the bug ship and these were placed in an open carrier. Mai was put in charge of carrying the tiny crew. As instructed, the negotiation party traveled to the lower levels of the ship and what certainly would have appeared enormous to the tiny crew was the earth-moving equipment. Videos were shown of excavation work as well as the Gate in operation.

When this was completed, Raman reported, "There is good news and bad news. The good news is that Engineer understands the wormhole transportation, but he has no concept of how it works. He just trusts that it does work."

"And the bad news?" asked Kristie.

Raman continued with, "Well, they are absolutely horrified with what our machines are capable of doing to any portion of their planet. They have no idea how the Tall Ones will react to their report."

Kristie was pretty sure she knew what the reaction might be, and she wasn't wrong; it didn't take long before the response from TCe's surface came back as a resounding "No."

Chapter 24

Polyarnaya

Captain Gigory Kazakov and CASO Alexander Pushkin were quite pleased with themselves. Star Ship Russia was heading towards TCf without the rest of the fleet. Their clandestine analysis of the planet indicated that it was actually better suited for human habitation than TCe. If they were correct, they would claim it for their own. They didn't care about any wormhole Gate reconnecting to Earth. They also didn't care to share the planet with anyone else and were willing to fight to keep it that way. Unknown to the rest of the fleet, the Russian shuttles had been outfitted with weapons. Though crude by Earth standards, they would certainly be effective against unarmed ships. The hope was that this serendipitous opportunity to leave the fleet would culminate in the completion of the secret mission the crew of the Star Ship Russia had from the day they were removed from their village in Polyarnaya.

When the frightful results of the pandemic of 2071, known as the Death Flu, became understood, those that could, looked for a place of refuge. Russia was no different, but something a little different happened there. The little town of Polyarnaya, on the island of O. Belyy in the very north of Russia, had already become a refuge for a handful of intellectuals who were fed up with Russia's heavy-handed treatment of everyone who was outside the upper-echelon of government—a government that had completely succumbed to the corporations that had made themselves too big to control. The government was, of course, aware of Polyarnaya, but as it was where dissidents went on their own and where the government might have sent them as punishment anyway, the town was left alone.

When the pandemic started to spread, people world-wide looked for places to go to get out of its deadly path. For most, they weren't able to move fast enough, resulting in the loss of nearly ninety percent of the human race. For Russians, Polyarnaya looked like a good place to go, but those already in Polyarnaya were not about to open the city's gates wide open and invite death.

In short order, they set up a perimeter, and no one was allowed in unless they passed two tests. The first test was survival. On the mainland, a series of isolation camps were set up. If a family didn't die or contaminate others, they were allowed to move to the next level, where they were held in isolation for two weeks. If everyone survived, they were moved to a third level and kept there for two weeks as well. If anyone died in level two or three, the rest of those in isolation were moved back to Level One. Few that made contact with anyone with the Death Flu ever survived.

The second test to be met was what people could contribute to the town. Those allowed in could come in with their immediate family if they had a high level of education and could also perform tasks normally associated with those who worked in the trades. There was no room for academics that needed to be waited upon. For those trying to get in, treatment was all very harsh and sometimes brutal. But once inside, they were welcomed and integrated into the community.

Polyarnaya had become a community of about 7,500. The Mayor was Alexander Pushkin, who had been a university professor of Astrophysics years earlier. An engineer, Gigory Kazakov, who had been a Naval Commander, led the village's equivalent of the Department of Public Works. These two actively, but quietly, encouraged others they knew to move to Polyarnaya with their families. The promise was that the town was so far removed from mainstream Russia that they could count on being left alone. Isolation was its sole attribute, but it worked.

The children who had migrated there during the pandemic were now grown and had themselves become highly educated by the older generation who lived there. The town thrived, though very few children were born there due to a general lack of interest. The lack of trust in the government prevailed, and by an unspoken agreement the Russian government was ignored. The government left them alone, but they were not forgotten.

Polyarnaya had been left alone with no outside government interference until 2106. It was then that the Russian government now found itself with a lack of qualified candidates for the new mission of the Star Ship Russia. Polyarnaya presented an opportunity.

When asked if they would ship out on the Star Ship Russia, the collective answer was a resounding "NO." This so infuriated the central government, and not wanting to be embarrassed by the world they rounded up the entire town of Polyarnaya and all but the most disabled were brought to the Earth's Gate and marched through. A few had escaped along the way but not many. Those that didn't escape were escorted by an armed guard and told they would be executed if they returned to Earth before the mission was completed.

Somewhat resigned to the circumstances, the new recruits were given assignments and put through rigorous training on the ship's systems. The village's Head of Public Works, Gigory Kazakov, was named ship's captain. The town's mayor, Alexander Pushkin, was named the ship's Chief Academics and Science Officer (CASO). Most of the ship's crew fell into line, but only after the captain and CASO quietly told each individual that this heavy-handed approach was going to cost the powers that be when the time was right. They promised to do whatever they could to establish a new Polyarnaya somewhere where they would forever be left alone. Until that time, they would do their assignments and keep the ship running.

When the Admiral learned the part of this story on how the crew was "recruited," it explained a lot of the attitude witnessed on the Star Ship, referred to by the crew as Polyarnaya and not Russia. Still, Captain Kazakov kept a tight ship, and while no one went out of the way to aid the Admiral, all did whatever was required for the mission.

What the Admiral didn't know was the secret mission of Russia's crew. If he had known, different decisions would have been made—not because he might be concerned about the Russia crew breaking away exactly, but because some key components for the proposed wormhole Gate for this solar system were only on Star Ship Russia. While efforts had been made to have backup components spread out among the four Star Ships, there were some that couldn't be duplicated when sent through the Gate to New Hope

Island on EEb. On top of that, it had been determined before the mission that four ships had a calculated better chance of making this shorter trip successfully than the six ships that were sent off on the original mission to EEb. That is to say, the UNSC didn't have enough resources to do things correctly, so the Commissioners said, "Good enough." Both the UNSC Science Director and Operations Director had been overruled when their concerns had been expressed.

Shortly after Russia had left the fleet to explore TCf, Raman made a prediction before blacking out once again. When Sharon heard him say "Star Ship Russia will fail and put the mission in jeopardy," she reported this to the Admiral. The Admiral contacted Captain Kazakov with the intentions of recalling the ship. After a long conversation, Captain Kazakov convinced the Admiral that with this new information he would be even more diligent than usual to avoid any problems. Always with cautious optimism, the Admiral relented and let Russia continue on its way.

If Captain Kazakov had actually taken the warning to heart, things might have turned out differently. Even though he was aware of this so-called ability of Raman's, he didn't really believe it. Besides, Captain Kazakov had an overriding desire to create a new Polyarnaya, causing him to act somewhat irrationally when it came to his secret mission.

Chapter 25
Tau Ceti f

Captain Gigory Kazakov continued to feel quite smug. His ship was free of the fleet, at least for a while. But if things went the way he and most of the crew hoped, they would never again have to see Admiral Dodson or anyone else they had left behind at TCe. With the Admiral's blessing, Russia was now off to see if there was a better planet in the Tau Ceti solar system on which to build the Gate. The operational plan was that if a better planet was found, Gigory would send a message and the rest of the fleet would join him. That was the Admiral's vision, but it was not the plan for those on the Russia. *Ha!* thought Gigory, *I have outsmarted Admiral Dodson.*

Gigory knew each of the Star Ships carried part of what was needed to build a new Gate. While Gigory was anxious to be away from the rest of the fleet permanently, it was never his plan to go out of his way to cause them great harm either. He knew, or thought he knew, that there was enough redundancy built in that the three Star Ships left back at TCe could still build the Gate, if everything went well that is. In any case, it wasn't Gigory's overriding concern. The resources he had on board would be more than enough to build a colony for his people. They could live and prosper and be left alone to design their own destiny. He would keep his options open, though, just in case a suitable location couldn't be found.

What he didn't know was that in their desire to do something grand with the fleet, the UNSC had decided to take a chance and not build in much of a safety margin. The UNSC planned, or hoped anyway, that the four ships would all make it to their destination and be successful in building a new wormhole Gate, establishing a colony, and eventually moving on even further to build more Gates. Unfortunately, the result was that without the critical components stored on Russia, there would be no functioning wormhole Gate in the TC solar system.

As Star Ship Russia got closer to TCf, things were looking better and better, almost too good to be true. Gravity was 1.3 g. The atmosphere was close to what it had been on Earth in the late 1600s. There were oceans, two large continents with what appeared to be fresh-water lakes, and large polar ice caps. The landmasses had rich vegetation in most areas, with what looked like grassy plains. The plains had some kind of grazing animals on them. There was no sign of any civilization of any kind, but that was also the case for TCe when they first arrived. Still, this first view was very hope-inspiring, and the crew was starting to get excited.

Everything was looking so good that Pushkin insisted that there would be no problem truncating part of the UNSC protocol. "We'll take the high-level flights for a while and then drop down closer and then land," he said. "I see no reason to spend the amount of time those pompous asses have been using. They are much too cautious. What do you say, Gigory?"

Gigory wasn't too sure about this, but he begrudgingly agreed with his scientist and former boss. "OK," he said. "Launch all three shuttlecrafts. Let's get this moving!"

Within three TCf days, each one the equivalent of 5.5 Earth days, Russia Shuttlecraft 3 had landed on the surface. In spite of Gigory's instructions, the crew wasted little time and removed their helmets after reporting that everything had checked out. "I think we have found paradise," the lieutenant reported. "With your permission, we would like to stay on the ground for at least one TCf day and do a more thorough study of the soil and the surroundings."

Gigory was as anxious as everyone on board to set up shop on the planet's surface, but still his training and self-discipline made him uncomfortable with this proposal. "I don't know about that," said Gigory. "You have already violated protocol and went against my orders." Then with a great deal of sarcasm added, "I hope you geniuses know what you're doing."

Siding with the landing party, Pushkin said, "Look, they are already down there. This is a great opportunity to really check things out." And then with the microphone off said, "And if something goes wrong, we only lose five people in the learning process. They wanted to do this."

Nothing said made Gigory any more comfortable. He was especially unhappy with the crew of the shuttlecraft who took it upon themselves to expose themselves to whatever might be down there. *But,* he thought, *I suppose we're better off if something does go wrong with the five that are down there then having them bring something back to the ship that might affect everyone.* So Gigory said, "OK. You are to set a watch, and you are to check in every four hours."

"Understood," said the lieutenant.

The next 5.5 Earth days later, the shuttlecraft returned to the ship and reported to the CASO. Through a video link to the shuttle bay, Gigory could see that the shuttlecraft's crew members were smiling so much that he thought they might hurt themselves. The lieutenant could hardly contain himself. "The soil is rich. There are some kind of animals that are about sheep-sized and are grazers. These animals didn't seem to care one way or the other that we were there. We saw nothing that looked like a predator. The air was so fresh it was like a tonic. The vegetation seemed varied and there was no indication the trees were intelligent or going to attack us. Thought you'd like to know that for sure. I can't wait to get off this pressurized cylinder and start a new life. Freedom at last!"

"That's great news," said Gigory cautiously, "but we have got to slow down a bit. This is all moving way too fast. We don't want to make mistakes in our enthusiasm to settle down. Besides we still have three ships full of people waiting to hear from us. If we want this planet to ourselves, we need to be clever. We need to decide what we're going to say and then be prepared for any backlash."

The shuttlecraft lieutenant said, "We should tell them to stay where they are and figure it out. Leave us alone or we'll shoot them out of the sky. We can do it, too."

"Great," said Gigory, "Did you learn those diplomatic skills from our government? You know, 'Shoot. Ready. Aim.' I'd rather not shoot, but if we have to let's be ready and then aim before shooting. Got it?"

"Yes, sir," was the unconvincing reply.

The next day, the shuttlecraft's exploratory crew all reported to the sickbay. All of them complained of body aches, fever, and throbbing headaches.

On Day Two after the shuttlecraft's return, the crew was in intensive care with no understanding what was happening to them. Vital organs were hardening, thus keeping them from functioning properly. The CASO and the medical team that had had been treating the shuttlecraft crew were starting to get body aches, fevers, and the throbbing headaches as well.

Gigory was outraged. He was angry with the CASO and the shuttlecraft crew for appealing to his weak side, but he was especially angry with himself for being so weak and not insisting on doing what he knew to be correct. All he could say when heard the news was, "Shit."

Gigory ordered the sickbay to be sealed off and for anyone that had been in contact with anyone else that showed signs of the illness to report to the sickbay. Those were good orders, but some who had been in contact with an infected person thought, *Well, I wasn't very close. I'm sure I'm OK. I don't want to go down to the sickbay, where I know everyone is contagious. I'll just stay in my quarters.*

In addition, whatever the cause happened to be, it was already in the ventilation systems, so it would eventually spread throughout most of the ship. Only the engine room's pods that were external to the main part of the ship could be truly isolated.

On Day Four, the shuttlecraft's crew all died within a span of one hour.

On Day Five, the first responding medical team died. Others also died in their quarters because the illness was spreading

135

throughout the ship. Gigory ordered the engine room's pods to be isolated, and no one was to be allowed through the airlocks, which were ironically designed to keep potential contamination in the engine room pods from reaching the main part of the ship, not the other way around. The operating engineers on duty were to remain behind closed doors. Of the four operating engine room pods, three were compromised when the engineers allowed their families in. Only the functioning Engine Room 2's pod stayed isolated. As luck would have it, the on-duty staff of fifteen operating engineers were all single, eliminating the family factor.

One of the non-operational engine room pods also became a site of refuge. Pods 5 and 6 were backup pods that could be rotated into place should one of the operational engines fail and have to be jettisoned. In the meantime, some enterprising individuals had turned one of these into a kind of clubhouse. It was completely clandestine, with only a handful of individuals aware of "the club." This group was in Pod 5 when the order was made to seal the bulkheads, so they did. At least for the short term, they were well situated after having previously stashed considerable food and alcohol supplies in the pod. With the autonomous air-recovery system functioning, they could survive for some time. Seventeen people were in Pod 5. Of the thirty-two people in Pods 2 and 5, eleven were men and twenty-one were women. Ages ranged from eighteen to fifty-six. They had intercom connection, and by default a fifty-six-year-old woman, a senior engineer named Natasha Smirnov, took charge. In charge of what, she had no idea.

Back on the Bridge, Gigory resigned himself to the inevitable. He put on his pressurized suit and helmet knowing that if this, whatever it was, didn't get him then he would eventually starve to death. He had an alternative plan, but first he had to make the call to Admiral Dodson. Besides being duty-bound, he was also ashamed of his arrogance.

The Admiral was surprised to see Captain Gigory appear on screen wearing a space suit but waited for Gigory to speak. "Admiral, I have dreaded this moment, but time does not allow me to put it off. First off, do not try to settle on TCf. It appears to be a paradise, but it is a Trojan horse. We do not know what it is, but it is deadly. One shuttlecraft landed, and against protocol the crew was lulled into a false sense of security, perhaps by the planet itself. Anyway, the crew removed their helmets against my orders and convinced me to stay on the planet for one solar cycle. They then returned to the ship with incredible enthusiasm.

"Dreadfully, they apparently brought back something that eventually killed them. Whatever it is, it is contagious, and within a few short days nearly everyone on board was dead or dying. I will also succumb if I remove this suit, so I suspect I will starve to death. There are thirty-two people isolated in two of the engine room pods. One has food, and the other has very little to keep themselves going. I don't know if rescuing them is an option."

It took all his strength, but Admiral Dodson remained calm, in spite of the gut wrenching within his body. His first question was, "Why did it take so long for you to report this?"

"All of our resources were aimed at trying to get a handle on this. There was nothing you could do anyway."

"Didn't you take Raman's warning seriously? You should have been even more diligent than the usual protocol, not less."

"I have no excuse. I was negligent. I will be paying the price, and worse, so will my crew. Sorry is pathetically inadequate. As long as I can, I will do whatever I can to rescue my people who are still with us and to reduce the damage I have done to the overall mission."

"Are you all right for the short term?"

"I should be all right for a couple of days at least."

"I assume you can communicate with the people in the engine room pods."

"Yes, everything on board seems to be working."

"Do you have control over the ship?"

"At the moment, yes. I have a stable orbit and all systems are functioning. Obviously, we have zero gravity, so everything, including me, is floating around."

"It took you a week to get there. I think if we push it, we could have a ship there in about six days. The question would then be, what could we do? I'll get back to you in an hour or so. Is there anything we can do here in the meantime?"

"Yes, Admiral, there is one thing. Please pray for us."

Chapter 26
Rescue Mission

Admiral Neil Dodson was filled with a mixed bag of anger, fear, frustration, and helplessness when he called an emergency meeting. All the senior officers in the remaining three ships were either in the Admiral's briefing room or linked in via video. He also had Raman in the room along with Sharon to help Raman through what seemed to be an increasing number of rough spots.

After filling everyone in on what was *obviously* a bad situation, Neil started with, "Raman, in your vision, is this what you saw?"

"I don't remember. I remember losing touch with what is going on around me and getting more of a premonition of something rather than a vision, but I don't remember the actual premonition. Everything went blank when I blacked out."

"So, if no one is around when you get a premonition, it goes unnoticed?"

"Yes, but not always. Sometimes I remember. I never thought about it, but sometimes I have blacked out in my quarters and don't know what happened leading up to it."

"What about when you're in Sharon's quarters?"

"Well, then, she remembers."

"Hmmm! Have you been working on controlling this better? Can you tell what's in store for the Russia crew? Anything at all?"

"Not yet."

Begrudgingly, Neil asked Shinya if he had ideas of what to do, and Shinya did not disappoint.

Shinya said, "Well, this is all fascinating. I'd like to collect some samples from the planet so we can study what has caused this problem on Star Ship Russia. Maybe we should set up a study group on the planet itself!"

"No, you idiot. I want to hear your thoughts on how we can save the remaining crewmembers," Neil barked and without waiting for a reply turned to Kristie.

Kristie said, "I think the rescue process is straightforward. The engine room pods can be separated from the main body of the ship and transferred to another ship. We could use at least one to replace the one we lost on the United States. Each pod has an external airlock in case repairs are needed on the exterior of the pod, so we could have a shuttle to extract the crew. The captain is another matter."

Ling Zhao, the CASO on China, asked what should have been on everyone's mind, "How do you know we won't be bringing this deadly thing onto our ships?"

Lillian Westgate, the CASO on United States, trained as a medical doctor replied, "I feel sure that the isolated crew members are not contaminated. And if they were, based on what Captain Kazakov told us they would all be dead by the time we reached them. Kazakov is another matter. He is in the contaminated area. He is isolated in his suit, but I don't see how he could get from the inside of the suit to anywhere else without either exposing him or us to the danger."

Neil said, "No matter the solution—even if there is no solution—time is passing. I'm thinking we send one ship on a rescue mission and work out details while it's on the way. The rest of us will stay in orbit and continue efforts to erect a Gate here, which brings me to another minor detail: there are some key components for the wormhole Gate on Star Ship Russia that were not duplicated. Without those components, we'll have a pretty-looking structure that does nothing. Give some thought to that detail."

Raman whispered to Sharon, "That doesn't sound like a detail."

"I'll explain it to you later."

At the same time, Captain Yue nearly yelled, "What? I thought we had backups built into this mission."

Neil said, "Well, it turns out the Commission didn't think this was going to be a difficult mission, so they believed that four ships with parts spread out among them would be fine."

"I can't believe that Dawn and her brother Richard would approve a plan like this after they spent all that time on the first mission."

"Our UNSC Directors are administrators and follow orders. They did tell me when we left that they weren't thrilled about the decision, but they felt the risk was small. They felt confident that the four ships would reach TCe, and they were correct. Whether intentional or not, our friends on Russia have created the problem. Now we need to figure out what to do next. But I need a volunteer ship to head for TCf."

Captain Monteiro said, "The United States will go. It makes sense because we are down to one spare engine room pod. We can make the rescue of the survivors and transfer the inactive engine pod. Now, that will leave five engine pods on Russia. What do we do with those? Also, do we risk pulling the Gate components off Russia?"

The Admiral said, "I don't have all the answers yet, but you should go. Leave as soon as you uncouple from the British Commonwealth and China. We'll work out the details as you proceed to TCf. I think that's all for now. Everyone put on your thinking caps and we'll reconvene in twenty-four hours."

Raman whispered to Sharon, "Do you have a thinking cap? I don't."

"I'll explain later."

Neil asked Kristie to stay as everyone else left the room or signed off. Once alone, Neil contacted Captain Gigory and informed him the United States was about to leave on a rescue mission. Details were left out for now. He then sent a message to New Hope Island on EEb. It was lengthy and concluded with a request for instructions from UNSC. Once the message reached New Hope Island, it would be sent through the Gate so not much time would be wasted, but it would still take over a year for the message to reach New Hope Island. That was faster than the speed of light, but New Hope Island was a long way off.

Chapter 27
Abandon Ship!

Captain Kazakov knew there was no way out of the mess he helped create. Even if there were a way for him to be rescued without contaminating the crew of the United States, he wouldn't be able to live with the knowledge that except for a handful of survivors, at least 9,000 fellow Russians from his village of Polyarnaya were dead. "Admiral Dodson, I have given orders to the remaining survivors on Russia to abandon ship when the United States arrives. I don't think that was actually necessary, but I wanted that to be my last official act as Captain of the Star Ship Russia. I know it is customary for the captain to be the last to leave, but I don't want to place anyone in a difficult position, so I am abandoning my ship shortly. I will take a shuttlecraft to the surface of the planet. I will remove my suit and enjoy the false promise of a paradise planet for as long as I am able. I will plant the village flag of our hometown of Polyarnaya, Russia, as a tribute to those that have died hoping for a new beginning. I have taken measures to avoid a painful ending when the time comes. I am not asking your permission but pray that you accept this as an honorable solution, which I know you must have been contemplating. I ask for prayers for my crew, now gone, my remaining crew's successful rescue, and for me. May God have mercy on my soul. Over and out."

There was nothing for the Admiral to say except a short prayer, as requested. Deep down, he knew of no means to rescue Captain Kazakov, who must have already been suffering from dehydration and hunger. The Captain had elected to take a heart-wrenching but honorable end. Going down to the planet's surface was something he actually had not considered, but it seemed fitting that a captain should do so. Maybe at some future time, humans may go to the surface of TCf and find what might be left of the Captain entombed in the shuttlecraft.

Before leaving the ship, Captain Kazakov loaded up with supplies from the Galley. When he got to the planet's surface, he landed in a meadow on top of a knoll. As soon as he landed, he removed his space suit and fixed himself a hearty meal. It was not anything a gourmet chef would find appetizing, but Gigory found it more than fine after not having anything to eat for days. The large glass of vodka helped make the food taste even better. He decided to get the most out of the time he had left. He unbolted a seat and dragged it outside. He positioned it so it would face the sun when it came up. He wanted to see at least one more sunrise. After eating more of his rations, he let a warm gentle breeze lull him into a peaceful sleep as the sun set for the night. He suspected it was the planet that was lulling him, because he certainly had many regrettable thoughts to deal with.

It was a long night so Gigory woke under the stars. He was more than a little startled when in the dim light he noticed a group of the gazing animals that the first landing crew noticed. They were standing near him watching. One creature came closer, but Gigory didn't move. He felt a little uneasy but stayed in his chair and felt, rather than heard, the creature "say," *I will stay with you, so you won't be alone.* It came right up to Gigory and sat next to him. It was shaped similar to a sheep, but instead of wool, it was covered with what appeared to be feathers. Cautiously, Gigory touched and then stroked the creature. It felt incredibly soft.

Gigory did see his sunrise and one more, and still another, and another. He felt no ill effects; in fact, he felt better than he had in a very long time, except he was running out of food and was hungry. He had planned on being dead by now, so while he wasn't exactly disappointed to still be alive on this very pleasant planet, he wasn't sure what to do. Not really thinking about it, he said to the sheep-like creature that stayed near, "Well, now I wonder what I should do?"

He was more than a little surprised when the creature looked at him, and he once again "felt" an answer, *You cannot leave. Follow me.* As the creature walked off, it looked back to see if Gigory was following, and then meandered on further. After being guided by the creature for almost two miles, Gigory came to a pond. It looked like good water, but how could he tell? He looked at the creature that was looking at him, and once again he felt rather than heard, *It is safe.*

Gigory didn't know what to think. He should be dead, but instead he was somehow communicating with this creature that seemed to be watching out for him. Gigory looked at the water—if that was what it was—shrugged, and took a taste. It was delicious. He would revisit this spot later with containers to bring some water back to the shuttlecraft. "Well now, little buddy, what about food?" he asked only half expecting an answer.

But he did get an answer: *we eat grass.*

As good as the grass looked, Gigory had to come up with something else if he was destined to remain alive. Back on Russia, there was plenty of food, and there were seeds and rootstocks that would probably grow pretty well on this planet.

Then the creature had said, "*You can't leave.*"

Gigory laughed. This was like a big joke. He was alive when he thought he should be dead. He was not only alive, but also in a sort of paradise—although a paradise without anything to eat did come up a little short. He had a random thought that maybe the creature was edible, but that seemed like a really bad idea. He then had another random thought, but this time he said it out loud, "Well, if I'm not going to eat you, I guess I'll need to call you something. How about Downy? You certainly feel Downy-soft." And Gigory chuckled at the thought.

You cannot eat me.

"OK, OK, I wasn't really considering it!" responded Gigory quickly as he stood stock-still, suddenly realizing he might be going mad talking with this creature.

Hunger makes a person do things they know they shouldn't. In Gigory's case, he was coming to a realization that whatever killed his crew was perhaps only deadly when it was away from this planet. Whatever it was, it lulled humans into a state of mental tranquility, but it was like a drug that you had to take continually. He had no way of knowing if a gradual withdrawal would be possible, but whatever "it" was it certainly proved deadly when not on the planet.

Hunger, though, made Gigory wonder what would happen if he made a fast trip to Russia to get supplies and equipment for the long haul. He decided to give it shot. After all, he had been on the planet's surface for some time now and thought, *At this stage, every day is a bonus!*

Gigory took off the next morning for Russia. As he approached the ship, he remotely opened the shuttle bay doors, flew in, and landed. When the bay doors closed and air pressure stabilized, he left the shuttlecraft and entered to the main part of the ship. The smell of decomposing flesh was overwhelming. He grabbed a facemask and oxygen tank and put it on. Gigory was grateful that most people had gone to their quarters to die in bed, so he didn't have to look at death at every corner. He spent hours grabbing everything he could think of to make long-term survival possible, and being Russian, that included a large quantity of vodka. However, with each passing hour, he felt increasingly more ill and wasn't sure he would actually live for the long term, but he at least had a goal.

Back on TCf, Gigory landed closer to the pond that Downy had shown him. By the time he landed, he was in terrible pain and curled up in a fetal position on the shuttlecraft deck. As he passed out, he thought, *It had been worth a try.*

Gigory awoke in the dark a while later and considered for a moment, *I'm still here!* He had no idea how long he had been out, but he felt good and couldn't be more pleased that his experiment had worked. His risk had been worth it. He needed to send a message to Admiral Dodson.

Back on Russia, the two groups of survivors had been in communication. They did not know anything about their Captain's survival. Their more immediate issue was getting some food and water from the reserve engine room pod to Pod 2. Natasha Smirnov, who never seemed to fear anything, volunteered to set up a lifeline. She put on her space suit and rocket backpack, went through the air lock, and shot herself over to Pod 5 with a light line in tow. When she reached the other airlock, she pulled the light line, which was attached to a heavier line, and connected the two pods together.

Using this line, food, water, and much better-tasting near beer was shared. That short-term crisis was averted.

Days later the United States was on the scene and started the rescue. It wasn't really necessary, but Natasha repeated the order to, "Abandon ship." All thirty-two survivors were ready to leave. That went smoothly. Everyone was confident, to some degree, that the survivors were not contagious. But to be safe, the surviving crewmembers of Russia were placed in quarantine.

The trickier issue was the transfer of one engine pod from Russia to United States. In theory, it was straightforward; after all, it had been done once before. "All you need to do is uncouple the pod, unplug the connecting wires using the quick disconnect couplings, and move it to United States and reconnect." Then ending with those famous words, Natasha said, "Easy. What could go wrong?"

In this case, nothing went terribly wrong. It did take days to detach and then both move and reconnect it using a shuttlecraft. But finally, the pod the size of a city block was safely in place. "Well, that's once in row!" an engineer quipped. The United States once again had two spare engine room pods.

There wasn't much that could be done to the rest of the once proud Star Ship Russia. Except for the one operating engine room pod that wasn't contaminated, entering any part of the ship would likely mean certain death. The four operating engines were in idle mode, but they couldn't be shut down. The one spare, according to the rescued crew, was contaminated, but no one knew for certain. The rest of the ship was certainly contaminated with whatever had been brought up from the planet, and according to the rescued crew it was one very large morgue. Every man, woman, child, dog, chicken, finch, and honeybee were dead.

Still, no one could bring themselves to destroy the ship, not yet anyway. The island mentality of the fleet of making do with what was at hand kicked in with "maybe it will come in handy some day." With that in mind, two of the United States shuttlecrafts were used as tugs and pushed the Russia into a safer higher orbit around TCf.

147

In case one of the unattended but functioning engines went critical and blew up, destroying the rest of the ship with it, the greater orbit was protection for the planet.

From the time the United States left TCe and returned, nearly a month had passed.

Chapter 28
Star Ship Africa Mission

In 2114, the new Star Ship Africa had been launched. The UNSC did design a mission for the ship. The ship carried the four working engine room pods and its two spare pods, plus it was fitted out specifically for this mission to carry an additional six engine room pods. The purpose was to meet up with Star Ship South America at Epsilon Eridani so that it could be refitted for service.

Everything that could be sent through the Gate to the New Hope Island Gate had been sent in advance of the Africa's arrival so that all work could be completed beforehand, except for the engine room pods. The radioactive material required for fission/fusion engines could not be sent through the Gate. There had been discussions about building the engine room pods at EEb and then just bringing the fuel onto Africa and fueling the South America on site. This turned out to be far more complicated than building the pods and fueling them in Earth's orbit, so it was decided to turn Africa into a freighter of sorts for this portion of the mission.

The Star Ship Africa looked a lot like the other Star Ships, if the extra engine pods were ignored. It was also slightly smaller in length at 2,500 feet. It didn't need the extra space for construction equipment or the materials for a wormhole Gate. Once the extra engine pods were transferred to South America, the vision for Africa was to be less encumbered. Future missions might require the ship to explore without the need to bring a lot of "stuff." This also meant the crew could be smaller, with a focus on the proper operation of the ship and due to not having to carry all the additional personnel required to establish a colony. A crew of 4,500 was more than adequate for this long journey, even with the need for more hands-on operations due to simplified computer programming.

The number crunchers had been asked if the trip to EE could be shortened. Anything less than the twenty-eight years that it took for the original mission would be a plus. With the experience of space travel better understood, some changes that were less conservative were implemented. The Africa would be allowed to exceed the arbitrarily established three-quarter light speed limit used on the original mission.

The ship would be allowed to accelerate slightly faster than the 1.5 g limits at the discretion of the captain and the onboard scientists. Reversing the ship, decelerating, and providing 0.5 g's would be the same, but turns would be more frequent. The ship would turn gradually until it was facing backwards and then decelerate, just as all of the other ships would. But this would be done more often with the Africa maintaining a greater overall speed towards EE.

When Captain Chiku, who only went by one name, first learned how much of an arc was needed to turn the ship around, he made the same observation made by others on the first mission, "Wow, we need a lot of room for the turns."

To which he got the same answer, "Yes, that's true, but guess what, there is a lot of space out there in space."

It was now fourteen years after the launch of the Star Ship Africa. There were no major issues with the ship. Most of the crew remained in high spirits, keeping busy when off duty with hobbies, parties, and continuing education. As always, there were the few that were the exception, especially with a crew this large, but most of the people problems were small. There was one jealousy-based murder that really dampened spirits for a time. The murder was brutal, and there was no question of guilt, so the trial was quick and followed military court martial protocol. This was followed by a quick execution. The guilty party chose to be ejected into space as a means of execution.

In 2128, Captain Chiku intercepted a message being sent to UNSC headquarters. It had taken three years to reach him, so even though the news he received wasn't new, it was new to him. The Star Ship fleet mission to Tau Ceti had not gone well. Russia and its crew had effectively been lost, leaving the remainder of the fleet without critical components for the wormhole Gate on TCe.

150

So far, the planet's indigenous population was balking at all overtures from the humans. Apparently, there was a lot of negotiating, so the Admiral remained optimistic that eventually a Gate could be built. Star Ships British Commonwealth and China were remaining in orbit around TCe, but Star Ship United States was heading back to EEb. It was on track to arrive at EEb about the same time Africa would arrive. Once South America was fitted out, the three ships would head for TCe. South America would have a new crew. The United States and Africa crewmembers that wanted to return to Earth could. New crews would be ready to go as needed.

The three ships together would carry everything needed to complete a Gate on TCe. For now, there was nothing for the Star Ship Africa and their crews to do except get to EEb without delay or mishap.

There was one other piece of information that really got the Captain Chiku's attention. Apparently, the fleet had rescued a castaway along the way. Before leaving Earth, the Captain had been taken aside by Princes Charm-E-Ine's advisor, Adio Mwanjuma, and was told in confidence a little about the Princess being part of some Order. The castaway, it seemed, appeared to be part of perhaps the same Order. Captain Chiku could only think, *Is this a coincidence? I don't think so.*

Chapter 29
What Now?

While the United States was on the rescue mission, some other decisions were made. There had been a break, or more like a crack, in the negotiations with the Tall Ones and Mobile Ones on TCe. It was just enough of a break that the Admiral believed something positive would eventually be worked out. He just had to find the one thing to win them over. He determined that it was worth staying in the Tau Ceti solar system rather than simply giving up and returning to EEb and New Hope Island. That said, there was the not-so-small issue of not having enough wormhole Gate components to complete a project.

Almost all agreed that attempting to take the components off Russia wasn't worth the risk, at least for now. So, to get what was needed, the United States would return to Epsilon Eridani and then bring the missing resources back. Of course, this wasn't like going down the street to a hardware store to pick up a few nuts and bolts; it had been a thirteen-year journey to get to Tau Ceti. At that rate, it would be twenty-six or twenty-seven years before the United States would return. Modifying the acceleration and deceleration protocols, the trip could, at best, be reduced to twenty-one years.

Even if negotiations failed on TCe and the entire fleet ended up returning to Epsilon Eridani b and New Hope Island, sending one ship in advance seemed prudent. Yes, it was a little risky sending one ship alone, but something had to be done and this seemed worth the risk.

All crew members of the three ships, however, were in consideration for the return trip, not just those on United States. Those that would be at sixty-seven years old by the time United States returned to TC had the first option to go back to EE and then back to Earth through the New Hope Gate. They would be replaced with a fresh crew from Earth. At least that was the Admiral's plan.

All others that wished to return home had their names placed into a lottery. However, a large number of people in the lottery who weren't selected threatened to make trouble. Eventually, the United States was filled with 18,356 people. This was a little over the design capacity, leaving better than 17,000 people on British Commonwealth and China combined, which was about the design limit for one Star Ship. Many of these people were not pleased to be left behind. They felt they also had been on this mission for too long and were now facing at least another twenty-one years of waiting. A lot could happen in that time.

The Admiral routinely sent updates of the fleet's progress back to EEb. But since it took over two years for the messages to reach EEb and relayed back to Earth, no one outside of those within the fleet knew what had happened. As a result, the United States would be a quarter of the way back to EEb before UNSC would have any idea of the fleet's situation.

At the same time, Admiral Dodson only had old news from Earth. One piece of news that really piqued his interest was the launching of a new Star Ship funded by what was called the Union of African Nations, which was led by a charismatic Nubian princess who seemed to emerge out of nowhere. This turn of events was all certainly surprising, but what wasn't surprising was the name of the new Star Ship, Africa.

Star Ship Africa was heading to EEb while being overloaded with engine pods. It had enough new engines to outfit the abandoned Star Ship South America. This was, of course, interesting, but Neil was having a very difficult time trying to understand what the UNSC had in mind and how this all came about, especially since it was the UNSC that said a fleet of four Star Ships was all they could support. So now why was there a push for putting two more ships into the fleet? Or did the UNSC have other plan for the two ships? Was it a new mission to yet another solar system perhaps? None of this made much sense to Neil, but since he had more immediate concerns he put his questions aside. Anyway, it wasn't as if they were going to be answered right away, if ever.

In the midst of his cogitations, he was interrupted by a call from the Bridge: "Admiral, this is Captain Parks. You need to come to the Bridge as soon as you can. We have a new message from Captain Kazakov."

"Kazakov? Are you sure?"

"Yes, sir. It seems he is still among the living."

When Neil made it to the Bridge, Captain Parks played the message: "Admiral, this is Captain Kazakov. I can only guess at what has happened. But until, or if, this is ever understood, I am forced to take this at face value. What has affected, or infected, my crew and me appears to be something like a drug addiction. The drug is somehow the planet's ecosystem. The planet provides a peacefulness that seems new to me without affecting judgment. I don't think it has affected my judgment anyway. When it appeared as though I wasn't going to die right away after being on the planet for days, I went back to Russia to get food and supplies and started to suffer what I'll call withdrawal. The symptoms then disappeared completely after returning to the planet's surface.

"I have seen only one species of animal so far. As reported previously, it is about the size of a sheep but covered with what looks a lot like feathers. One of these creatures seems to have adopted me and is able to communicate. I talk and then I get a feeling of a response. I wouldn't call it mental telepathy, but maybe that's what it is.

"So far, I have not witnessed any severe weather. Soils here seem to be fertile, probably from these grazing creatures. I'm going to plant some seeds and hopefully something other than grass will grow. The creature that has adopted me—I call Downy—doesn't seem to object to the introduction of non-indigenous species of plant, or me for that matter. It is quite docile.

"I've had some time to think. In fact, more time than I like. I don't believe building a wormhole Gate here would be possible without severe consequences. This drug contamination would probably go through the Gate. On the other hand, it looks like humans could thrive here as long as they never left. I suppose some would think this would be a perfect penal colony, as no one could

154

ever leave, but this place should be reserved for those who would appreciate it.

"Please send messages so I don't go mad. If there are any thoughts on how I might be able to understand the planet better, please let me know. I realize now I should have been more helpful in the past. Perhaps in my exile I can make up for that shortcoming. Over and out."

Even those that had heard the message already still stood as stunned as the Admiral was. If only this revelation of the planet's power had on people had been known before, Star Ship Russia would still be an integral part of the fleet. True, the shuttle crew that landed on the planet would had to have stayed on the planet. Even if they hadn't exposed themselves to the environment, it now seems apparent that even the shuttlecraft carried whatever affected people back to the ship. He had no idea how this new information would affect the future of the fleet, but he felt certain it would. He didn't need Raman to tell him that, but perhaps Raman could offer up something.

Admiral Dodson left the Bridge without saying a word. He went directly to the briefing room and called in Zanck, Raman, Sharon, Kristie, and reluctantly, Shinya. Even while they were gathering, word of Captain Kazakov's survival started spreading throughout the two ships. It didn't take long before some started thinking that being exiled in paradise would not be a bad option.

In the briefing room, Neil repeated the message from Captain Kazakov and immediately turned to Raman and Sharon. "Is it possible to focus your attention on TCf and offer something? Anything?"

"Actually," said Sharon, "Raman did have a spell. He saw a population on TCf before blacking out. We thought maybe it was the population of those grazing creatures, but maybe it was humans? I don't know."

"I thought you were to tell me or Kristie if there were any episodes."

"No," said Raman. "You didn't think it; you clearly said it."

Pursing his lips, squinting, and looking over the top of his glasses squarely at Sharon, who was rolling her eyes, he said, "And?"

"This happened less than an hour ago. You were busy," Sharon responded just as Raman went into a trance.

Raman said, "United States will have…" But he blacked out before he could finish. Sharon tried to catch him, but Raman was just too big and fell to the deck, adding more black and blue marks to those already on his body.

Neil shook his head saying, "Now what?"

Chapter 30
Breakthrough

Admiral Dodson was certain that some long-term agreement could be made with the Tall Ones. They had been interested in the concept of an atmosphere exchange, but they were less than thrilled with what was involved in order to build the wormhole Gate. Something more was needed.

In the meantime, there had been progress with short-term arrangements. The concept of hundreds of tiny bug ships lifting China's Shuttlecraft 2 into the upper atmosphere and somehow transferring it over to another shuttlecraft, only to be towed back to China, was considered for perhaps a nano-moment before being rejected. It was the transfer part that created the angst. It was simply too precarious.

Instead, it was determined that some emergency repairs were possible. The crew would have to wear their space suits, because the hull had too many holes in it to hold any atmosphere. Parts were dropped and then brought to the shuttlecraft by the bug ships. Engineers onboard China took the shuttlecraft crew through the repair procedures until there was some level of comfort. Engine testing was out of the question for fear it would ignite a massive fire.

Instead, several hundred bug ships did connect to the shuttlecraft and lifted it to above a safe elevation of 35,000 feet. The engines were started, and the bug ships released the craft. It dropped slightly as momentum built and without incident made its way to China. There was no incident, that is, related to the actual shuttlecraft at least. However, more than one crewmember had serious laundry issues after the flight.

On another front, Pilot, Engineer, and Fire Control had reluctantly agreed to stay on board British Commonwealth when asked by the Tall Ones. Neil saw this as a good sign that the Tall Ones wanted to maintain communications, so Neil decided to give the bug ship crew more access to the ship. They were always carried, of course, by one of the biologists. Usually, Raman went as well to maintain an open dialogue. During one of the tours, Thanos, filling a conversation lag, casually asked, "So what is the biggest issue facing your people?"

Fire Control responded immediately with, "Short term, it is the Stranglers. They have become very aggressive and will not even discuss any possible resolutions to the common problem we all face: not enough CO_2. Our waters can no longer sustain any quality of life, as dissolved CO_2 is nearly depleted. Many Stranglers have evolved enough to reach out of the waters and in their search of a source of carbon attack the Tall Ones. The Stranglers grow around the Tall Ones, sending roots into the Tall Ones and extracting carbon. Once the Tall Ones are reduced to dust, the Stranglers move on and branch out. Losing any Tall One this way is serious, but the Stranglers have been spreading out at an increasing rate and have stopped all communications."

Thanos, looking puzzled, said, "I thought the yellowish-green acid goop you used to shoot down our shuttlecraft killed the Stranglers."

"It did, but they have been adapting fast. The advanced branches are now almost completely immune. The Tall Ones haven't come up with any new weapon that we, the Mobile Ones, could use. We are mobile, but we are quite small in comparison to the Tall Ones and the Stranglers, so there are limitations."

"And there is no other plant species or other life form on the planet?"

"I don't understand the question. What is plant life? There has always been the Tall Ones, the Mobile Ones, and the Stranglers."

"Plants where we come from are... well, that's not important." Thanos had started to explain plant life but quickly decided that was a bad idea. He had suddenly realized that perhaps with no recorded history, even if there had been some other life on TCe, the current residents might not know it. If this were true, then there might have been some other species of some kind that used to thrive on oxygen, like humans do, creating the CO_2 the three species of life on TCe now need. On the other hand, there was a time in Earth's history when there was no oxygen. As oxygen had become a byproduct, oxygen-breathing species developed. This was a very interesting question, and it was an answer he hoped Shinya was working on.

Thanos shifted to, "So, what would be the ultimate solution for the Stranglers if it could be reached? Killing them all off?"

"We kill for self-preservation. The collective intelligence of the Tall Ones can't be compromised. Ideally, the Stranglers would give up their aggression and go back to the sea that was their home. We don't see that happening. Unfortunately for the Stranglers, if they continue as they are, they will eventually kill off all the Tall Ones. The Stranglers will then die off, too, leaving only the Mobile Ones, but we will be without purpose or direction."

This last comment about purpose and direction got Raman's attention. It was, after all, the lack of purpose and direction that led him to the Order. He guessed that all species needed purpose and direction, even if they didn't realize it.

When the tour ended, Thanos asked to meet with the Admiral and the two Vice Admirals. While too much oxygen and not enough carbon dioxide was the overall long-term concern, it was the threat of the Stranglers that was the immediately pressing concern. If the humans could propose a way to deal with the Stranglers, it might be the breakthrough needed to eventually set up a wormhole Gate and small colony. Besides being a way station for more missions to other solar systems, it could eventually become the final solution for carbon neutrality on Earth.

In fact, Shinya had been able to focus on one issue. It was a single issue that invited his need to drill down into the smallest detail. Other issues that he didn't care to consider were left to the senior academics in his department. Not surprising, they assumed the work on some peripheral issues without being specifically assigned. They knew these other issues were important, and having nothing else to do, they just went ahead meeting in small groups to self-assigning these tasks. Zanck and the other Second People worked in one of these groups. Neil had no idea this was happening, but that was about to change.

"Well, Shinya, do you have anything you'd like to share?"

"Yes."

After a very long moment, Neil nearly shouted, "Well, what is it?"

"Oh, I've been studying the bug ship when the crew was touring to try to understand how it works."

"I don't suppose you got permission to do that."

"Huh? Well, I was trying to understand what the power source is, because as we know anything that might spark a fire is avoided. The mechanics that make it fly are very complex and don't matter."

"They don't matter?" asked Neil.

"What matters is the power source…"

At this point Raman whispered to Sharon, "Shouldn't Shinya be listening to the Admiral?"

Sharon repeated her usual phrase "I'll explain later."

As Shinya continued, "…which is fascinating. The power source, as well as the ship's controls, is the crew. The ship itself is very light, as there is no built-in power supply or controls. The crew, when seated, uses their lower appendages, or I guess we'd call them roots, to communicate with each other and the ship. Power also comes through this connection. As the ship is light, it requires little power. That said, the flight time is comparatively short, as the crew needs to recharge by settling into soil and absorbing or breathing in CO_2. It's rather fascinating I think."

"Fascinating!" barked Neil. "This sounds incredibly unbelievable. What else?"

"Oh, I want to take one of the crew apart to see how they function."

Somewhat stunned by this comment, Neil said in calm voice while looking over the top of his glasses, "You can want all you want, but it ain't gonna happen. Got it? You're not to touch one hair, or branch, or whatever is on those little guys!"

"I just want one," pleaded Shinya.

"No! And to be sure you get it, hell no! What else do we have? What about the Stranglers?"

"What about them?" asked a now confused Shinya.

"Shinya," said Neil. "You or somebody in your organization was supposed to figure out a way to control the Stranglers."

"Is that important?"

"Unbelievable. Anybody else have anything?"

Raman whispered to Sharon, "Is the Admiral upset?"

"I'll explain latter."

Zanck put up his arm and started signing, "Some of us formed a task force to look into the Stranglers. Obviously, we don't have any first-hand experience with them, but with Raman's help we floated an idea across Fire Control."

Raman looked at Sharon and mouthed, "Floated?" Sharon just shook her head.

Zanck continued. "As we have been told, the Stranglers have developed, or evolved, a means to neutralize the effects of the goop the Mobile Ones have been shooting at them. A flame-thrower would work, but the consequences of using a flame means that is out of consideration. It may sound crude and old-fashioned, but we think hacking at them with cutting tools should be a deterrent. If we can heat the cutting edge to cauterize the ends, it would stop growth—at least in that direction, we think. We discussed the use of what you humans call "herbicides" and rejected that as generally bad for the environment, but also because it might somehow affect the Mobile Ones and the Tall Ones. The cutting idea would have to be done by Star Ship crew members, as the Mobile Ones are simply too small."

"OK," said Neil. "If nothing else, that would certainly get their attention, and maybe Raman could open a dialogue. So how do we get a task force down on the surface to start cutting and hacking?"

Kristie chimed in, "Our shuttlecrafts can make it to the surface by gliding down. They aren't really designed for that, but engineering is confident that some auxiliary wings would help. It would still be a rough ride and there would need to be a clear area to land."

"That gets us down there, but what about getting back?" Neil asked.

"Ah! That's easy. We use the same approach we used to get the China shuttlecraft back. Hundreds of bug ships towing the shuttlecraft to the upper atmosphere where the engines can be ignited," replied Kristie.

"This is a lot to take in. I think I'll float this past the Mobile Ones and Tall Ones," said Neil.

Raman mouthed to Sharon, "More floating?" before going into a trance saying, "Our numbers will soon diminish." He then blacked out, slumping in his chair.

Chapter 31
War

The Admiral presented everything he had to the Tall Ones and Mobile Ones. In the short term, he would send down squads to put an end to the Stranglers. This would be done either by cutting them away or by negotiating some sort of an agreement. When the Stranglers were dealt with, the humans would be allowed to begin a settlement. The settlement would be in a location that was uninhabited and conducive to constructing the wormhole Gate. A plateau had been identified that would work. It was at an elevation of about 14,000 feet where nothing grew. It was not ideal for a settlement, but it was potentially workable for a Gate.

Eventually, the Gate would be constructed and somehow an atmosphere exchange would be implemented where TCe would get CO_2-rich atmosphere from Earth, and Earth would get TCe-rich O_2 atmosphere in exchange. A second settlement nearby the first one, but at a lower elevation, would be needed to support the Gate operations and the staff needs such as farming. This was understood, but there would have to be a wait-and-see period. Neil suggested a trading post, but he couldn't figure what might be traded. If nothing else, this new Gate would be a supply depot for future exploration missions by the fleet.

The Tall Ones made it clear that they didn't fully trust the humans, but they were willing to move forward one step at a time. For now, that meant going after the Stranglers. The Tall Ones could see no drawbacks with the humans engaging the enemy.

With that settled, Neil set up a conference with the Captains and CASOs on both ships explaining the deal. He hardly finished when Captain Ying Yue said, "I'd like my marines to be the first to engage. We are ready."

Captain Parks said with a smirk, "You've been looking for a fight. You know this probably will be more like tree-pruning rather than fighting. You think your marines can handle that? Might be pretty risky."

Sharon knew what was coming when Raman whispered, "This doesn't sound too risky to me."

But before she could say anything, Raman went into one of his trances again and said, "Mourning is on the horizon," and then went face down on the conference table.

Everyone had learned that it was wise to listen to Raman's warnings, but in this case they all heard "morning," not "mourning," so they were confused. After all, morning was always on the horizon.

China Shuttlecraft 3 carried twenty-four marines from the Star Ship armed with axes, machetes, handsaws, and anything else they could think of that could cut the vines without creating a spark. There was a lot of joking as the shuttlecraft headed for the planet. After all, the marines had been a police force on the ship with almost nothing to do for years. So while they wouldn't be able to fight like real soldiers, at least they were going to do something. Someone joked they were the "cutting edge" and all agreed that would be their platoon nickname. In addition to the marines and shuttle crew was Raman, whose function was to communicate with the Stranglers with the hope they would back off.

As expected, the landing was rough as the shuttle glided down and plowed into an area that the Stranglers had already left desolate before moving—or growing—on. There was very little there to indicate anything had ever lived there. It was about two miles to where the Stranglers where attacking the Tall Ones. Once on the ground, the marines put on exoskeleton suits to counter the increased gravity of the planet. The marines noted with quiet envy that Raman didn't seem to need one. The marines and Raman headed off, instantly noting the fresh oxygen-rich atmosphere. "This will be fun," quipped one of the marines.

Raman reminded everyone, "We're to try and get them to back off first. Unnecessary death is to be avoided."

"Raman, you know we're talking about vines, not people or even critters."

"Yes, perhaps, but let me talk first," Raman answered.

As the group approached the area of destruction, things started to look a little different. First witnessed by Raman were the creaking sounds of the Tall Ones, which could be translated as screaming as the Stranglers, encircling the Tall Ones at a rate that was easily seen, strangled and then feed off them. The leading ends of the vines were nearly microscopic, but further down the vines were more than three feet in diameter. From the "trunk," multiple branches fanned out. The ground was so covered by the Stranglers that there was no place to step, but 100 feet or so back from the destruction was nothing but bare soil. The Chinese marines looked at their leader, who said, "This looks like a bit more than a pruning job."

Raman moved to the front of the group. Making creaking sounds as loud as he could, he asked who was the leader of the Stranglers. All movement by the Stranglers stopped and Raman heard, "We are one with each other. We are of one purpose, deciding and acting as one. What are you, and what do you want?"

Raman did the best he could to explain who and what he represented, and he concluded with a demand that they stop what they are doing in exchange for a future reclamation of their home waters. This explanation, punctuated with questions from the Stranglers, went on for nearly two hours. Raman confirmed the Stranglers were a subspecies of what still survived in the sea. The Stranglers had rebelled against the rest and somehow were determined to evolve into a terrestrial version of the ocean life. This took only a few decades to do, and they continued to become more resistant to the Mobile Ones' attacks.

Raman said, "We are committed to defend the Tall Ones if you persist with this aggression."

The Stranglers snapped back, "Go away you annoying creature. We will dominate this land by ridding it of these self-righteous Tall Ones and their puny little Mobile Ones. You will not stop us."

Raman wasn't sure he got the exact language, but he certainly understood the context and relayed it to the marines, who with one voice said, "It is war then!"

As the Stranglers went back to their path of destruction, the marines moved forward. Their strategy was to hack off the leading ends of the vines as far back as their cutting tools would allow. They would approach from the leading areas of the Stranglers' attack and work back towards the thicker sections of the Stranglers.

The first two marines to start hacking were only seconds into their work when leading vine edges, released from the Tall One being attacked nearby, suddenly lashed out and speared them both. The other Marines stood horrified as their two companions were reduced to powder in minutes.

Raman heard the Stranglers say, "These are good. Send more."

The platoon leader ordered a retreat. Plan A was not going to work. Even worse was the fact that some of the vines' leading ends slowly moved off the Tall Ones, and they started following Raman and the Marines in their retreat. Fortunately, the vines' progress was slow, allowing plenty of time for the survivors to get back into the shuttlecraft and for the fleet of little bug ships to lift it off towards Star Ship China.

Absorbing what had happened, the Admiral realized that Raman had actually said "mourning," as there was now a general sense of grief within the ship for the two dead marines. Captain Yue's eagerness for a fight was raised to a new level after losing two warriors. "To plants for heaven's sake. This shall be avenged!" she cried out!"

"Yes," said Neil, "but we're not sending more people down there without a better plan. We were too cocky by underestimating our opponent. It is obvious that we were thinking we were dealing with plants like we have on Earth, not some kind of plant-like creatures that can think, reason, and adapt. Raman, Zanck, and Kristie have talked with Fire Control from the bug ship. He confirms the behavior we saw was not expected; the Mobile Ones never got close enough to trigger that reaction. I have assigned them," and with a sigh, he added, "and Shinya to devise a new plan. I'm hoping our Vice Admiral of Academics and Science can use his multiple degrees in Botany to devise something clever. We need a solid Plan B."

Chapter 32
Mutiny

The thirty-two crewmembers rescued from the abandoned Russia had been brought back to the British Commonwealth with all hopes of New Polyarnaya gone. At first, they were thankful to be saved. Then many suffered from survivor's guilt when they thought about the loss of most of the crew. This was coupled with the realization that their Captain had decided to expose himself to whatever had killed the crew and die a quick death rather than die from starvation. When they then learned that their Captain was actually doing quite well on TCf, they weren't sure what to think.

When the United States left to return to EEb, the remaining Russians as a group decided to stay behind. They really had nothing to go back to on Earth, and the thought of leaving their Captain didn't seem right even though he was on another planet. Communications weren't constant, but their Captain did get to communicate from time to time with his remaining crewmembers. It seemed the Captain had indeed found the perfect place to establish a new Polyarnaya. It was heartbreaking to think that every one of the Russia crew could have lived their dream if only it had been realized that they simply needed to go to the planet's surface and stay there. When one the crewmembers commented, "We should join the Captain," it started many to start thinking along those lines.

All of them knew the remaining two Star Ships were staying behind with the hopes of establishing some kind of an outpost on TCe, but in order for that to happen the Admiral had to make good on a commitment he made to battle these so-called Stranglers. The first encounter proved that conquering these creatures wasn't going to be as easy as first imagined. And assuming they could even be conquered in the future, the humans' reward would be a less-than-ideal outpost on the planet, with the long-term hope that a wormhole Gate would be built. At best, it would be another twenty or so years until the Star Ship United States returned.

The more the Russians thought about it, the vision of being "trapped" on TCf with Captain Kazakov seemed like a rather pleasant way to spend the rest of their lives. Gradually, the Russians started to share their once secret mission of creating a new Polyarnaya and the possibility of doing it on TCf. It didn't take long before some non-Russian crewmembers started sharing the same vision. This was especially true among those who were denied the opportunity to go back to EEb on the United States.

The Admiral became aware that there was some grumbling among the crews, but he was preoccupied with negotiations and war with the locals. At one point, Raman went into one of his trances and announced, "Trouble will lead to a new settlement." Unfortunately, anyone who heard this proclamation assumed it meant a settlement would be established on TCe after the Stranglers were defeated. Time would reveal the true meaning of these words, however.

As the plans for the war began escalating, the Russians petitioned the Admiral to be brought to TCf to join their Captain. This was not expected, of course, and the Admiral didn't take this seriously, so he said, "No." He did think about it, however, but only from a logistics point of view. *How could we even do that? Any shuttlecraft we would use could only make a one-way trip. If it returned and docked, it would contaminate the entire ship.*

The conflict on TCe was originally thought to be almost a joke by the marines, with many of them acting more like arborists than a fighting unit at first, but it had turned into something much more sinister. The Stranglers weren't passively allowing the humans and Mobile Ones to eradicate them. Instead, the Stranglers seemed capable of establishing a rather robust defense. The Stranglers had shown that they were able to quickly evolve physically in order to ward off attacks. At the same time, they were being aggressive when an attack was threatened. It didn't help that the Stranglers apparently found the carbon-based humans tasty and were hoping for more. This was an enemy far different from anything the marines had ever trained to encounter. It was jungle warfare, where the jungle itself was the actual enemy.

As new battle plans developed, the number of disgruntled crewmembers grew and became increasingly more belligerent.

Interestingly, most of the troublemakers were on the British Commonwealth. The China crew, for the most part, passively attended to their duties, but not all. Captain Yue and her CASO Ling Zhao issued harsh punishment to anyone accused of disloyalty. Unfortunately for Captain Yue, that type of behavior was adding to the disloyalty.

The Admiral did note that the discontent might lead to something more serious and remembered Raman's vision. "Trouble will lead to a new settlement." Considering possible solutions, Neil reasoned that if he could orchestrate a defeat or retreat of the Stranglers and establish a settlement on TCe, then everyone would be happy. If not necessarily happy, then at least they'd be content. Maybe.

As it turned out, the momentum was too great. Fifty-five China crewmembers took over the shuttlecraft bay, with another 137 outside the bay who were armed with clubs, knives, axes, fire extinguishers, and anything else they could find short of guns. As much as they wanted off the ship, they didn't want to risk shooting holes in it even if they had access to firearms. Their demands were clear, though: "We want to be brought to TCf and join up with Captain Kazakov."

Captain Yue was furious and ready to send her marines in to throw them all in the brig, but before doing anything she called the Admiral. "Admiral, we have a situation here. Some of my crew want to leave. They have taken over the shuttlecraft bay and want to be brought to TCf to join with Captain Kazakov. That is a long trip for a shuttlecraft, and one ship wouldn't be able to handle the number of those who want to go. I think they might take the remaining two active shuttlecrafts and make the trip, though I suspect they don't have any pilots among them. I want my marines to go in and bash some heads and lock them up. Looks like a couple of hundred people."

"Yes," said Neil in response, "I'm sure you would love to knock them around." Captain Yue was surprised when the Admiral continued with, "It seems worse here. This mutinous activity must have been festering for some time. This action was obviously coordinated. We have over 300 on the shuttle bay deck, and I've been told there are others who want off the ships as well. They won't identify the ringleader, but they do have a spokesperson. Lock down the shuttle bay outer doors, set up a perimeter to keep this isolated, but don't confront them. Oh! And at least for now, don't provide them with any food or water."

"I'd love to give them something, but it wouldn't be food or water."

"Understood. Maybe later, but for now sit tight until I can figure something out. Out."

It was Sara Brown who was designated as the mutineers' spokesperson. The Admiral, Vice Admiral Marshal, Raman, and Sharon met with Sara in the Admiral's meeting room. In addition, Neil had set up a communications link with Captain Kazakov. While there was the long-time delay for the signal to reach the Captain, the Admiral wanted feedback. The Admiral started with, "Sara, this mutiny isn't going to get you anywhere. What do you think is going to happen?"

"Admiral, with all due respect, we don't want to take over the Star Ships. We just want to get off. We are a long way from home, the plan to set up a Gate is many years into the future, this war with those vine things doesn't look like it will be going well, and we have a perfectly good place to settle on TCf. We just want to go there."

"First off, if you really had respect, we wouldn't be sitting here now having this conversation."

"Perhaps, but we wanted to get your attention."

Looking over the top of glasses, with tight lips and squinted eyes, the Admiral said, "Well, you succeeded. Let me explain a few things. First off, you will not be taking any of the shuttlecrafts. Second, assuming we somehow get you to TCf, there is no telling what you will encounter. Captain Kazakov seems to be doing well, but there is no understanding of what might happen in the long run.

You might all end up dying from whatever affected the Russia crew, but later. Third, while the climate conditions seem perfectly fine now, we don't know what the seasonal changes are. Fourth, how do you think you are going to set up shop and thrive? You'll need to grow your food and build shelters. That doesn't just happen. You know that. It is precisely why we have what we have on the ships. Oh! By the way, does the good Captain Kazakov know about this?"

Raman was a little confused with "good captain," but for once said nothing.

"Admiral, Captain Kazakov is not aware of any of this. We are aware that there are risks, but they seem worth it to us. Remember, not everyone that wanted to go back to EEb and New Hope Island were allowed to go." Then turning red and raising her voice, Sara said, "And your pig-headed decision to have only the United States return instead of the entire fleet was wrong. Many of us thought that was a stupid decision. We should have all gone back, but you wanted to be a hero and finish the mission."

Kristie could see that Neil was about to blow up, so she said, "Sara, you can leave now."

"But we're not finished here."

"Oh, yes we are. For now anyway. Dismissed. Now!"

Sara was red-faced, and stood up quickly, overturning her chair, and stormed out of the room, only to be stopped by the two marines at the door. Kristie said to them, "Take her back to her traitor friends." Then turning to Neil said, "That went well."

Raman said, "That didn't seem to go well to me."

Sharon rolled her eyes saying, "I'll explain later."

Neil tried to ignore this little exchange, but it did direct his attention to Raman. "I didn't have you here because you have a pretty face. I want to know what you were sensing from Sara Brown. I need some of your intuitiveness."

Raman's first thought was, *I have a pretty face? What's that got to do with anything?* But after a long minute of thinking, he said, "Sara was very nervous. I think she represents accurately the feelings of most of the troublemakers. They, like most people, are afraid of the unknown. They are aware there are unknowns on TCf but believe the worst on TCf is better than the best being faced on TCe."

"Do you sense the number of people that want to leave?"

"It is far more than the numbers at the shuttle bays. I sense they are in the thousands."

"Thousands!" shouted Neil. "Good God save us."

"I'm pretty sure we'll need to save ourselves," said a very innocent Raman.

Hours later, Neil received a response from Captain Kazakov: "Admiral, Sara Brown was correct. I knew nothing about this. I will be honest and tell you that I certainly wouldn't mind having human company. Downy and his, or her, or whatever it is, friends are nice to have around, but they aren't my kind. You are correct that neither of us have any idea what long-term effects this planet might have on people. I have only experienced the most perfect weather, but I also don't know what seasons are like here. The seeds I planted are doing well. In fact, everything is growing faster than expected. At the moment, I don't expect ill effects from whatever matures, but who knows. I don't. Assuming you let people come, I think they will do well here. The calming effect of the planet should allow me to keep order. That also assumes that there is a way to get people here without compromising British Commonwealth and China. I'll cooperate as best I can. Over and out."

Over the next couple of weeks, The Admiral, Kristie, and the three Captains developed a plan. In the short term, Neil allowed the mutineers food and drink in exchange for a list of all that wished to leave the Star Ships. Next to each name was an "M" if they identified themselves as a mutineer, an "F" if they were related to a mutineer and wanted to leave, or an "A" meaning they weren't part of the mutiny but also wanted to leave. This system wasn't perfect, as not everyone was going to be truthful, but it gave the command an idea of what they might be dealing with. The bottom line was that a little more than 1,500 wanted to leave China, much to Captain Yue's shame. She felt better, when it was learned that over 4,400 wanted to leave British Commonwealth. Included in that number were all but one rescued from Russia.

This many people leaving the fleet would have both good and bad ramifications, but in the end, it was decided it was better to get rid of the malcontents now. Neil made a one-time offer to the crews of both ships. He would allow people to go to TCf. This was understood to be a one-way trip. Those leaving would take their personal possessions, enough food for six months, hand tools for building shelters, and growing crops. They were to leave the local indigenous creatures alone. They would be allowed a small flock of chickens, with the idea that the flock would be providing eggs and chicken meat for the long term. The one shuttlecraft operated by Captain Kazakov could be used to retrieve more materials from Russia, but anything Gate related, including all construction equipment, was to be left behind with the hope that it might somehow be used in the future.

When Neil, through Sara, told the mutineers how they were going to get to TCf, a little less than 500 decided that staying behind was a better option. Everyone that wanted to leave was transferred to the British Commonwealth. The Star Ship would go over to TCf. Captain Kazakov would fly his shuttle up near the British Commonwealth, but he would not dock. A line would be shot from the Star Ship to the shuttlecraft, and once secured those departing would put on their space suits and take themselves along the line to the shuttlecraft into the airlock. Three people at a time could go through the airlock. When about a twenty people were on board the shuttlecraft, it would bring them down to TCf. This process was to be repeated over and over until everyone that wanted to leave with their supplies had been brought down.

There was some discussion about using the remaining two shuttlecrafts still on board Russia, but there were no qualified pilots, so Captain Kazakov had to do all the work. In all, it took nearly a week before all the transfers were completed. Those that had changed their mind did so when they realized they would be doing a spacewalk.

The British Commonwealth was away from TCe for over a month. While it was away, the China crew was left weightless, as it took at least two ships tied together at the bow to rotate and create centrifugal force. China was also left to renew the fight on TCe. Captain Yue was both pleased to be left in command of this effort and annoyed with the reasons.

Gigory Kazakov maintained his title of Captain and rightfully assumed command of the new settlers on TCf. He assigned tasks prioritizing shelter and farming. He did allow a small group to do exploring, but he kept the settlement boundary restricted.

Gigory did communicate with Downy to try to ascertain if there would be problems with what was happening to Downy's planet.

Downy communicated, *No.* But he added with no further explanation, *We also are not native.*

Gigory Kazakov was left startled and thinking, *What does that mean?*

Admiral Dodson was now down to a little more 13,000 crewmembers on two ships designed for 36,000. If this kept up, there would be no one left to build anything.

Chapter 33
I Hear You

With everything that was going on, the Admiral had nearly forgotten that he asked Raman to try and get his premonitions under control. It wasn't good that Raman was potentially causing physical injury to himself, but from a selfish standpoint Neil wanted to have as much advance information as possible.

However, with Sharon's help Raman had been working on it. It wasn't clear how much actual work went into it, as Sharon was now extremely close emotionally and physically, with this "work" now exclusively taking place in Sharon's quarters. The game plan was to isolate Raman from distractions and to meditate. The end goal was to have the same premonitions, but it would be in a controlled setting. Neither of them was sure this would work, but nothing would be lost in the effort.

Also, neither of them knew that another distant being was receiving many of Raman's thoughts. Though they were not all of his thoughts, they were those which had any anxiety associated with them.

On Earth, Princess Charmy had occasionally heard what she thought were people talking in her vicinity. It took some time to realize that she wasn't a schizophrenic and was in fact picking up messages from someone else. It was something buried deep in her memory banks that came forward, reminding her of what she had been told so many year ago about her DNA: "Don't worry about it, but you have an extremely rare condition, a unique configuration of your DNA, that gives you the ability to communicate over unknown distances with someone else with the same DNA. Documentation of this condition indicates that it is so rare that you'll never be able to use it."

Somehow, someone else had this ability and was transmitting alarming messages to Princess Charmy. It wasn't clear that these messages were directed to her, but she was certainly receiving them. In any case, it seemed important that this communications link be established somehow. To that end, Princess Charmy would take time from her busy schedule to sit quietly and meditate. What she found initially was that she should have been doing this anyway. She felt so much more relaxed and focused after each meditation. It was only a few months before it finally happened.

Raman was in Sharon's quarters after their shift in the Lounge. Even though he had the lofty title of Ambassador of Foreign Affairs, he still needed to keep busy. Besides, while working in the Lounge or making beer, he was able to eat and drink as much as he wanted without anyone noticing, except Sharon. They had just taken a little "nap" and Raman was resting with his head in Sharon's lap. Sharon was gently rubbing Raman's temples, and his thoughts were wandering. Raman was trying hard to put his mind at ease, but with the fleet now down to two ships, the mutiny, the war on TCe, being so far removed from his original mission, and the general sense of uncertainty, his mind was far too active. At one point his thoughts were, *What am I supposed to do?*

He did more than startle Sharon when he bolted upright. He certainly hadn't expected the response, *Who are you?* Raman got up and looked to see who was in the room with them. Not seeing anyone, Raman asked, "Did you hear that?"

"Hear what?"

"Someone wants to know who I am."

"Ah, noooo. I didn't hear a thing. Are you all right? Is this another of those premonition things you have?"

"No, this is something completely different."

"Maybe you should answer?"

Raman thought about this for a few minutes. *How can I answer?*

Not seeing any action on Raman's part, Sharon finally suggested, "Why don't we go back to what we were doing when you got the message or question or whatever you think you heard? What were you thinking at the time?"

"I was thinking about everything that's going on and just wondering 'What am I supposed to do?' I certainly didn't expect a response."

Trying to lighten the moment, Sharon said, "Well, why ask a question if you don't expect an answer?"

"What?"

"Never mind, come lay back down and focus on a response. I don't know how this might go, but can you possibly try and project your thoughts? Like aiming them somehow?"

With that, Raman lay down on the bed and once again put his head in Sharon's lap. He initially was too keyed up, but eventually with Sharon rubbing his temples, he was once again able to relax and focus his thoughts. *I am Raman-I-El. I am on the Star Ship British Commonwealth in the Tau Ceti solar system. Who are you?*

I am Charm-E-Ine on the planet Earth. Your name tells me that we are from the same home world. I have many questions for you.

As do I for you, thought Raman, *but this effort is taxing. Can we continue later?*

Yes, very taxing. I am excited to have contact. Let us do this again in twenty-four hours.

Yes, twenty-four hours. And with that, Raman passed out.

Sharon didn't move. She could not hear this thought conversation, but she could tell from Raman's rapid eye movement and tenseness in his body that something was going on. When

178

Raman came around hours later, he was extremely excited. He didn't go into the home-world scenario. Instead, he only said he was communicating with someone like himself who was on Earth. Sharon stared at him and exclaimed, "That's impossible. Earth is twelve light years away!"

Raman considered this. "Yeah, OK, but she—I think it is a she—said she was on Earth. We agreed to communicate again in twenty-four hours. I don't think we can do this for more than a few minutes at a time. It is exhausting. This is exciting, even if it turns out not to be true. Can we go and get something to eat?"

"Is there anything you do that doesn't require food and drink?"

"Well, yes" said a smiling Raman as he gently removed Sharon's clothes.

Chapter 34
The Impossible

Sharon and Raman decided not to tell the Admiral about this very intriguing and strange contact with Earth until they could somehow verify it was in fact contact with Earth. The whole thing was impossible, but over the next week and a half, with communication sessions occurring every twenty-four hours, it was starting to look like the impossible was actually happening. Still, this person calling herself Charm-E-Ine needed to be confirmed as someone actually on Earth and not someone who was pretending. They finally concluded that the Admiral or someone on his staff could ask the right questions to get the needed confirmation.

Raman fortified himself with several strong beers, and with Sharon at his side they met with Admiral Dodson and Kristie.

"Raman," said the Admiral almost smiling, "do you have some new premonitions for me?"

Not letting Raman speak right away, Sharon said, "Actually, we think we have something quite different to report."

"Oh really! Like what?"

"We think Raman might be communicating with Earth."

The Admiral, remembering the communication device used on the first mission, said, "So where did you two get a communications device? We didn't take one when we rescued Raman, and he certainly wasn't hiding one in the clothes he wasn't wearing when we rescued him. And what do you mean, 'might be?'"

"Well," said Sharon, "Raman has been making contact on a schedule—in brief spurts every twenty-four hours. The communications are not lengthy. Also, the information isn't anything we could verify as actually coming from Earth, so we're suspicious. We thought that perhaps you or the Vice Admiral could give us some questions that might confirm the origin."

180

"OK, so get me up to speed here. How is this possible?"

Raman spoke up, "I was doing what you asked, trying to control my premonitions. My body was very relaxed, but my mind was very active trying to understand what I should be doing. In my mind, I actually projected that very question and heard an answer. I thought someone had entered the room and was speaking to me, but no one was there but Sharon, and she heard nothing. With Sharon's help, I have been placing myself into the same relaxed state each night and have been having a conversation with someone called Charm-E-Ine claiming to be on Earth, but we can't prove it."

"So you're telling me that you are having instantaneous communications across twelve light years of space with no help from any equipment. Is that right? Well, buddy, old pal, that's impossible."

Raman was puzzled with the "buddy, old pal" comment, but he kept quiet. Instead, Kristie said, "You know, Neil, the impossible is only impossible until it happens."

"Really?" said an increasingly annoyed Admiral. "I don't believe any of this, but just to keep this in the impossible department, we will attempt to dispel this crap once and for all. In the meantime, can you enlighten us mere mortals as to how you think this might be possible?"

Raman said, "You remember how I said we weren't supposed to be in stasis for more than a few hundred years? More than that amount of time, and anything could happen to the body. And you figured out I had been in stasis for thousands of years? We already know it has caused me to see danger. And I know I get confused. I can only guess this newly discovered side effect is also a result."

"I'm still not buying it, but so what if it affected you? Are you telling me someone else has been in stasis too long and it affected them the same way?"

181

"That was actually a question I asked. Apparently, this Charm-E-Ine had been told that she was born with an odd DNA configuration, giving her the ability to communicate telepathically with another with the same DNA configuration. However, she was told that it was such a rare thing that there was no one alive with the same condition, so she was advised to forget about it. When my first thoughts of distress went out as I was coming out of stasis, she received them having no idea where they came from. Apparently, I've been sending her messages without knowing it since you rescued me, and she has been trying to identify me. What more can I say? Well, actually I can say more. This Charm-E-Ine, with help, has unified the African nations, and she is their leader with the title of Princess Charm-E-Ine—or Princess Charmy, as many call her."

"Good grief!" said Neil as Kristie winced. "This is getting more bizarre with every passing minute. How can you top that?"

Not realizing that Neil was not serious, Raman said, "Well, in addition, apparently the Union of African Nations has built a Star Ship and it is on its way to Epsilon Eridani."

Sharon was feeling more and more uncomfortable as Raman kept blurting out what he knew, or thought he knew, with absolutely no filtering. It was more than Neil and Kristie could take all at once. They were dumbfounded. After a moment, Neil asked, "Are you pulling my chain? Or maybe your brain is so screwed up you actually believe this crap. Just, just leave."

"Admiral," said Raman, "I'm not pulling any chain. I didn't know you had one!"

"Leave now. I mean it!"

And with that, Raman and Sharon left and went to the Lounge, where Sharon said after pouring a couple of beers, "That went well."

"Gee, I didn't think so."

"I'll explain later."

Meanwhile, Neil, who was still sitting with Kristie, said, "Do you believe any of that?"

"Well, he did mention the Union of African Nations, Princess Charmy, and the Star Ship Africa. We knew about all that. And even though it wasn't made news to everyone, it is conceivable that he heard about it and perhaps thought it was communications with Earth. I think we've all noticed that he is gradually getting less clear in his thinking. Anyway, let's prove it. Since this Charm-E-Ine person is reported to have some power and a Star Ship, she must be involved with the Space Commission somehow. Can we come up a few questions that only the Commission Operations and Science Directors could answer? I'm sure you and the twins know a few things that very few others would know."

"Yes," said Neil, "except the twins are no longer in charge. Shortly after the Star Ship Africa was launched, Richard and Dawn retired. Remember? I don't know the new people, but I'm sure we can come up with something."

Kristie was right, of course. There were some things shared that only a few people would know about. The first one that came to mind was the warning Neil was given about the Star Ship Russia crew and Captain Kazakov. That night, Neil couldn't sleep thinking about this and came up with couple more questions. *That's it,* he thought. *We'll get to the bottom of this nonsense tomorrow.*

The next day, Raman was called to the Admiral's quarters and three handwritten questions were given to Raman. Raman, in turn, was to communicate the questions to Princess Charmy that night, leaving Neil with the expectation that he would have answers the next evening.

At the other end of this communications link, Princess Charmy found the questions creative. She had also wondered if this person calling himself Raman-I-El was for real. The very nature of the questions confirmed that he was and she wasted no time in talking to Richard and Dawn, the retired Science and Operations Directors from the United Nations Stellar Commission. The new directors wouldn't have a clue on this subject. Not surprising, Richard and Dawn also believed what they were hearing was impossible, but they played along. Something this crazy was a good distraction from sedate retirement.

By the fourth day, Neil and Kristie, who were in the Tau Ceti solar system, along with Richard and Dawn, who were twelve light years away on Earth, reluctantly had to believe that the impossible was reality. The impossible was apparently possible after all.

Chapter 35
Plan B

The initial assault on the Stranglers hadn't even been close to going as planned. It had been hoped that Raman could negotiate with the Stranglers, but they didn't want to hear anything, so the Chinese marines attacked with axes, machetes, and anything else they could find with a sharp edge. However, the Stranglers were not vulnerable to their "pruning" attacks.

The Stranglers defended themselves with an offensive move, which was completely unforeseen. The leading ends of the vines had rapidly disengaged from strangling the Tall Ones and, at a speed never expected, strangled two marines. Within minutes, the vines had turned them into dust. Adding insult to this major blow, the Stranglers, as translated by Raman, said the marines were tasty and wanted more. This pronouncement made it clear that the carbon-based human life forms were viewed only as a potential food source.

This turn of events put everyone on edge, but in the case of Captain Yue there was complete outrage, and she wanted revenge as soon as possible. The new plan had a far more serious overtone than the first plan, especially with everyone knowing just how dangerous the Stranglers were.

The idea of using flamethrowers was reconsidered. The fear was, though, that once the Stranglers were burning, the high levels of oxygen would make the flames too intense to contain and move onto the Tall Ones.

Attacking straight on toward the leading vines that actually did the strangling no longer seemed like a good idea, even if the marines could move out of the way fast enough. The trailing ends of the Stranglers appeared vulnerable, but this part of the vine shriveled up and died off as the rest advanced, so it would make no noticeable difference to attack there either.

In the past, the Mobile Ones had tried to stop the Stranglers by attacking the leading ends, but it slowed them only marginally as new leading ends would come forth. Also, shooting at the leading ends as they were wrapped around the Tall Ones would result in damaging, or even killing, the ones they were supposed to be protecting.

That left the three to four-foot-thick middle sections of the vines. There was a belief that the leading ends couldn't reach back quickly enough to ensnare the marines if the marines could move fast enough. However, the bark, or whatever the outer layer of the Stranglers happened to be comprised of, had evolved into something quite difficult to penetrate. It was why the Mobile Ones yellowish-green defensive acid goop wouldn't work. It would work, however, if the outer layer could be opened up, and that is where Plan B started to develop.

The concept was to have four-man teams attack the midsection of each identified Strangler vine. They would have to move quickly while hacking a small area with axes. To do this quickly, each marine would strike a blow, and as soon as he lifted the axe again, the marine next to him would strike. This process would continue rapidly within the team of marines until a hole was opened up.

The marines would quickly move away as the strangling parts of the vines moved towards them in defense. As the marines moved away, two or three Mobile Ones would fire their yellowish-green goop into the opening, inflicting damage. Multiple openings might be needed per vine to kill it off, but no one knew for sure. In fact, no one was sure this plan would work at all. Captain Yue, however, was aching for a fight, even though she would be monitoring from the China Bridge. She pitched this proposal to the Admiral, who, through Raman, relayed the message to Fire Control, who was still onboard British Commonwealth.

Fire Control conferred with those higher in authority. The general feeling was that the plan had merit. If the marines could open a wound, the yellowish-green acid goop should cause significant damage. With agreement from the Mobile Ones and the Tall Ones, the Admiral gave his approval. "Proceed with caution."

Before actually attacking, the marines practiced at the stern of the China as it was rotating around the connecting point with British Commonwealth, thus producing a gravity force similar to that on TCe's surface. Even though they would be wearing exoskeleton suits to counter the gravity, it was still deemed important to be in the best physical condition possible. Every available advantage was to be used. With whatever could be found for satisfactory chopping, the marine teams practiced for a week, building up stamina and perfecting coordination.

None of this was a secret, and word soon filtered through the two tethered ships regarding how the new plan was shaping up. It didn't take long before those that would eventually be assigned to constructing the Gate and support facilities heard the plan. George Miller, the construction superintendent, shook his head when word reached him and thought, *This is B.S.!* And with that, he headed off to see the Admiral.

George was a rather gruff, no-nonsense individual. He had overseen some of the most challenging civil construction projects on Earth before signing onto this mission. He wasn't afraid of charging in when circumstances warranted, with the unfortunate result being the loss of two fingers on his left hand and a portion of his right foot, resulting in a rather pronounced limp. Combined with a thick, graying, black beard and rather broad shoulders, he could be scary.

Neil knew George, of course, but only as someone who eventually would be the point person in charge of construction. As a result, Neil was a little surprised when George insisted on seeing him immediately.

"Hello, George," said Neil as they shook hands and then sat down across from each other at the conference room table. "What can I do for you?"

"Admiral, I have just heard about the plan to deal with the Stranglers. Sending marines down there with axes to cut openings in those creatures is one dumbass plan."

A somewhat annoyed Neil Dodson responded, "Well, gee, George, don't hold back now. Just go ahead and tell me we have a dumbass plan."

"I just did. Now listen, we have the best construction equipment on board these two ships. Why isn't it being used? If we got just one of the big excavators down there with a toothed bucket, we could rip into the stupid vine creatures like nobody's business. We might not even need the Mobile Ones to shoot them up with the yellowish-green goop."

Up until now, Neil had been sitting, but after George's verbal assault he stood up, put his hands on the table, and said, "First off, we don't want anything going on down there that might start a fire we can't control. Second, we need the machinery and the fuel to build the Gate."

"Admiral, you're a smart man. These machines were picked because they are powered with old-fashioned, very reliable internal combustion engines. The key word here is "internal." Something would have to go horribly wrong for an external fire. And if a fire did start, the high oxygen levels would only feed whatever was burning, making the fire more intense. But once the fuel was used up, the fire goes out. So, we keep the machines back from the leading ends of these creatures and use the Mobile Ones for a fire watch. Oxygen, by itself, won't burn. Secondly, didn't we send the United States back for more supplies and equipment so I can build the Gate? We're not going to use up any precious resources with this approach. And finally, we ain't gonna build anything if we're not allowed down there. We can sit up here and twiddle our thumbs, but that ain't gonna get us anywhere."

Keeping his composure, Neil said, "Anything else?"

"Just one little thing. We have already modified the fuel injection systems on the machines to compensate for the high percentage of O_2. At high altitudes, we usually have to lean back on the fuel to compensate for the low oxygen. Much less power that way, but here on this planet these machines are going to be awesome!"

Neil wanted to put George in his place, but he couldn't. George was right. Neil had listened to the appeal of Captain Yue, who wanted a fight. George's approach would be far less of a fight. Still, it seemed a bit too simple, so Neil said, "OK, George, let me think about it. In the meantime, prepare the details for your plan. Keep in mind that whatever equipment goes down in the shuttlecraft will likely have to stay. I don't think our little Mobile Ones bug ships can lift a heavily loaded shuttlecraft back up to a safe altitude. I'll get back to you."

Without another word, George got up and walked out of the room. He'd made his point.

Chapter 36
Attack

The Admiral considered George Miller's plan. It was simple. Sometimes simple was the best, but was it too simple? He took his time getting input from everyone that he trusted. He did run into a temporary roadblock with the Mobile Ones and the Tall Ones, as they remembered with shock the images of what the humans' machines could do to the landscape. With the Tall Ones population under increasing stress from the Stranglers' assault, they finally agreed that while they considered this approach drastic, it was worth it.

Captain Yue was at first annoyed that her plan of attack was being questioned. "Who does this George Miller think he is to question my authority?" she barked. But as she envisioned the excavators inflicting serious damage, she warmed up to the concept. "This could be awesome," she relented.

George chose two Caterpillar 325 hydraulic excavators for the mission. These weren't the latest design or the biggest machines ever made. They weren't even the largest pieces of equipment on the Star Ships, but their size would allow them to be transported to the surface by the shuttlecrafts. The larger machines would have to be assembled on the surface and the time it would take to do that might allow the Stranglers to have the upper hand, so to speak.

The Mobile Ones were fascinated with these monster machines. They were certainly monsters when compared to their own physical size, but what really fascinated the Mobile Ones were the tracks that allowed the machines to crawl along the ground. It was the same fascination that caused one observer to say they moved like a caterpillar, and of course the name stuck. Since there were no caterpillars on TCe, the reference meant nothing to the locals.

China Shuttlecraft 1 and British Commonwealth Shuttlecraft 3 were assigned the duty to bring "the Cats" to the planet's surface. The descent was a little fast with this heavy load, but a safe landing was made. In addition to the machines and shuttlecraft pilots were George Miller, Raman, and the two operators.

At a safe distance, the machines and a few hundred Mobile One bug ships were readied for the attack. When the Cats were fired up, the carbon exhaust caught the Stranglers' attention, and some leading-edge vines looked towards the source. The Cats crawled towards the tangled vines, and with hydraulically powered force drove the teeth of the excavator's buckets into the vines and ripped them open. The bug ships fired their yellowish-green acid goop into the wounds. This scene repeated itself over and over.

While individual Stranglers were mortally wounded, they weren't dying immediately. Along with the vines that hadn't been attacked yet, they disengaged from the Tall Ones and aimed an attack on the Cats. The leading ends of the vines started to encircle the Cats and try to suck the life out of them. To say the equipment operators were nervous would be a huge understatement. However, it was soon discovered by everyone involved that sucking the life out of a machine wasn't possible. The operators continued to swing the machines around, slamming the buckets down on the vines while the vines were puzzled over how to stop the damage.

With a speed not expected, the vines would encircle the excavators and squeeze. The cabs did buckle a little, but the machine held firm. In fact, they held up better than the operators, whose vision was sometimes blocked and whose nerves were being shattered. The initial attack lasted nearly four hours before George had the excavator operators back their machines off to a safe distance. The Stranglers directed their attention towards the attackers, setting up what looked from a distance to be a huge hedge.

Raman could tell that the Stranglers, who had always been the aggressors, were considering what had just happened and what they might do next. He took this time of apparent confusion to ask the Stranglers if they were ready to consider going back to the sea and leaving the Tall Ones alone. The answer was "no."

With that, the excavators moved forward once again. The going wasn't quite as easy this time, as the operators were facing the leading edges of the vines instead the back. It was nerve-wracking, and it took some time, but eventually one of the excavators made it through the leading vines with a combination of smashing the bucket down, swinging the bucket back and forth, and simply running up and over the vines. Once behind the "front lines," this excavator went back to gouging the main trunks, and the Mobile Ones shot their weapons into the wounds.

The second excavator didn't fare as well. Two of the Stranglers managed to get a strong hold of the excavator. It was not enough to actually stop the machine, but it was enough to crush the cab and break the windows. Once the windows were broken, the leading ends of the vines strangled the operator and turned him into dust, just as they had done to the marines on the first engagement. Raman and George immediately ordered the other excavator to retreat and watched in fascination as the vines seemed to be making an extension of the doomed excavator's exhaust stack.

George said, "What are they doing?"

"I think they are feeding on the exhaust emissions," Replied Raman.

"Everything with these creatures is so bizarre. And poor Henry. I don't look forward to telling his wife how he died."

The other excavator made its retreat successfully. This one's operator, Melinda, was clearly and understandably upset. Still, she managed to say, "Are we giving up?"

"No," said George. "We going to fortify the cabs and anything else that might be able to get crushed and go at it again. You won't have to be involved anymore unless you want to."

"Oh! I want to. Henry was a friend."

"Good. You are now our only veteran in this campaign. I watched you out there and saw how you modified your approach as you gained more experience with these things. I want to bring down another machine, and maybe we can even get Henry's machine back after it runs out of fuel and those vines creatures leave it alone. You'll need to tell the new operators what you learned."

"OK. What do we do now?" Melinda asked.

"The shuttlecrafts seem to be far enough back that we should be safe from the Stranglers, at least for tonight," said George. "We'll stay behind with one shuttlecraft, and the Mobile Ones will get the other shuttlecraft back up in order to get another machine as well as what we will need to armor your machine. It'll be a day or two before we can get back into it."

Chapter 37
Again

George Miller contacted an anxious Admiral and staff as soon as he got back to the shuttlecraft. Everyone onboard the two Star Ships was pleased that there now seemed to be an effective way to deal with these vine-like Stranglers by using machines instead of manpower. At the same time, all were in shock over the death of Henry.

No time was wasted, as another excavator was fortified and loaded onto the shuttlecraft along with armor for the two machines already on the planet's surface. This time, there were multiple operators being sent down with the revised plan to maintain an extended period of attack. With three machines operating at all times, one would rotate out of the attack for maintenance, fuel, and operator relief while the other two continued to battle.

The Stranglers did, in fact, abandon Henry's excavator after it ran out of fuel. All the Stranglers had slowly returned to attacking the Tall Ones, perhaps thinking the yellow attacking machines had given up.

Even when two excavators headed towards the Stranglers, the vines continued their destruction of the Tall Ones until the excavators started in once again with the ripping of the main trunks. That was when the vines returned their attention to the machines. Their numbers, however, had been diminished from the first attack, and they were less effective this time against the invaders. For the next thirty-two hours, there were at least two excavators continually pounding away on the vines with no let up until the last vine stopped moving. The Mobile Ones kept at it as well with the yellowish-green goop, making sure that "dead" meant "really dead."

The Tall Ones were extremely grateful for this outcome, but at the same time they reminded the ground force that this was just one attack by the Stranglers. The Stranglers were attacking at twenty-eight different locations. Some attacks had been in progress for quite some time, and as a result the Stranglers had become numerous and even larger. Some of the newer attack areas were quite small, as were the vines themselves. No matter the size of each assault, however, it had to be neutralized before the Tall Ones and Mobile Ones could rest—and by extension, before the humans could rest as well.

The next area that needed to be liberated was less than two miles away, so the three excavators lined up and moved through the "forest" to the next battle zone. Along the way, there was a tremendous amount of very loud creaking wood heard by the operators and the new additional support staff riding in the open vehicles. This was extremely disconcerting to the humans. There was a thought that the heavy machines were somehow damaging the "root" system used to communicate and that the Tall Ones were upset. There was a tremendous collective sigh of relief when Raman informed everyone that the Tall Ones were trying to show their gratitude and were actually saluting the task force for their efforts. For the operators who had been cooped up in the Star Ships for so long, this provided a major sense of pride, though they were too proud to show it!

Liberation efforts in the next zone went quickly. Then it was time move on once again. With each new encounter, there were new challenges, sometimes proving to be extremely difficult. It seems the Stranglers had found a way to communicate from destruction zone to destruction zone, allowing some zones to receive advanced warning and put up a formidable defense. The Stranglers would sometimes gang up on an excavator, strangling so hard that the machine couldn't move until a second, and sometimes the third, excavator would attack the creatures from the back.

With each encounter, more support staff and equipment were brought down from the Star Ships. Fuel trucks and bulldozers were brought down, and a kind of mobile headquarters was set up in a tractor-trailer, adding still more support staff to the battle.

In perhaps half of the cases, the destructions zones were far apart and the Mobile Ones had to use the bug ships to lift and carry everything. It was hard to tell what looked stranger: the bug ships carrying the shuttlecraft to higher altitudes or the sight of excavators being lifted by "bugs" over the treetops? Many pictures were taken.

Fortunately, most of the Stranglers' activity was concentrated in one sector of the massive continent. Still, there were a few cases where it took days to move the task force to a new attack area. While the bug ships were numerous, there were limits in terms of both numbers and the duration that they could carry the heavy machines. On these long trips, stops were frequent so the bug ship crews could recharge. Even so, it was becoming obvious to the humans that the Mobile Ones were starting to suffer from fatigue. There was general concern that if the task force couldn't convince the Stranglers to give up and return to the sea, eventually more would rise up and establish new attack areas.

That didn't happen. At the end of five months, with two destructions zones left to liberate, Raman was finally able to get the Stranglers to agree to go back to the sea. In exchange, the humans promised to help get the carbon cycle more in balance within the sea itself. How this was to happen wasn't discussed, but it would be "in the future."

That was the good news. The other good news was that the Tall Ones were very appreciative of what the aliens had done for them. And as hoped, the humans would be allowed to construct their wormhole Gate. More good news was that an agreed-upon location was found. A plateau was identified that was devoid of anything green. It was very close to the ideal forty-five-degree latitude between the magnetic poles, and it was large enough for the massive array that would be both above and below the ground. The plateau was named "High Point," being selected from hundreds of names nominated. It was, after all, a high plateau. And with the humans now having a place to build, everyone generally agreed this was a "high point" in the mission.

But where there is good news, there is often bad news. The five-month battle that went on almost around the clock took a toll on the equipment. The wear on the machines wouldn't have been quite so bad if the always wet and damp conditions hadn't existed. In addition, a large quantity of fuel that was to be used for the wormhole Gate construction had been consumed. Even under ideal soil conditions, there would have likely not been enough fuel. The construction site was also mostly ledge, hence one of the reasons it wasn't occupied. The ledge meant even more fuel would be needed to install the underground array, tunnels as well as the underground portion of the Gate itself. Plus, equipment would certainly be breaking down more frequently.

The Admiral wasn't going to be discouraged, however. It was full speed ahead until they couldn't go any further. What remained of the construction crews of the Star Ships was assembled and sent down to High Point with the goal of building a settlement and laying out the eventual wormhole Gate. Actual construction of the Gate would have to wait until the Star Ship United States returned.

Chapter 38
Star Ship United States

Captain Carlos Monteiro was having a difficult time maintaining a positive outlook. The United States was now into year three of the trip back to New Hope Island on EEb. With 18,356 people on board, it had started out a little over-crowded, but it was manageable. Things were changing, however. The CASO, Lillian Westgate was in the briefing room as well.

"Lillian, what can I do for you on this extremely pleasant day? It is so nice outside. I'd thought I'd go for walk. Would you like to join me?" asked the Captain.

"Yeah, sure, very funny. After I tell you what's going on, you might want to take that walk without a space suit!"

"Oh great! I can hardly wait to hear your glad tidings!"

"Carlos, have you been drinking?"

"Not yet, but I suspect what you want to tell me might cause that to happen."

"Carlos, this could be serious. We have a food-production problem. We're not sure what's going on, but some food crops are failing. Mostly root crops like potatoes, beets, and carrots. They seem to be rotting from the inside out. We're also seeing some of the beehives failing."

"Well that ain't good! What about the chickens? Are they still doing their thing? You know, laying eggs?"

"So far. The only critters having a problem seem to be the honeybees."

"Outside of the gang down on the agriculture decks, who knows about this?"

"Not many. I was going to tell them to keep it quiet, but..."

"Yeah, I know, the fastest way to get a message out is to call it a secret. We already have a morale problem. This isn't going to help. Most of this crew we have feels like they are returning home having wasted decades in a failed mission. Many didn't really want to be on this mission in the first place. I can hear the grumbling all the time. We need to find a way to keep everyone so busy they forget the other stuff."

Lillian, wincing as she said it, asked, "Do you want to hear the rest?"

Carlos, who didn't sit still very long under the best of circumstances, stood up and while walking around the room said, "All right, you might as well finish my day. What is it?"

"The engineers haven't been able to stabilize the Engine 1 fission/fusion reactions. We're not at a critical state yet, but power is fluctuating."

"Yes, I'm sure everyone has noticed the changes in g-force. What are the operating engineers thinking?"

"They don't like the idea of jettisoning the engine pod this early in the trip, but if it goes critical or they can't stabilize the reactions, it will have to go and we rotate one of the spares into position. This is your area of expertise. I'm a medical doctor. Remember? But I have to say, we need to listen to them."

"Yeah, they are a good bunch out there in the pods. If they think Pod 1 has to go, then so be it. You got anything else to brighten my day?"

"The Lounge is open!"

"Of course it is. It's always open, but we probably need to make sure it is functioning properly. Something has to be. Let's go."

Chapter 39
Communications

While communications between the remaining two ships in the fleet, the Star Ship United States, Earth, and New Hope was faster than the actual travel time to each, it still took months and years to receive a message depending on the distance. Now, almost five years into the United States return trip to EEb and New Hope, the Admiral received the message from Captain Carlos Monteiro that crops were failing and he was having engine problems. Using the ship's communications array, the message would take even longer to reach New Hope. In the meantime, only those onboard the Unites States knew what was going on, and now so did Neil.

The Admiral called a senior staff meeting. He had his two Vice Admirals, Captain Parks, CASO Shawn Murphy, Raman, Sharon, and Zanck sitting in his conference room. Captain Yue and CASO Zhao were video-conferencing from their ship.

Neil laid out where he thought things stood. "The United States seems to be having problems. Or at least that was the message Captain Monteiro sent out, but that's over a year old. He continues to update, but as they are moving away from us, the messages are getting even older. Bottom line, I'm praying none of the issues turn out to be something they can't handle.

"We now have nearly 1,500 hundred people on the planet setting up shop on High Point. We don't have a lot of equipment fuel left. Turns out we didn't have enough with us to begin with based on the soil conditions, or lack of soil, down there. There is fuel on Russia, but I'm currently reluctant to try and retrieve it. Even with that, however, we burned up so much fuel fighting the Stranglers that there still might not be enough. I might change my mind later if I can be convinced we can do it safely. I suppose the same is true for the Gate materials left on Russia, too.

"So we started out with over 45,000 people on four ships. As it stands today, we have two ships, limited construction resources, and a few more than 11,000 people onboard British Commonwealth and China. On these two ships, we have the only food source. High Point might be able to grow something to eat someday, but not in the foreseeable future.

"We are currently 100 percent dependent upon the Mobile Ones and their bug ships to get our shuttlecrafts back up to us. This is what I think we all knew, or at least should have been able to figure out.

"Here are some newer facts. The continent of Africa has a new leader they call Princess Charmy. She has brought the Africa nations together to form the Union of African Nations. The new union is feeling pretty good about itself, and under the sanctions of the Stellar Commission has built and launched Star Ship Africa towards EEb and New Hope. It's stated mission is to bring new engine room pods for Star Ship South America so it can be put back into service."

Captain Yue and CASO Zhao looked at each other and in unison said, "How can you possibly know that? That's impossible."

Neil smiled at this obvious opening, saying, "Well, you know our friend here, Raman, has been predicting events, or giving warnings, from time to time. It turns out he has another ability that even he didn't know he had. That's the ability to communicate over incredible distances instantaneously. It is a rare condition, even for his people, but it turns out this Princess Charmy is like Raman. They have the same rare ability and have found each other. They have been communicating almost every day. Raman tells me that it is extremely taxing, so only brief exchanges occur."

Captain Parks chimed in with, "Come on, Neil, you don't expect us to believe this, do you? He has to be making this up."

"Nope, we have had test questions answered that only Kristie, the former Directors of the Stellar Commission, and I would know."

Like the rest, CASO Zhao remained unconvinced. "I still think this is not possible, but just assuming for a second that it is possible, how is this possible?"

Kristie answered with what she and Neil had already expressed. "The impossible is only impossible until it happens. How it is done is something I don't think anyone will ever understand. Consider for a minute that before it was done, the concept of communicating using radio waves would have been considered impossible. Now, I'll bet most people still only have a vague concept of how radios work, but we accept the fact that they work. For us, right now, it doesn't matter how Raman and Princess Charmy are able to communicate the way they do— or for that matter, if this is something that is even going to be long-lasting. What does matter to us it that we can tell the Stellar Commission what is going on and they can make plans to help us out. Does that make sense?"

Captain Yue shook her head but said, "I guess so. We have nothing to lose."

Back on Earth, Princess Charm-E-Ine was having a similarly difficult conversation with the new Directors of the UNSC. These were people that had no history with any of the individuals that made up the Order.

"What do you mean you've been talking with the space fleet?" asked the Director of Operations.

"Not 'talking' exactly," responded Princess Charmy, "but exchanging thoughts. You remember they rescued a fellow called Raman while on the way to Tau Ceti? Well, it turns out we both have an altered DNA that allows us to transmit thoughts over any distance, instantaneously."

"You know, Princess, you are a very weird person. We know you went to the former Directors asking specific questions about information they had only shared with the Admiral. I thought that

202

was odd. But now, if I'm hearing you correctly, those questions came for the Admiral through this guy they rescued. Have you listened to yourself? I mean really!" said the Operations Director.

"Hold on. This sounds a lot like that guy Sherman Hamer who was on the ships when they went to EEb. Supposedly, his buddies and cousins had some sort of device for communicating," said the Science Director. Then turning to Charmy, "Do you know what I'm talking about? Is that what you have?"

Avoiding a direct answer, Charmy said, "Well, yes, something like that."

"Well, I still think it's far-fetched, but we'll try to be open-minded. So, do you plan to keep us up to date with the fleet activities?" said the Operations Director.

"I will," said Charmy. "I will contact you every day."

"The same way you communicate with this Raman person? Or are you going to use something more conventional?"

Ignoring the smart-ass comment, Charmy said, "No. I will call you on our secure line once a day. You can then let me know what you want relayed."

From that point, the rest of the conversation was just Charmy telling the Directors what was happening light years away. It was very distressing to hear about the status of the fleet, with Russia out of commission, the United States heading back to Epsilon Eridani, the conflict on TCe, the mutiny, and the status of their fleet's supplies.

When Charmy was finished and had left, the Directors sat back to absorb what they had heard.

"You know, when Richard and Dawn retired and the Commission asked us to take these jobs, I wasn't expecting any of this. Not knowing what was going on has made for a much more pleasant job. I thought all we had to do was go and make a speech once in a while. I was going to get out of here as soon as the wormhole Gate on TCe was operational. It now looks like that is a long time off."

"Yeah, I have no intention of hanging around. This job is starting to be too much stress."

"I'm not sure what we should do. Let's call a meeting of the Commissioners."

And that is what they did, because few actions can deflect clear leadership when it's needed like a meeting.

Chapter 40
Support From Earth

Reports from the fleet through Charmy to the Directors were sometimes positive, but mostly they were distressing. As a result, the new Director of Operations and the Science Director resigned. The Commission members, realizing that they had hired a pair of incompetents, readily accepted the reasons for leaving as "stress-related." The Commissioners hoped new appointees were more suited to the tasks ahead.

The business with Star Ship Russia was especially disturbing to the Commission because they had all been warned that there was something not quite right about the crew that had been assembled. All, that is, except the Russian Commissioner, who already knew of the "recruitment" circumstances. Even with that concern, however, a complete loss of the ship and crew had never been imagined. When confronted, the Russian government blamed Admiral Dodson "and his little girlfriend Vice Admiral Marshal." Since there was nothing gained by arguing the point, the disparaging remark was filed away with shrugs.

The former Directors Richard and Dawn had initially been concerned about Vice Admiral Shinya Ishikawa. Their fears were confirmed, but it appeared that the Admiral had been able to handle him for the most part, even though the Vice Admiral had caused problems.

It would be an understatement to say that informing the commissioners of what was happening to the fleet was interesting. The Commission, when convened, was naturally interested in the actual issues. However, the real interesting discussion that came first was when the commissioner from Brazil sat back and, after trying to solve the puzzle, finally said, "I'm confused. I thought it took years to get messages back and forth. Now we are hearing about things that just happened. What am I missing?"

The newest Operations Director was trying to wing it, but having had anticipated what was an obvious question had prepared an answer. It wasn't the complete truth, but it was close enough and a bit more plausible than the actual truth. Besides, there was a need to avoid any possible focus on Princess Charmy. That distraction wasn't necessary at all. "The scientists in the fleet discovered a way to make a kind of miniature worm hole, which we call a portal, that would accommodate a signal. Imagine a thin wire that can transmit a signal over long distances. The portal they would make is smaller than the wire."

"That still makes no sense. We all know our wormholes only work when there is a sending and a receiving gate. This miniature portal you're talking about has only one gate or portal. Right?"

"That was true initially, but the first message was picked up by our Earth Gate in South Dakota. From there, a new communications portal was built to better accommodate the signal."

"How come we're just hearing about this now? This sounds like a real game-changer!"

"Well, we're not sure; this is all that new. The last Directors resigned without telling us very much. But maybe it is new if you're just hearing about it now. For our part, we didn't want to get anyone's hopes up until we were sure this was for real."

Charmy listened to this exchange with amazement. *The Director is saying this with a straight face.*

Another commissioner chimed in with, "And where is this portal located? I'd like to see it."

"The portal is near the Earth Wormhole Gate, but there isn't really anything to see, as it is a sealed room with only a few wires coming out." The Director hoped that would put an end to this uncomfortable discussion. Not that the real agenda was going to be less difficult, but it would at least be without any white lies.

"Look. Can we get back on topic? We have a number of things to discuss and some decisions to make."

206

This did get the discussion away from the portal, but now, the focus went from this new means of communication to a blame game. This continued for a little while, but finally Charm-E-Ine said, "Enough already, there are some serious issues that we have to deal with. Far more issues to deal with than we ever anticipated.

"Remember, before I became a Commissioner, this Commission thought four ships would be OK? It is not the fault of the fleet for believing that. Deep down inside, I am quite sure most knew that the Commission was sending off a fleet with a far less motivated and skilled crew than the first mission. Yet, they have overcome some major obstacles, not the least of which has been establishing favorable relations with the locals. An indigenous species we could never have thought might exist. So what do we do now? The Admiral had determined to stay at Tau Ceti, and in so doing sent the United States back to EE for more equipment and a new crew. I believe what the fleet needs now is more than what one ship can provide."

Then with a smile, she added, "Aren't you all geniuses to anticipate this turn of events, allowing the UAN to build Star Ship Africa and send it off to EEb to recommission the South America? So now we'll have three ships to send back to Tau Ceti!"

The commissioner from Great Britain said, "We know you're being more than a little sarcastic, but I'm not about to tell everyone back home that there was a screw up by previous Directors."

"Excuse me! This project was vetted and approved by everyone and placed Richard and Dawn in the position of implementation. Don't blame them now that they aren't here to defend themselves."

"OK, 'we' screwed up, but my point is that I plan to tell everyone the mission remains on track, if not exactly on schedule. Just a little additional support is needed from us. And we have the resources to make this all happen! Isn't that right?"

The Commissioners were more than willing to agree to this scenario.

"Well, not quite," said the Science Director. "It is true we can make this happen, and our newest ship is certainly going to play a large part in the success. Calculations indicate that the United States should reach Epsilon Eridani about the same time as Africa. That will be in about seven years, around 2133. It will take six months or so to refurbish South America before the three ships can head for Tau Ceti. That gives us some time to get what we need through the Gate at New Hope, including three new crews. I'll assume all the Commissioners will help with the recruitments.

"A bigger issue may be the Gate components. We salvaged what we could for the Gate at Tau Ceti from the abandoned Gate on Mars, as it was thought to be in the best condition. We don't have spare Gates kicking around here. We can make some of what is required here on Earth, but the highly technical stuff will have to be salvaged. I currently have no warm and fuzzy feeling that we're going to be able to get everything we need from either our Moon or Saturn's moon Titan. That means we'll have to send crews off to both and ask them to bring back everything they can. From that, we'll ship through the Gate what we know the Admiral will need. We'll also ship whatever we think they might need for some redundancy. The goal would be to have everything ready at New Hope Island when the ships arrive."

This time it was the Japanese Commissioner who said, "So we've got to send our current Earth-bound shuttle fleet off? How long will that little effort take?"

"Oh, about four years."

"Four years? Good grief. All of a sudden we're looking bad again."

"Ladies and Gentlemen, you are all skilled at spinning the truth to something palatable. I'm not suggesting you don't tell the truth. Just leave out the unpleasant details."

"These are more than details, but I get it. I think we all get it," said the British Commissioner. There were unhappy faces, but affirmative nods proved this to be the case.

The Science Director reminded everyone "This isn't going to be cheap."

Princess Charmy was finding it hard to be quiet but once again found she needed to be assertive. She finally spoke, "If cost is the issue, the Union of African Nations will cover the costs."

Not wanting to take a back seat to the UAN, a loud chorus rose up, "No, no. We're all in this together. Support will be from Earth, not just Africa."

Princes Charmy looked at the two Directors, and the three of them smiled.

"Is that it?" said the Japanese commissioner.

"Yes, for now," said the Science Director. "But there is a potentially a large issue that will have to be faced. In this case, however, it needs to be solved by the Admiral and his staff. By the time the ships leave Epsilon Eridani and finally reach Tau Ceti, the crews on China and British Commonwealth are going to be well along in years. The Admiral will be eighty years old, assuming he can hang in there that long. The Vice Admirals are right behind him in age as well as the rest of the crews that signed on originally. The exceptions, of course, will be the children that shipped out with their parents and the kids who were born on the ships. Along with everything else we went over today, keep this in mind as well."

"Let's see," said the commissioner from Scotland. "We have a planet with smart trees and too much oxygen. We have a colony of sorts on TCf with people that can't leave. We have a ship orbiting TCf with critical equipment we can't use. We had a war that used up too much fuel fighting smart vines on TCe. We have two ships in orbit around TCe that are basically waiting to be rescued. We have another ship, the rescue ship, between Tau Ceti and Epsilon Eridani that may be in trouble. We have another ship heading to Epsilon

Eridani with engines but with no idea of what's going on. We are, hopefully, going to get spare Gate components from abandoned Gates in our solar system; that's only a small mission of about four years. Frankly, I don't see what could possibly go wrong! I need a stiff drink."

Chapter 41

2134

The year 2134 had a lot going for it. The newly made-up fleet of Star Ships United States, South America, and Africa were on their way back to Tau Ceti after being refitted and getting new crews. Star Ship Africa had a reasonably uneventful trip from Earth. There were the usual conflicts among the crew and one engine room pod had to be jettisoned along the way, but it arrived with its one spare engine room pod plus the six new ones for the South America recommissioning.

Some of the Africa crew decided they would stay on for the trip to Tau Ceti. Many of whom were those who had been born early on the trip from Earth or were quite young when the trip started and had subsequently been educated onboard. A few crewmembers decided to stay on New Hope Island, and the rest went back to Africa and became local heroes.

The work on South America went as planned. Thankfully, the plan had included dealing with unexpected problems and delays. One problem never should have occurred, though. The original fleet of six ships had all been built with interchangeability built in. So whatever was on one ship could be transferred and "plugged" into another ship. This was especially true for the engine room pods in case one ship had to "donate" to another. Africa and the twelve engine room pods that were attached to it were constructed nearly fifty years after the first ships were built. Whether it was due to an inability to follow the original designs, or more likely the result of some genius who thought an improved design should be incorporated, the net result was that the engine room pods brought over for South America didn't fit.

When the first engine pod was being readied to attach to South America, a very long string of colorful metaphors could have been heard across the galaxy as the engineers, awkwardly working in space suits and shuttlecrafts, discovered the problem. Things simply didn't fit together.

After some considerable head scratching, the lead engineer, with a casual wave of the hand, suggested removing the entire mounting assembly for the pod on Africa and using that to replace the one on South America. The brackets on Africa were no longer needed, so it made sense. It made sense until the amount of work required was determined, however. In the long run, this was the fix and all the engine room pods were moved. This caused the retrofit to take a lot longer than anticipated, by nearly three months. Meanwhile, everything that needed to be done was being worked on. This was just about the same time that it took the United States to arrive from Tau Ceti.

The United States did not have a good trip. It had to jettison one engine room pod, leaving just one spare. The bigger problem it faced was the crew's overall health. Though loaded with more people than the design capacity, it was believed this would not be an issue, assuming no other issues arose. Unfortunately, the breakdown of "assume" to "ASS-of U-and-ME" was the one thing that didn't fail. The horticulture decks were compromised. No one figured out what went wrong, but the crops failed to produce enough food. This included the usual ingredients needed to make the near and full-strength beers. This in turn reduced the drinkability of the water to a very low level. All the canaries that were onboard, which were intended to be a pleasant distraction and an early-warning poisonous air-detector, died on certain decks. This forced Captain Monteiro to close off those decks and cram more people onto the remaining decks.

Rationing was put in place, and though no one actually died of starvation, the overall health of its people was so severely diminished that other health issues took the lives of over 3,500 members of the United States crew. Those that survived the trip were emaciated. No one from the ship opted to stay, and all were sent back to Earth though the Gate. Very few of the crew had much to say. Even Captain Monteiro, who always displayed enthusiastic energy, was quiet. In addition to the ship's logs, he gave his verbal report, but it was obvious that he was depressed and only wanted to leave. He never sent a message back to the Admiral. He never even mentioned the ships and crew left behind at TCe.

212

The United States was completely cleaned from top to bottom. No one wanted to take any chances, so all soils and plants on the horticulture decks were incinerated and disposed of. It took a little scrambling, but within a month the horticulture decks were starting to flourish once again. Still, the first arrivals of the new crew were a little nervous. The new Captain and new CASO met each new arrival and spent some time with them in the Lounge, where the new Bartenders were in full customer-service mode.

Captain Katherine Hickey stood at exactly 5'1" and weighed in at 100 pounds even. She usually wore her hair in a ponytail, adding to her appearance of a teenager, even though she was thirty-three years old. The new Captain only spoke when she had something to say, which was usually in the form of an order or demand. Katherine had been an Earth-based shuttle pilot and had been in charge of the Gate-salvage operation on the Earth's moon. She had heard that new crews were being put together and demanded to be included.

With all the personnel changes within the UNSC headquarters, the UNSC Operations Director of the month wasn't sure Katherine was a good choice. He thought that maybe she wouldn't present a figure of authority, but when he interviewed her, he quickly changed his mind. "So Kathy, why do want this job?"

"First off, my name is Katherine, not Kathy. I have been involved with the space program long before our latest effort. Did you know that I was born on the United States when it was on the first mission? None of this new mission will be new to me. In fact, by being Captain, I will require far less technical knowledge than what I've been using, because I'll have a crew to delegate..."

This went on for forty-five minutes, completely exhausting the Director. When she finally finished, all he could say was, "OK. You have the job."

The CASO was Kendrick Foreman. He was a big contrast to Katherine in every way. He had a doctorate in astrophysics, but he had never ventured far from his research at the California Institute of Technology. He stood at 6'1", a foot taller than the Captain, and weighed in at a somewhat hefty 230 pounds. Ken, as he liked to be called, was extremely gregarious and would eventually become a favorite on the Lounge deck.

Another senior member of the crew was Dakota Bickmeier, age thirty-three, the son of Leonard Bickmeier and Summer Snow Bickmeier, the previous operators of the Earth Wormhole Gate. Dakota grew up with the Earth Gate very much in his life. As a child, he was fascinated with the machine. As he grew older, he went off to the Massachusetts Institute of Technology, where he discovered he knew more than some of his instructors. He absorbed as much as he could, earning a PhD in Electromechanical Engineering, and he then went back to South Dakota and delved into every last detail of the Gate. He was recruited at the age of twenty-eight to salvage the Gate on Titan. He was then asked to go to TCe to be the technical expert for the new Gate. Rightfully concerned that the Gate's parts were coming from multiple sources, the UNSC wanted someone who could put the thing together correctly. Dakota was the obvious choice, and he was given the title of Gate Specialist.

Dakota and Katherine knew of each other, but as they had different salvaging missions they never actually met. And now for different reasons, but with the same goal, they were on United States as shipmates. They weren't shy when it came to their responsibilities, but socially they were both surprisingly inept. The result was a close working relationship, which might have blossomed into something more if their natural attraction to each other wasn't pushed aside.

The Directors and Commissioners were more careful overall with the crew selection this time. Since there were already crews on British Commonwealth and China, sheer numbers weren't as important as the quality of the crew. As a result, the crew sizes were smaller than what design capacity allowed. Africa, which was smaller than the other ships, maintained a crew size of 4,500. The United States had a crew of 10,350, and South America had a crew of 10,751.

The new Star Ship Africa Captain was Adeyemi Kanayochukwa. He was born in Nigeria to a wealthy family who sent him off to Heidelberg University in Germany, where he received a PhD in Mathematics and Statistics. Princess Charmy had recruited him to manage the UAN treasury. While he was recognized for his incredible ability to manage the economy, he wanted adventure, and Charmy put in a favorable word for him. Adeyemi wasn't looking to become Captain, but after numerous interviews and tests, his name rose to the top. His presence was quite imposing, with a trim body, shaved head, and styled uniform. His one major drawback was his name. Few could get it right, so eventually he was known as "Captain AK."

By contrast, the CASO was Lebechi Gilbert. Her mother was also Nigerian, but her father was an expatriate from Scotland. She was considered to be brilliant in the world of physics and as an instructor. Most people who saw her for the first time were rather unimpressed by her frumpy clothes and strange mannerisms. But Lebechi sort of grew on people. While she was considered brilliant based on her accomplishments, no one knew where she had received her education, and she never enlightened anyone either. Only the Directors and Charmy knew she was home-schooled and then further self-taught ultimately obtaining the equivalent of a four-year degree.

The South America Captain was Jose Cabello. Jose hailed from Argentina. He had been a pilot and then squadron leader for the Argentina Air Force. His ability to focus was only disguised by constantly telling jokes. One of his favorites was, "My father is a Fireman, so he named me and my twin brother with the only names he could think of. I'm 'Hose A,' and my brother is 'Hose B.'" Of course, there was no twin, or even a brother.

The CASO was Camila Garacia. She was a very serious individual. She did not want to be on this mission, but the President of Columbia convinced her that it would be an honor for her and her country. So even though she was Chancellor for one the most prestigious universities in South America, she relented, becoming one of the most dedicated members of the crew.

For the trip back to Tau Ceti, Captain Hickey was also given the title of Vice Admiral of the Second Fleet. This wouldn't mean much when the fleet was within shouting distance of either Eridani Epsilon or Tau Ceti, but when the Second Fleet was too far away from either one, she had full autonomy.

Admiral Dodson was kept informed with the progress of the second fleet through Raman and Charmy. Daily reports were sent back to Earth through the Gate. These in turn were reported to the Directors and Charmy. Charmy would then give a summary though her mind connection with Raman. Long communications were still too exhausting, so they were always brief, but it was more than enough.

One message sent to the Admiral was at first distressing, but he quickly came to realize that it made sense. Neil was almost seventy years old. He never really thought about his age. Oh sure, he knew how old he was, but he was always too busy to think about what it meant. His philosophy had always been, "If you keep moving, they can't bury you, or at least they're not supposed to!" The fact that no one actually got buried in space wasn't relevant.

By the time the Second Fleet made it back to Tau Ceti, he would be 80. His two Vice Admirals weren't far behind, and none of the ships' officers were getting any younger. The fact that the Directors who had sent the fleet off in the first place had also already retired highlighted the issue for Neil. It was the long-term view that prompted the Directors to tell Neil that he needed a succession plan. He was not being ordered to step down, but he needed to groom people to step in when it became necessary. The Directors were sensitive enough to avoid any reference to mental capacity or death. Neil would give this serious consideration. After all, once the wormhole Gate was built on Tau Ceti e, there would likely be a new mission for the fleet. Neil thought, *And there will be a Gate on TCe, damn it; there absolutely will be a Gate!*

Though Raman and Princess Charmy only knew each other through their telepathic connections, their connection was becoming more than just about important communications. They knew they were from the same planet, though they were separated both by distance as well as some 3,000 years of birthdays.

After many years on Earth, Charmy had become what many would consider "worldly." When she understood Raman's history, she felt sorry for him. He was extremely naïve. She was grateful that he had found a friend in Sharon Hooding, but she was also distressed to learn that it was a friendship with special benefits; that was something completely forbidden by the Boss. Still, she could not blame him. Intentionally or not, he had been abandoned, and he was rescued by the same species he was supposed to guide. It was only natural that he would seek comfort and friendship from the only source available.

As communications continued, there were more and more details about each other shared. Slowly, Raman felt closer and closer to Charmy, though still light years away. The naïve Raman naturally shared his growing feelings with Sharon. Sharon listened and gradually realized deep down that they weren't destined to be together forever. At the same time, at 50 years of age, she never considered she might get pregnant.

When Dr. MacFarland confirmed that she was with child and not dying from cancer or some other disease, in tears Sharon asked, "How can this happen?"

"It's biology, Sharon. Shall I explain it to you?"

The year 2134 certainly had a lot going for it as the Second Fleet departed Epsilon Eridani for Tau Ceti.

Chapter 42
Mid Way

In the greater scheme of things, there wasn't much to report when the Second Fleet had reached the halfway point of the trip back to Tau Ceti. The engines were running smoothly. The skid steers when the ships went from acceleration mode to deceleration mode and back again also went smoothly, though the crews were a little disoriented on the first cycle. That was nothing new, except to those experiencing it for the first time.

With her Vice Admiral hat on, Katherine called for a small celebration, similar to what ancient mariners would do when they crossed the equator for the first time. Each ship made up a skit of some kind and it was broadcast throughout the fleet. She also transmitted the skits to EE and TC. The lounges were filled with special food samplings, and the Bartenders brought out brews they had prepared for this event. It was party time.

At this point in the trip, Katherine and Dakota, who had now spent a few years working together on the same ship, still hadn't overcome their social shyness. They were work colleagues, and both were uncomfortable at the thought of insinuating anything different. However, what they both didn't know was that the other person would like their relationship to be more than just professional. Both were now 38 years old. Both had never had a serious relationship with anyone. Neither one knew what to do about it.

This day or night, or whatever it was if you didn't look at the clock, was shaping up a little differently. Katherine was talking with the Head Bartender, Terry, while Katherine was working on her fourth pint of ale. Terry said, "You and Dakota have something going on?"

"What do you mean?" responded Katherine quickly.

"Well, Dakota keeps looking this way, and it isn't me he's looking at. Maybe it's your pint of ale he's eyeing, but with the women that are surrounding him and engaging in less-than-subtle flirting, I'm thinking it's you he's looking at. Maybe he wants to be rescued."

Katherine looked over at Dakota, and he smiled. Katherine said, "You really think he wants to be rescued?"

"My God in heaven! You two are unbelievable. NO! He doesn't want to be rescued, dummy. He wants you!"

"You know, Terry, calling your Captain a dummy isn't a smart move."

"Well you ain't gonna fire me and send me home."

"No. I was more thinking of sending you outside for a while without a space suit, but I think this last pint you gave me has some forgiveness in it."

"Well, now, ain't you just such a sweet thing?" said Terry, and they both laughed.

Katherine then sat for a minute, staring at her ale while Terry went off to take care of more customers. Katherine suddenly felt every muscle in her body become tense. She quaffed down the last of her ale, stood up, and marched over to Dakota with a menacing eye. Dakota saw her coming, and at first, he was smiling until he saw the look on her face. The smile was completely gone by the time she arrived in front of him. Looking up into his face, she said, "You and I need to get something straight. Right now. Come with me."

At this point, everyone within range of this confrontation stopped what they were doing and watched somewhat dumbfounded as Katherine and Dakota left the Lounge deck. Katherine found a small empty room and they went inside. She said, "Do you have something you want to say?"

Dakota was baffled and said, "Did I do something wrong?"

"No, you idiot, you didn't do anything wrong. You haven't done anything at all, and now I guess it is up to me to do it." And with that, she put her hands up and around Dakota's neck and pulled him down for a kiss. Actually, it was more like a peck really.

For a minute, Dakota stared at her, making Katherine think she really screwed up. "I'm sorry," she said.

Then Dakota picked her up, said "shut up," and planted a lip lock on her so hard she thought she might pass out.

Now it was her time to stare for a nanosecond before grabbing his hand as they went to her quarters. On the way, he thought, *It must run in the family. Dad told me this is how my mother broke the ice with him.*

Two months later, they had an old-fashioned marriage, and everyone in the fleet celebrated. In the reception line, most either said something like "finally" or "took you two long enough!"

Nine months later, they produced a daughter. In keeping with his mother's family tradition, Dakota wanted an appropriate name. His mother was born in the summer during a freak snowstorm, so she was named Summer Snow. He was born in South Dakota, and he was so named. It seemed logical to Dakota, and with Katherine's blessing, that their daughter was named Celeste.

Still light years away back on British Commonwealth, Sharon's and Raman's son was now four years old. Dr. MacFarland remembered that when he first examined Raman, he declared that Raman was human. Since that time, the good doctor had been convinced that Raman was certainly not human, in spite of what he thought he saw way back when. The doctor knew about Raman's premonitions and the communications with Earth. And no human that he knew of could pack away the amount of food and drink Raman did. With that understanding, Dr. MacFarland had been concerned about the birth of the child.

When Sharon went into labor, the contractions had been more intense than anything the doctor had ever seen or even heard about before. He was afraid he was going to lose Sharon. If she hadn't been such a strong woman to begin with, in spite of her age, he might have lost her. Like his father, Raman, the baby boy wasn't small, weighing in at just over thirteen pounds. His eyes were open and he didn't cry. He wanted to eat. Sharon did the best she could, but her body wasn't capable of meeting the demand alone. Soymilk was added to the diet.

When Dr. MacFarland examined the baby, he saw two eyes, two arms with hands, two legs with feet, two lungs, two kidneys, two hearts—*What a minute,* he thought. *Two hearts?* With that, he was more careful with his exam and found a number of abnormalities. That is, they were certainly abnormalities when compared to a human body. The baby certainly acted and looked healthy. He decided this was something most didn't need to know, but he did tell the parents. Sharon wasn't sure what to think, but she was satisfied that the baby appeared to be healthy. *Can an extra part here and there be a problem?*

Raman seemed rather blasé about the whole thing, much to the annoyance of Sharon and just about everyone else involved. It was as if he didn't understand how any of this might have happened or that he was even a central figure in this event. He didn't really understand human anatomy, except the parts he had explored on Sharon. He didn't know much more about his own anatomy, so any so-called abnormalities meant even less to him.

Sharon knew anything that looked like marriage was out of the question. In fact, Raman was becoming less and less interested in Sharon while the communications with Princess Charmy continued. Sharon tried to convince herself that this was OK with her, but she was more than disappointed.

However, it made the naming of the child a lot easier, as she decided she didn't need to ask for Raman's consideration Sharon considered names like Starman, Starchild, and Solar, but the names either sounded like something from an old movie or were completely dorky. Since her baby was now the brightest thing in her life, she named the child Astron Hooding, knowing most people had no idea what it meant. It just sounded cool. And as Astron became a larger part in Sharon's life, Raman spent more time in his own quarters.

The Admiral and Vice Admiral naturally monitored all of this as a somewhat pleasant distraction from the issues at hand. Another piece of information came in and was placed directly into the hands of Vice Admiral Shinya Ishikawa. It was coming from Captain Gigory on TCf. The settlement on the planet was crude, but it was suitable for their colony's needs, at least for now. There was still a degree of uncertainty about long-range weather patterns and how that would affect life on TCf as they continued building their settlement of New Polyarnaya. Part of the reason for giving it to Shinya was that since everyone on TCf was a mutineer of some kind and had chosen to be on the one-way trip to New Polyarnaya, the Admiral had little sympathy for anyone there. The other reason was more scientific.

The settlement was growing food. Everything seemed to thrive and matured faster than anyone expected. That alone was worth trying to understand, and Neil hoped Shinya might be able to get information from the settlement to help understand how they had been doing it.

However, there was something else going on down on TCf. At first, it meant nothing. A few people picked grass and chewed on it, and it was not unlike chewing on a piece of hay like some farmers did in years past. But it seemed that more and more people were not just chewing on the grass, but they were actually eating it.

And there was one other thing that was startling. An exploratory party had been sent off and reported finding what they believed to be some kind of spacecraft. Details were sketchy, but it appeared to be large, centuries old, and it likely crash landed. There was no sign of any crew alive or dead, nor even clues as to what they might have looked like. Was the ship actually occupied? Did a crew survive? Were they rescued? There were so many possible scenarios.

Closer to home, Neil had been more than just considering what the UNSC Directors had told him. He needed a succession plan for himself and most of his senior officers. Who might take over if one of them could no longer perform their duties?

It didn't really seem that long ago that the fleet had left EEb, when he was 43 years old. How did he suddenly become almost 70? *They were right*, thought Neil. *The older you get, the faster time goes by.*

Star Ship China was actually in pretty good shape. The crew was younger. The CASO on British Commonwealth was also on the younger side. Captain Parks was another story. He was older than the rest, and he was also was in very poor health. That would have to be the first priority.

Neil had already decided that Zanck should succeed Shinya. Both agreed, even though they both didn't really consider this a pressing issue.

For Kristie and for himself, Plan A would be to hang around long enough for the Second Fleet to show up and then promote Vice Admiral Hickey to Admiral. She would then be allowed to pick her Vice Admirals, though by that time it was hoped the new Gate would be completed and the Directors could figure it all out.

Plan B was a little trickier. Kristie and Neil looked to the operating engineers for answers. There were the engine room pod crews that reported to the head of engineering and his lieutenants. Pod crew chiefs and all the senior engineers would be watched closely before any interviews would be set up.

At least everything on of TCe's surface seemed to be under control. Support facilities for the Gate were nearly complete, and most of those on the surface seemed satisfied with what they had accomplished. They had come up with some creative ways to grow food, but they still depended heavily upon the ships for most of their food.

The Tall Ones and Mobile Ones were at ease now that the Stranglers had returned to the sea. The Tall Ones, in particular were fascinated with the stories of the huge diversity of life on Earth and how carbon neutrality was still an issue for the planet. They had taken it upon themselves to try and solve the problems of both planets with one solution. They had a lot of work to do.

Neil had one other thing of a very personal nature that was laying heavy on his mind. When he learned about the marriage of Katherine Hickey and Dakota Bickmeier, along with the birth of their child, it had an impact on him like no other, and he didn't understand why. It defied logic, but it triggered something inside of him.

The impact on him intensified when Sharon and Raman ended up with a child. Something had tipped on some unseen scale. In the case of Sharon and Raman he reasoned, it was because he knew them so well. The Katherine and Dakota thing might have had something to do with their age. He simply didn't know and decided to stop analyzing his feelings. Neil planned a nice dinner for Kristie and himself in the Lounge, and when the place was packed, he said, "Kristie, will you marry me?"

When Kristie became conscious once again after fainting to the floor, she looked up at a concerned Neil Dodson and said, "I guess. Though we shouldn't rush into anything!" Then she yelled at Sharon, "Go get the Pastor before he changes his mind!" And before Neil even had a chance to change his mind, Neil and Kristie were married in the Lounge at ages 75 and 73, respectively. They had over 700 witnesses.

The crew was bewildered as the happy couple went over to China for their honeymoon.

Chapter 43
Ship to Shore

The Admiral was certainly grateful that there was communication between the crew of the Star Ships and the indigenous population on TCe. But while there was communication, it was limited through the ability of one person, Raman. Eventually, this would likely become a serious problem. It wasn't Raman's fault, but Raman not only had to interpret thoughts, he sometimes needed to describe technical concepts that he didn't understand. Confusion and misunderstandings were inevitable. Neil thought, *If I could just pick up a radio microphone and call the Tall Ones direct and have a conversation in real time...*

And while ship to shore conversations without the need for Raman would be a huge next step, there was far more the Admiral wanted. He wanted to more readily "ship" things to the "shore" of TCe. This included the significant problem of getting the shuttlecrafts functioning autonomously. Modifications had been made so the ships could glide in for a landing on the planet's surface, but getting off the planet required a fleet of bug ships to lift the shuttlecrafts high into the atmosphere before blasting off to dock with the Star Ships. This was OK in the beginning to get things started and when battling the Stranglers, but it couldn't continue. There was too much to move and the bug ships' efforts certainly weren't sustainable.

In one of his rare moments, when he wasn't focused on some minutiae, Vice Admiral Ishikawa wandered onto the Bridge in his usual trance-like state and randomly asked, "Why do we use the little bug ships?"

"Well, the locals are afraid the exhaust from the shuttlecraft will ignite the oxygen-rich atmosphere. Remember?" asked Neil.

"You know that can't happen, right?" said Shinya.

"What do you mean? Why not?"

225

"Oxygen doesn't burn. It's an oxidizer that allows other things to burn. So only if something that was on fire were to make it to the ground would there be a fire. And then with this rich oxygen atmosphere, the fire would be unbelievable. But with some kind of spark arrestor, which could ensure that only a clean exhaust was expelled, and with the shuttlecrafts only going to the High Ridge plateau, where there isn't anything there to catch on fire, the shuttlecrafts could just come and go without the bug ships."

"And you just thought of this?"

"No."

"Well then Dr. Ishikawa, why didn't you say something before?"

"Umm, well, I don't know. I guess because no one asked? I thought maybe you wanted to have something for the bug ships to do."

"You thought? You are really are unbelievable. Do you even know why you're here in the first place?"

"Oh sure. My father made me. I think he's dead now, so I can go home when the Gate is completed. I'm going back to my lab."

When this brief conversation between Neil and Shinya concluded, Shinya suddenly wandered out just as he had wandered in. After a few minutes of enduring a now very silent Bridge with all eyes on him, Neil asked, "Am I the only one here that feels like an idiot?" And suddenly, everyone on the Bridge became very busy.

Neil's face turned red as he turned to Kristie and said in a very controlled, calm voice, "Have Raman confirm this approach with the Tall Ones and Mobile Ones. Have engineering do another modification on the shuttlecrafts. And finally, lay out new protocols for the pilots to follow for landing and taking off that will avoid anything down there that could catch fire." After a long pause, he added, "I want to cause severe bodily harm to that man. I want him to go home more than he does!"

Then, like a bolt of lightning, Neil thought, *I really am the idiot here. George Miller said the same thing about the excavators. The only difference is his machines are internal combustion, and the shuttlecrafts aren't.* Then to Dr. MacFarland he said, but not really expecting an answer, "Doc, when do you think it is time for someone to stop pretending he can still remember things and let the younger generation take over?"

Trying to be clever, Doc said, "I used to know that, I think. I do know there are two things that happen when you get older. One is you start to lose your memory."

"Great. What's the other thing?"

"Oh! I don't remember."

Neil just looked at him over the top of his glasses and went off to lick his wounded pride.

The Tall Ones did, in fact, understand the attributes of oxygen. It was what they saw in the shuttlecraft exhaust that was the concern. Any ignited particle that might make to the planet's surface would be enough to put their world on fire. They couldn't rely solely on the very wet environment to keep things under control. That was why they had empowered the Mobile Ones with air ships and flame suppressors. These aliens from Earth were introducing something they had never seen and certainly didn't understand. It appeared as a threat, and it was treated as such.

Reluctant at first, the Tall Ones were gradually becoming more comfortable with the humans. The humans had helped them with the war, and they weren't demanding anything. They did want to form a colony of sorts, and while the Tall Ones and Mobile Ones were initially opposed, they had finally agreed to allow the construction of a settlement and a Gate on a piece of land that was not suitable for much of anything else.

The Tall Ones maintained a 'trust but verify' attitude toward the humans, and in doing so, they were taking things one step at a time. The promise of the humans helping with the carbon issues on TCe was something the Tall Ones found intriguing, and it was certainly an inducement to foster further cooperation, but they weren't going to rush into anything.

Zanck, who was not from Earth and who was certainly not human, reinforced the notion that the humans could be trusted, but they needed to be watched. The actions by the crew of the Star Ship Russia and the subsequent mutiny had not gone unnoticed by Zanck and his fellow Second People. They had watched carefully and came to the realization that trust only went so far. While individual humans might be completely trustworthy, that didn't mean the entire human race could be completely trusted. With this cautionary preamble Zanck's believed that the Admiral could be trusted.

While translations between Zanck and the Tall Ones were exclusively through Raman, he did not share with Neil the full extent of the thoughts that went on between the non-humans. He remained naïve enough to not consider these exchanges as anything significant, so he only provided Neil with what he needed to hear. The Tall Ones eventually agreed to a trial run of a modified shuttlecraft following an agreed-upon landing and takeoff protocol. Hundreds of bug ships were launched and prepared to put out any fire for this test run.

China Shuttlecraft 2, under the command of Lieutenant Wang, was given the honor of this first test flight to make up for being the only shuttlecraft to be shot down by the Mobile Ones. It was a success. Lieutenant Wang navigated down through the clouds on a perfect trajectory to High Point. More importantly, he piloted the shuttlecraft back into orbit under its own power! It was a perfect landing and perfect launch. A collective sigh of relief was expelled from all concerned. Perhaps the greatest relief, though they didn't actually sigh, was felt by the crews of the bug ships, who were becoming quite fatigued from all the heavy lifting they had been doing.

This latest ship-to-shore activity was very reassuring to the Admiral and his staff. It had taken a long time, but each breakthrough with the locals was getting them closer to the goal of building a functioning Gate. All of this, of course, remained contingent upon Raman's ability to communicate with the Tall Ones. Rescuing him and using his unexplained abilities had certainly made possible so many impossible things. *What forces, Neil thought, could have created such a serendipitous encounter?*

While Neil felt blessed to have Raman at his disposal, he kept coming back to the realization that any long-term relationship with the inhabitants of TCe would require a broader ability to communicate. The barrier had been breached with the Second People on EEb with sign language. Something different was needed to communicate with the Tall Ones and Mobile Ones.

The ability of the Tall Ones to design technology like the bug ships and the ability of the Mobile Ones to build these ships was intriguing. Just like the bumblebees on Earth, these bug ships shouldn't have been able to fly. Not only did they fly, but they were also doing it with the power source being the crewmembers, who acted almost like batteries. Even more fascinating was the fact that this was all done with no written records. Every design detail of everything developed was stored in the consciousness of the Tall Ones.

Shinya's focused attention on the Tall Ones had helped him conclude, "The Tall Ones are interconnected via their root systems. They use this system plus their creaking language to communicate, but also to store information. It is more than just memory; it's more like how a computer stores information until needed. Apparently, the Mobile Ones can tap into this database for plans, enabling them to build what is needed. Pretty incredible, I think."

"Yes, incredible indeed," said Neil, "but how do we tap into this so we can communicate without Raman?"

"Is that important?"

"For crying out loud! It is only important if you want the Gate to be built so you can go home. What do you think?"

The wide-eyed Shinya only said, "Oh!"

It was Zanck who came forth with an idea, though it proved easier said than done. Via sign language, he proposed, "Some kind of written language could be developed—I suppose what you humans call English. We know the Tall Ones and Mobile Ones can see. They certainly understand images, or designs, or whatever. Otherwise, there would be nothing to communicate, no matter the medium. It seems to me that if they could see an image in the form of a word, they could translate that into whatever they use for language. The Mobile Ones know how to make things, so at least they should be able to make designs on something that we could understand. I'm suggesting the written English language. It would mean, of course, that the local population needs to be willing to learn this form of communication."

Through the bug ship crew, who had eventually returned to the British Commonwealth as ambassadors, the information was relayed to the Tall Ones. The concept of a written language was so foreign to them that it took them days to even respond with questions.

After some simple words were written and then translated, the concept was understood. It was Engineer that grasped the concept first and was enthusiastic to give it a try. The Tall Ones, who were the real thinkers, concluded it was something new that certainly couldn't hurt.

It actually took nearly two months to get to this point, but then the hard part started. The Tall Ones stored information as images, not words. Kristie said distinctly, "Remember, 'a picture is worth a thousand words.'" Without words, communication could only be done through images. And then there was the issue of human technology and concepts that the Tall Ones would have difficulty conceiving. So they not only had to learn to read human words, but also had to be taught what the words meant to form a proper image.

"Yes, I suppose that's true," said a thoughtful Admiral, "but let's not get too carried away with this. Let's start with the basics. I'll bet these Tall Ones are smarter than we might think. I'd like Mai Tran and Thanos Tzounopoulos to get this started. They have spent more time with our bug ship crew then anyone. And I suppose Raman should be involved as well until some basic understanding between us is established. Oh and by the way, we have just a little less than four years before we really need to have some basic communications without Raman. That's when the Second Fleet should be arriving and we can hopefully get the Gate done." With a smile, while looking over the top of his glasses, he added, "No pressure!"

As this was all going on, Raman was still having daily ship-to-shore communications with Earth. Some of it was business-related, with the aim of providing progress reports. Some was of a personal nature between Raman and Princess Charmy. With each communication, Raman was feeling closer to Charmy and more distant from Sharon. In that context, Raman didn't seem to understand that Astron was his child. As frustrating as it was, Sharon knew she was losing Raman; in actuality, she realized she never really had him at all.

On Earth, Charmy was feeling closer to Raman, but not in the same way as Raman. Charmy could sense that something was wrong with Raman, likely the result of being in stasis for an unbelievable period of time. He was acting far more like an automaton than could be considered normal. Raman had made it clear what he thought his relationship with Sharon had been. This had also disturbed Charmy, but Raman acted as if this was normal. But it wasn't normal for his people and forbidden by the Order!

More disturbing was the business of Astron. Raman casually mentioned that Sharon had a baby. Charmy knew exactly what had happened, even if Raman was oblivious. While Raman wanted to be on Earth to be with Charmy, Charmy wanted Raman on Earth to care for him as a lost soul before it was too late, if it wasn't already.

Chapter 44
Arrival

It was a glorious sight when the Second Fleet came into view. The lead ship was the United States. Within hours, Africa and South America also came into view. It was January 11, 2144, exactly thirty-seven years from the time when the First Fleet had left EEb and New Hope. Neil would be eighty years old in a couple of days, and he saw this as a fantastic birthday present.

Over the next couple of days, the Second Fleet slowly maneuvered into position so that the bows of all five ships were connected and a synchronized rotation was established. The Admiral declared a day of celebration. All the Captains, CASOs, and special quests assembled in a crowded Admiral's conference room to meet and get acquainted before retiring to the Main Lounge with the rest of the off-duty British Commonwealth crew.

The lounges on the other ships were full as well. Sharon and her other bartenders brought out "the good stuff." The Galley out did itself with food. Pilot, Engineer, and Fire Control were introduced to the new arrivals, as the bug ship crew was placed on the bar, along with their ship, for their own protection. Kristie thought it might be rude and considered bad form if the bug ship crew were to be crushed underfoot! At the same time, the bug ship crew found the whole affair rather bizarre.

Neil wasn't sure how it would be received, but he had determined that the mutineers on TCf should be made aware of what was going on. The delayed signal was received and the celebration onboard the ships was apparently met with mixed reviews. The hardcore cynics waved it off. They weren't interested, or at least professed to not be interested. Some were jealous and wondered why they hadn't had enough faith in the mission. Others were just curious. Captain Gigory shared all these feelings at once while at the same time realizing, for perhaps the first time, that he and everyone around him were separated from humanity forever.

During the long absence of the United States, the crews of the China and British Commonwealth had been rotating between the ships and High Point. Shuttlecraft flights were limited to save fuel, but it still gave everyone a chance to "stretch their legs."

The community on High Point was well established, with nearly 4,000 permanently stationed on the surface. They were also in a party mood now that they could visualize their very long mission coming to a conclusion. Even if they never went back to Earth, it would feel good to have that option.

Mai and Thanos had made progress with teaching the Mobile Ones and Tall Ones how to read and write. It had been an extremely slow and frustrating process just to get a few words assimilated. Written words were such an odd concept. Gradually, more words were added, and with each new word the next words came easier. There was still a very long way to go, but both Mai and Thanos believed that by the time the Gate was actually up and running, the aliens from Earth and the locals would be able to have basic conversations.

In the meantime, the Tall Ones certainly knew there were more arrivals orbiting their planet. They believed they had little choice in changing the way things were developing if they were to save their planet; at the same time, however, they were still concerned enough about the future and took precautions. To them, implementing precautions meant that a defense strategy was being developed, just in case.

Neil, as usual, had very little to drink. Even so he was feeling quite good. But then in a somewhat melancholy moment, he asked to see Katherine Hickey and her husband Dakota Bickmeier privately. When alone, Dakota winched when Neil started off with "Kathy…"

She cut him off with, "My name is Katherine."

"Of course it is. I'm so sorry, Admiral," as Neil smiled and looked at her over the top of his glasses.

"I'm only the Vice Admiral, and I'm guessing that title goes away now that the fleets have joined," said Katherine.

"Well, yes. The Vice Admiral title does go away. I'm retiring as of right now. I know age is just a number, but I've had enough. I will guide you as needed, because it is important for you not to lose what they used to call 'corporate memory,' even if my memory is fading. I'm about to go back into the party and announce your promotion to Admiral of the combined fleet. My Vice Admiral of Operations, and adding with a smile, my wife Kristie Marshal, will be retiring as well. You'll need a replacement. It should not be Dakota, at least for now. He has plenty to do to get the Gate built. You are stuck with Vice Admiral Shinya Ishikawa until the Gate is done and he goes home."

"You're telling me this, just like that? What do the UNSC Directors have to say about this?"

"Oh, they know. I told them a couple of days ago this was going to happen, and they agreed. I actually think the Directors are relieved they don't have to do anything."

"A couple of days ago? Are you telling me you can get answers that quick?"

"Yup. We have a secret weapon," said Neil with a laugh. "Do you accept?"

This was what Katherine wanted, but she had no idea the opportunity might just be dropped on her like this. She'd only just met the Admiral, and now she was in charge, though she didn't exactly feel like she was in charge. Even so, she had enough composure to say graciously, "Thank you, Admiral. It will be an honor. I accept with hopes and prayers that I can meet the extraordinary standards you have achieved."

"Excellent."

All three were beaming as they reentered the party and Neil made the announcement. The crews of the First Fleet were disappointed, if not surprised. Captain Yue put down her glass and left the room. It wasn't that she didn't know this was coming; Captains Yue and Parks had both been told. Captain Parks knew he was too old to be considered, but Captain Yue had maintained visions of being named Admiral, even if it was for a short time. Besides, she thought, *That scrawny little thing doesn't look like Admiral material.* The crews of the Second Fleet were thrilled and cheered. The free flow of alcohol prior to the announcement likely enhanced the cheering.

Serious work would start in a couple of days. For now, it was time to get the new folks oriented and to party!

Chapter 45
Tau Ceti e Wormhole Gate

Admiral Dodson was impressed with the new Admiral Hickey. Just like the UNSC Directors on Earth, he was initially concerned that her presence didn't project authority. Her social shyness didn't help that impression. Outside of official business, she seldom would approach anyone and initiate a conversation.

In her official Admiral role, however, she had a completely different take-charge personality. She made it clear that Dakota was in overall command on the planet's surface, but she also made sure that it was understood by everyone that George Miller was in charge of the actual construction—all construction.

Katherine had a religious upbringing, and with that she implemented some rules that she had implemented in the Second Fleet, which were actually easy to follow. Construction was to be continuous on a twenty-four-hour Earth schedule. The day and night cycle was far enough off from the Earth cycle maintained on the ships that it didn't matter too much for most people on the planet's surface once they got used to it. But once every seven Earth days, people were required to take a full day off to rest and observe religious activities, if they were so inclined. It didn't matter what day. Katherine was so insistent on this point, though, that she actually assigned a task force to make sure people would adhere to the rule.

Not everyone was able to fully adapt to the gravity on TCe. While the Star Ships were rotating in orbit providing a slightly greater than 1.5 g force in the sterns of the ships, it gradually weakened forward until it was nearly zero at the bows. Admiral Dodson had made it mandatory for those that would be working on the surface of the planet to spend time in the ship's sterns to acclimate. Many did not spend enough time doing this, and as a result some had a difficult time on the planet. These people were cycled back to the ships and received reprimands from Admiral Dodson initially, which now came from Admiral Hickey, but nothing more severe than that happened to them. Captain Yue, however, would often add some mild punishment if it was someone from her crew. Much to the embarrassment of the officers on board United States and China, the Second Fleet crews who had been experiencing the 1.5 g acceleration cycle already were performing much better on the planet's surface.

Acclimation to the gravity was deemed extremely important for the long term. In the short term, though, those that were working and doing physical labor wore the exoskeleton suits to counter the gravity. These weren't conducive to fine-detailed work, but most of that could be done while sitting on something. The same was true for the equipment operators. It was the machines that were doing the work. But while there was no question that the gravity of TCe was having an impact on the people of High Point, only the high oxygen levels helped counter the effects. In time, most got used to it.

Neil, who wasn't a drinker, was initially skeptical when Katherine ordered that pubs be set up in High Point settlement. There would be no hard liquor, but there would be good beer, some wine, and the best food that could be prepared. He did note that it seemed to allow people to relax, and it did help shed the rough and tumble atmosphere of an all-encompassing construction site. He noted with a laugh, "It is becoming so civilized down there!"

Dakota Bickmeier wasted little time. Two days after the welcoming party, he was on the planet's surface at High Point. Initially, he had concerns about adapting to the gravity on TCe, but the acceleration cycle of the Star Ships had made the difference. He, like everyone else, was appreciative of the unexpected benefits to his stamina from the high oxygen level.

Dakota spent the first couple of days with George Miller. Dakota wasn't sure what to expect, but considering the limited resources George had to work with, the amount of work that had been completed was impressive. Construction wasn't Dakota's strength. That was George's domain. Dakota was there to oversee the details necessary to get the Gate functioning.

When George was asked what kind of engineer he was, he would usually say, "Well, I'm supposed to be a Civil Engineer, but

I have a difficult time staying very civil." Not everyone got the word play.

He had proved his worth in the war with the Stranglers, and his authority was never questioned. While he would listen to anyone with an idea and would readily adopt good ones, when he made a final decision on anything it was understood there was to be no discussion.

Unlike Katherine and Dakota, he was extremely well-adapted to socializing. He was a big powerful man with hands that had a vice-like grip. When he entered a pub, or any social event for that matter, he seldom had to initiate a conversation. People just gravitated towards him. Part of the reason for this was his one strict rule when not on the job, "Thou shalt not talk about work. Anything else is fine, but not work!" Plus, he usually had a beer in his hand and loved jokes.

Though they were not fancy, Dakota found the residences George had built were comfortable. Well-equipped shops had been built as well, and the heavy machinery needed to build the Gate was ready to go. Some heavy construction had started on the Gate infrastructure, but when the fuel supply was nearly gone, everything stopped. A donated engine pod from China had been brought down and put in place in a remote underground bunker to provide power to the community and some of the tunneling machines. A second one would now be brought down for the huge power demand of the Gate.

With a fresh supply of fuel, the heavy machinery went back into action. The operators wasted no time. They had been spending most of their time trying to keep the very humid and even wetter conditions from eating up their machines. It was good to be back building something.

More construction people and technicians were poured into the project. At the peak of construction, there were nearly 3,000 workers, plus their families, in addition to all the people in various support functions. The High Point settlement population was approaching 8,000.

238

The ridge was solid rock in most places. Since half of the Gate needed to be underground, the rock presented both a problem and a solution. The problem was the actual work required to tunnel and excavate the ledge. Countering this was that there was little need for shoring as the tunnels were being constructed.

While the outer perimeter of the Gate was being prepared, the Gate core space was being built. This was completed first, and the actual Gate components were brought down in the order of assembly. George and Former Admiral Dodson noted with some amusement that Dakota seldom looked at any plans while directing construction. He knew the Gate so well; he could direct most of the work without plans, much the same way the Tall Ones seem to function. Plans were only needed when the hundreds of technicians were assembling components. This required extreme precision. It would be considered bad form if people entering the Gate for a transfer to Earth or EEb never made it. There was no room for error.

One thing Dakota had going for him was that the Gate components, for the most part, came from dismantled Gates that once functioned. When dismantled, assemblies were maintained intact as much as possible, thus reducing reassembly time and probable errors. Though there were some variations from one previous installation to another that generated some head scratching.

The Mobile Ones reported the progress to the Tall Ones. While neither species could understand what was being done, they were impressed with the degree of activity.

The Stranglers eventually devised a way to directly monitor the progress to some extent. They wanted to see how the promise of carbon being brought into the TCe ecosystem would come to fruition.

In 2146, just shy of thirteen months after the process began, the Gate on TCe was ready for testing. Katherine, using Raman's connection with Earth, let them know the first test was about to begin. Dakota's parents, though retired, still lived near the Earth

Gate and were on hand for this first test. They felt the same anxiety they felt when the EEb Gate first came online.

There was protocol for testing. Small inanimate objects would be sent to Earth and then returned to High Point. The same thing followed with an exchange through the Gate on New Hope Island on EEb. The transmitted items became increasingly more complex, and with each transmission testing was done to make sure the makeup of the items hadn't changed. When Scotch whisky and beefsteaks started arriving from Earth, the smiles on High Point started to get bigger.

Chicken transport tests were next, as the transmission got closer and closer to being actual people. After three months of testing, it was time for someone to volunteer. Just about everyone in the fleet who hadn't been born in the fleet had at one time gone through the Gates between New Hope Island and Earth. Still, this was a new Gate that was made up of old parts, so the list of volunteers for the first test was small. Actually, there was one volunteer: Vice Admiral of Academics and Science Shinya Ishikawa.

Katherine hadn't really taken the time to know Shinya, but of course Neil certainly knew him, and he was surprised that of all people Shinya would be the brave one. In fact, he wasn't being brave at all. He never considered this to be a test. He had confirmed that his father had passed away, so now the only thing he wanted to do was go home to Japan and his lab. He didn't know he no longer had a lab waiting for him after being away for forty-five years. It never occurred to him. He pictured everything as he had left it. He didn't see this as a test, with him being the actual test subject. He only saw a way home and a chance to get away from these annoying people.

Shinya never spent time trying to acclimate to the gravity conditions on High Point, so his frail body was naturally stressed from the gravity. That only made him even more anxious to get through the Gate. The Gate was fired up with Shinya inside, and off he went to Earth. Neil was as anxious as Shinya for him to leave the fleet, but he still didn't really want him to get hurt in spite of what

240

he had said previously. He made a silent prayer that all would go well.

With the Earth Wormhole Gate in South Dakota in receiving mode, Dr. Shinya Ishikawa appeared. He seemed to be in fine shape, and when asked if he was OK, his response was, "Can you get me home now?"

"Well, yes, after a thorough examination," said the resident medical doctor.

"I had one before I left, why do I need another one?"

Laughing at this, the doctor said, "We want to make sure all your body parts came with you."

"Oh. Then can I leave?"

"Yes," was the only possible response.

Shinya did pass the test. Word was sent to all concerned parties, and from then on Gate transfers started in earnest.

Chapter 46
Earth 2146

With VAAS Ishikawa safely back on Earth, there was a sudden surge of volunteers to go through the wormhole Gate back to Earth. Admiral Hickey talked this over with her predecessor, who had been thinking about this day for a very, very long time. After all, he wanted to go back the Earth as well.

"So Neil, we're inventing a protocol here. Here are my thoughts. The Second Fleet just got here. So, for the most part, the crews of the First Fleet should get first dibs to go home. But still, not everyone can go at once. We need people to maintain the ships and prepare for the next mission."

"Is there a 'next' mission?"

This simple question startled Katherine. It never occurred to her that getting to TCe would be the end of the road. After all, she had just been promoted to Admiral. Being an Admiral of a fleet of Star Ships that wasn't going to do anything never dawned on her. It should have, she realized, but it didn't. "Well," she admitted, "I guess, I don't know. I just assumed."

"Never assume," said Neil. "Besides, there is still a lot of work to be done here. The community supporting the Gate and interacting with the natives needs a firmer footing. I don't think it will ever be able to support itself in terms of food, but maybe in due time. We need to explore possible trade, mining, who knows, but High Point needs to move in that direction, and we're nowhere near that goal now."

"What do you think? One year or maybe two?"

"Probably two anyway. In the meantime, you need to go back to Earth and meet with the UNSC Commissioners and Directors. I'll bet they have some grandiose scheme their cooking up. This will be one of those occasions where you certainly don't want to assume. You'll have to prepare for the worst and hope for the best. For a best-case scenario, the UNSC will want to know your recommendations for the Vice Admirals, Captains, and Chief Academic and Science Officers for each ship to lead a new mission. Remember, lead, follow, or get out of the way. You should take the lead if they won't.

"You will need to have a plan for the High Point operation. Remember, while it is connected to Earth through the Gate, that connection disappears if the Gate fails for some reason. Along that line of thinking, we had the serendipitous benefit of Raman's ability to communicate with Earth. I think we need to talk to him about what he wants to do."

Katherine had a lot to think about. She made up an organization chart with new names in each of the senior officer positions for each ship. She would keep it to herself for now. Why recommend promotions into positions that would be meaningless if the ships weren't going to go anywhere? Also, it wasn't clear if anyone would want to stay with the fleet or on High Point. She might have all new faces. Then again, maybe she'd quit if the UNSC only wanted her to babysit a parked fleet.

There were three general categories of people in the fleet: those who wanted to go back to Earth to stay, those who were comfortable staying on the ships or on High Point, and those who wanted to go back to Earth but not stay. Of those that really wanted to go to Earth, or in a few cases New Hope Island on EEb, most of the operating engineers were held back until they could be replaced. It would take months to sort this all out.

Neil and Katherine talked to Raman and Sharon. The breakthrough in communicating with the Mobile Ones and the Tall Ones using the written word had an extremely slow start, but it was now accelerating at a rapid rate, to the point that Raman's unique ability to translate was almost never required. That meant he could, if he wanted, complete the trip to Earth that had started some 3,000 years earlier!

"Well now," Sharon quipped, "you shouldn't rush into these things you know."

Raman heard this, but as usual he didn't understand the sarcasm. Instead, he said, "I want to go now and meet Princess Charm-E-Ine."

"And what about you Sharon?" asked Neil.

Looking at Raman with a face that said it all, Sharon said, "Astron and I will be going to Earth, but we'll not be going with Raman." To this, Raman gave no indication that he cared.

Those who returned to Earth after so many years found many things had changed, yet many things had not. Sharon decided she had enough of "change" and went back to her home state of Iowa with her son. He would be raised without his father, but he was told often about him as well as the special relationship his parents had while in space.

To Raman, Earth should have been filled with wonder, but his increasingly dulled senses left him with only a vague sense of direction. Immediately upon stepping out of the Earth Wormhole Gate, he was alone.

Though they were no longer in charge of the Earth Wormhole Gate, Len Bickmeier and Summer Snow came by whenever possible, making it a point to greet those they deemed to be important. They hoped their son, Dakota, would be coming through to visit soon, but on this day, they had a special reason to be there; they wanted to greet Raman.

With them was a guest and friend from many years back who had led a group from the Order that had helped save the very first interstellar space mission to Epsilon Eridani back in the 2080s. Having just been brought out of stasis and rejuvenation, Gabe-Re-El had returned to age thirty-three, initially surprising Len and Summer with his appearance. When Gabe had contacted them, they had naturally assumed he would have aged. Instead, he was younger then when they first met him.

Gabe knew the encounter was going to be awkward, and he took it upon himself to tell them who he really was. He also told them more about the Order, with the understanding they were never to tell anyone else. Other people at the Earth Gate hadn't met Gabe previously, so they did not necessarily expect anything in particular. However, at 7'2" and 300 pounds, while wearing all-white clothing, he definitely attracted attention.

Raman exited the Gate with a large group. Everyone was quite animated and simply excited to be back on Earth—everyone, that is, except Raman, who stood out in the crowd, not due to his size so much as his demeanor. Gabe went directly over to Raman and told him who he was before saying, "Raman-I-El, you have had an experience I don't think anyone from our society has ever experienced before. We will be spending time together so that I can understand what you have experienced and report back to the Boss. They are quite distressed over the disappearance of your ship, and they now need to bring you back into the fold. You have missed a lot."

Gabe expected questions from Raman, but all he received in response was, "I want to see Charm-E-Ine."

Len and Summer had expected a happy reunion of sorts between Gabe and Raman. This interaction, however, was a little strange and awkward. Len and Summer looked at Gabe, who gave a little wide-eyed shrug and then escorted Raman out of the complex. Once outside and away from prying eyes, Gabe handed Raman an antigravity backpack and put on one of his own as well. Raman looked at the backpack and then at Gabe saying, "I know what this is, but remind me how this works."

This was another response Gabe hadn't expected, but he took the time to caution Raman that there was some guess work on the pack's calibration, as each one is designed for the intended user. After a couple of brief experimental flights, they allowed the antigravity panels to spread, and they flew towards Africa. The flight path would take many days, flying over the least-populated areas. They would stop only to eat and to sleep.

Gabe was used to people staring when entering an eating establishment because of what he wore, his size, and the amount of food that he would eat. Then there were more stares when he paid with gold and silver coins. Raman was a little less conspicuous in the clothing that was made for him on the Star Ship, but still people stared. Gabe noticed, however, that Raman took it in stride, or that he didn't care.

Charm-E-Ine knew that Gabe and Raman were coming. Raman had been communicating to her where they were each night. Now at the capital of the Union of African Nations (UAN) in Pokola, Princess Charmy greeted the new arrivals. Gabe gave a little bow to the Princess, but Raman went directly to her and embraced her, sobbing hard during a very long embrace.

Gabe was both appalled and moved by this, and it wasn't until later when Raman had gone off to bed that Gabe learned that Charmy had understood that Raman was damaged. And while this provided a means for them reach out to each other, Raman had increasingly lost all empathy towards others. He was now in a constant state of blurred thoughts, allowing him to be easily led by the actions of others. He functioned—and functioned well—with specific tasks, but he lacked enjoyment in whatever he was doing. Gabe filed that analysis away in his brain for future reference.

Gabe then turned his attention to the Charm-E-Ine. "So, Princess Charmy, you have been a naughty girl. It took the Boss some time to catch up with you, but now they want to reign things in. You have violated so many of the Order's guidelines and rules that it is difficult to know where to start."

Giving no indication that she was apologizing, Charmy said, "Yes, I went rogue. After my team was killed, leaving me alone, I at first wanted to join them in death. Instead, I found a calling that went beyond what our Order allows but maintained the intent. I have no guilt over what has happened. I was asked—no, I was more so drafted into unifying Africa in peace. I was actually held up as a benevolent dictator and have strived always to live up to the 'benevolent' part. After all, aren't we members of a benevolent order?"

"Yes, but we're supposed guide, not take charge and become head of state!"

"Again, I have no apologies. I was alone, and I alone determined the best course of action for me. I wanted to live out my natural life doing something good. I do care what the Boss thinks, but I also believe I have made a difference, a positive difference that will shape Africa for generations. Now you show up and you're going to give me a hard time? Nope, not going to happen. What do those three individuals want me to do? Undo everything that has been accomplished and let Africa flounder for another generation or two, or three, or whatever? Actually, I wonder if there is ever a disagreement between the three of them. Do the three of them actually think as the 'one Boss?' Yeah, yeah, I know, 'it is one of the great mysteries.'"

"Are you done?"

Smiling, Charmy said, "Maybe."

"Actually, what they want is for you and Raman to go into stasis, and when the time is right to come out and use the telepathic communication ability you two have. It is extraordinary and should be preserved for the betterment of all. You two would be a nucleus for a new team of six. You would be the team leader."

"I'm a team leader now. And it's a much bigger team."

"Yes, very cute, but if you don't go back into stasis and rejuvenate back to age thirty-three, the Order loses a lot for the long term. Also, there are thoughts that the damage done to Raman after such a long stasis period might be reversed."

"Wouldn't that also reverse his special communicative ability?"

"Maybe, but some DNA testing would need to be done first."

"Hmmm. I'll think about it."

And while Princess Charmy was taking her time to think about Gabe's less-than-subtle hint, Katherine Hickey had come to Earth for a meeting with the United Nations Space Commission members and Directors. She wasn't sure what to expect, but using her predecessor's guidance, she was prepared for the worst. Or at least, she hoped she was.

The previous Directors Dawn Cohen and Richard Sylva had an interesting perspective on the space missions. The twins had been made Vice Admirals during the first mission to EEb, so they had first-hand experience of being "out there." They had long since retired and recently passed away quietly within days of each other. They had led full lives, leaving behind a legacy that would be difficult to eclipse.

There had been a succession of Science Directors and Operation Directors since the Dawn and Richard era. Some had left soon after being appointed because they couldn't take the stress. The latest was Mei Ping as Science Director, and Rudolf Rottenfusser, who was in charge overall as the Operations Director. Both were well educated, but neither had ever been in space. They were armchair warriors who believed field experience wasn't necessary to direct the operations. The Commissioners wholeheartedly agreed, and all of them had a very high regard for themselves. In fact, they had such a high opinion of themselves that studying the history of the program was believed to be just a waste of time.

So, not surprisingly, when Admiral Hickey showed up for a conference to discuss what should be done with the fleet, Director Rottenfusser knew little about the Admiral and started the discussions off with, "Well, Kathy, welcome back to Earth."

"You may call me Admiral Hickey, Admiral, or Katherine. My name is not Kathy."

"Oh sorry. We can be a little informal here."

"Informal is fine with me, but my name is Katherine."

248

"Yeah, OK, got it. Anyway, welcome back. The Commissioners have been discussing the future of the fleet. We have six ships with not much to do."

"We have five ships, sir. Russia is off limits, at least for now, until someone figures out how to clean it." In spite of her knowing better, Katherine said, "Maybe you'd like to do it?"

"What? No. No. OK, so five ships." Taking on a lofty air, the Director continued, "The Commission would still like to establish a robust colony on a planet. Not just outposts like we now have on EEb and TCe but a new bold and beautiful mission."

"OK, that sounds good, and it's something I'd like to discuss. Where would the fleet go?" asked Katherine.

"Oh, that will come later. We're keeping it secret for now, but it will be bigger and more beautiful than ever. We might even split up the fleet."

"Really? You've thought about this, have you?"

"Oh yes, but we don't need to worry about that today. What is important is getting all of our ducks in a row for the next mission. To do that, we would want to establish a chain of command."

"Are you firing me?"

"What? No. That's not it at all. It's the other ranking positions we're concerned with."

The Science Director, Mei Ping, pulled herself up straight and tight to the conference room table and said forcefully, "We want Captain Yue to be promoted to Vice Admiral of Operations. There is to be no discussion."

Katherine thought this was interesting. The Science Director from China wants her countryman to be promoted. If the Commission had bothered to ask to see her list of recommended promotions, they would have seen Captain Yue was going to be recommended by Katherine for that very position. Thinking fast, Katherine said, "OK, I can live with that, but I'd like to make the recommendations for the other Vice Admiral position, most of the Captains, the CASOs, and a few other key positions."

Believing she had cornered Katherine, Director Ping felt satisfied and agreed. The self-satisfaction disappeared when Katherine handed over her previously prepared list and there at the top of the list was Captain Yue's name recommended to be Vice Admiral of Operations.

"Director Ping, if there is going to be a new mission, do we have another wormhole Gate somewhere?"

"No. We're working on it."

"Excuse me for asking, but who exactly is working on it? As far as I know, the only true expert on that matter living today is Dakota Bickmeier, my husband. He is at High Point fine-tuning the wormhole Gate there, so that leaves me a little confused. Also, before there are any plans to actually send ships away from High Point, what's the thinking about the ongoing relationship with the indigenous population? I'm certain you don't want an outpost with nothing to do. Admiral Dodson and I think there should be trade. When building the Gate, the geologists found deposits of rare elements that could be quite beneficial."

"I suppose that's true," said Director Ping. "But what would they want in exchange?"

"You're kidding, right? One thing they desperately want is carbon. Preferably, they'd like it in a gaseous form, though they aren't that fussy."

"Well, we have plenty of that, I suppose. What do they want that for?"

"Really? It's all in our reports. That's what the three species need to live. It is the same as oxygen is to us."

The look of boredom went over Director Ping face as she said, "Interesting."

Director Rottenfusser added, "Now, Kathy—I mean Admiral Hickey—don't worry about a thing, because we've got this all under control. We'll get back to you when we have more to discuss."

With that, a very baffled Admiral left the building. She would stay on Earth for a month, visiting others and generally relaxing. During that time, the Commission called no more meetings and she ultimately went back to her command. In confidence, she said to Neil, "Those people are idiots." She also added, "'If in the course of chaos and danger those in charge remain calm, perhaps they don't fully comprehend the situation.' I'm afraid we will be 'blindly' going where no man has gone before."

Chapter 47
Transplants

When Katherine was back on Star Ship United States, she was informed of a new development. This came seemingly out of the blue, but to the Mobile Ones and the Tall Ones they had been considering a new idea for some time. They wanted to explore the possibility of separating a cluster of Tall Ones and establishing a colony on Earth.

Their expressed purpose for this was to study the diverse ecosystem of Earth first-hand to get a better understanding of how carbon dioxide had altered the ecosystem. While humans were still working to reverse the long-term effects on the ecosystem from too much carbon emissions in the late-20th century, the Tall Ones wanted an increase in emissions, or at least useful carbon, to improve their eco-system. It was also believed that the Earth's ecosystem could make a huge positive impact on the overall health of their species. More CO_2 and less gravity would enhance growth. The Mobile Ones who would accompany the Tall Ones would be extremely mobile with less gravity than what their machines were designed to accommodate.

Besides, it only seemed right that if humans had a colony on TCe, why not allow a reciprocal colony for the Tall Ones on Earth? In the end, it was agreed that they would give it a shot.

Zanck was charged with the planning of this operation along with a team made up of Tall Ones, Second People from Zanck's planet, and humans. Younger Tall Ones were selected to be part of the study, as they needed to fit into the Wormhole Gate. To volunteer was a strange concept for the Tall Ones. Since they were communal, a decision by one was a decision by all, so those who were going to be transplanted were selected instead.

A place on Earth had to be chosen for this to take place. The climate could have wide swings, but it was believed that too much sun combined with high temperatures was something not usually seen on TCe, so that was to be avoided. A location not too far from

Earth's Wormhole Gate would have been ideal, but not everything can be ideal. There was concern about a non-indigenous species being brought to Earth to set up a colony, bringing with it, of course, the usual protests from the humans. Logic won out, though, for once anyway. Logic said humans now had two outposts on different planets in two different solar systems. These outposts were isolated from the local inhabitants, so wouldn't some sort of reciprocity be acceptable as long as the conditions established were similar to those imposed on the humans?

After a lot of discussion and exploration, a final agreement was reached. Coat Island, located in Hudson Bay, would be the place where the Tall Ones' colony would be established on Earth. No humans had lived there for nearly two centuries. It was home to a great diversity of wildlife, but that might be beneficial. It wasn't as if the Tall Ones were going to take over the entire 2,000-plus square miles of the place. Cold winters were not viewed as a handicap. Some Tall Ones did live in cold climates on TCe after all. The Mobile Ones didn't care either.

A small airstrip would be constructed on the island. A new permanent human research station would be established as well to collaborate with the Tall Ones on the goal of finding a beneficial solution for both planets in terms of dealing with carbon. Carbon neutrality was an issue for both those on TCe and those on Earth. A single solution might potentially solve both.

In the summer of 2150, forty Tall Ones were separated from the network. The stored information within the network was now split amongst two groups. New information would be stored only in the group that obtained it, but eventually there would be regular information exchanges. The separation was a little traumatic, similar to what they felt when the Stranglers were attacking. In time, however, the collective network would recover, and the new colony on Earth would expand. Ten bug ships and crews were also selected. In their case, though, there was a decision process that closely resembled volunteering.

The first immigrants were quite literally uprooted and brought through the TCe Wormhole Gate and sent to Earth. A military plane flew the Mobile Ones and Tall Ones to their new home, where the Mobile Ones set about making their counterparts comfortable. It didn't take long. The atmosphere was so refreshing and the soil was nearly perfect. Though unfamiliar bacteria, microbes, and things like earthworms were at first considered scary, the Tall Ones soon got over them. The Mobile Ones built their little community among the Tall Ones and were equally thrilled with the carbon-rich atmosphere. Only time would tell if this was going to work.

It was agreed that the TCe colony on Earth would be allowed to grow to about the same size as was allowed for the human colony on TCe. Tall Ones who grew to a large size were destined to live and die on Earth, but as younger Tall Ones got to be certain size, they were to be sent back to TCe. At the same time, as the mature Tall Ones died, other young Tall Ones from TCe could replace them. In this way, information would be exchanged between the colony on Earth and the Tall Ones on their home world.

There was a little humor in all this. There were a few trees on Coat Island, and the Tall Ones thought they might be friendly. When reaching out to the local trees, the Tall Ones were a little put out that they were being ignored. A species that looked something like them but had the intelligence of a post was not expected. Flying creatures fascinated the Mobile Ones, especially the ones who decided the Tall Ones were a great place to build nests. The Tall Ones were a bit apprehensive when that activity started, but in time the Tall Ones accepted this as a way to enhance their appearance. They were becoming vain! Climbing creatures were also fascinating, but they brought a fear factor with them. The first years on Earth had a very steep learning curve.

The Stranglers had not been forgotten. When they found out about Tall Ones and Mobile Ones going to Earth, the Stranglers wanted to be included. All, except the Stranglers themselves, agreed that the Stranglers couldn't be trusted. Introducing them to an aquatic environment with no way to monitor their activity was deemed a really bad idea. They would have to wait for carbon to be brought to them.

As suspected, the Tall Ones thrived. They actually thrived far beyond any expectation. They grew in height nearly six feet per year, and eventually they grew to heights only witnessed with the giant redwood trees. Mobile Ones also thrived. They could fly further with much more energy. One of their bug ships was offered to the humans for research. The plan was to reverse-engineer the ships and then reproduce them at a larger scale. It seemed like a good idea, but though the ships themselves were very light and could be replicated on a large scale, the power source and controls being the crewmembers was not a transferrable possibility. That symbiotic relationship couldn't be replicated on a human scale. The human scientists finally declared in a satire-laden report that, "The bug ships couldn't possibly fly, just like bumble bees can't fly. And by the way, the Earth is still flat."

Chapter 48
Abdication

Within two months of Raman-I-El coming to Earth, it was confirmed in Charm-E-Ine's mind that there was, in fact, something not right with him. She didn't think it was because he had been away from his own people for such a long time. She believed Gabe-Re-El when he surmised that it was likely due to damage caused by being in stasis for such a long stretch of time. Much of what Raman did could be considered normal. When he had something that needed to be done, he would do it, but with no emotion. It was very robotic, she thought. Probably everyone in the Star Ship fleet would have thought he was a little odd, but it was nothing outside of what they might expect from time to time in anyone else.

Translating while with the fleet would have required no effort of thought on Raman's part. Those abilities were something all their people had. It was as natural as eating and sleeping, and certainly in the eating department there was nothing wrong there.

When Charmy and Raman first started communicating, she hadn't noticed anything unusual. The communications were brief and went right to the heart of whatever needed to be discussed. As those communications became more regular, she had noticed Raman seemed to be reaching out for support—support that he could only get from his own people. Charmy understood and was more than willing to help someone who, like herself, was separated from her people.

When Raman started sharing more and more about his relationship with Sharon Hooding, Charmy started getting concerned. What Raman was doing was a long way from being acceptable. The concern became greater when it was apparent that Raman was either ignoring warnings from Charmy, or he simply didn't care.

Now with Raman hovering around waiting for Charmy to give him some direction, something had to be done. He was one of her people, who had originally been sent to Earth to help guide the people of Earth to their potential. Raman couldn't guide himself now, though, let alone guide others. On the other hand, Charmy knew she had crossed the line in the other direction and had become a leader, not just a guide.

Maybe Gabe-Re-El was right. Maybe Raman and Charmy should get back with the program and go into stasis, starting over when the time was right. Maybe! But what about her followers? What would they do without her? Then it hit her like a ton of bricks.

Her people didn't age the same way as the people of Earth. She had already lost many of her human friends and supporters. In Earth years, she was now over 95 years old. Her plan had been to live and die a natural death, but she actually didn't know how long that might ultimately be.

She felt fine and still looked amazing, though she did notice she was slowing down. While in her position, much had been accomplished in terms of bringing Africa to a position of admiration around the world. Her people loved her, and she loved them back. The Princess had been too busy to think about what might happen when she was no longer with them. *Perhaps it is time that I did step down. And if I go into stasis,* she thought, *I will come out at some time in the future, and besides being rejuvenated back to age thirty-three or so, I will be able to witness first-hand how Africa has progressed.*

When Gabe-Re-El came around again asking Charmy what she had decided to do, she first looked to Raman and then told Gabe she would be making plans for a successor as the leader of the Union of African Nations. She and Raman would rejoin the Order. Charmy said she needed some time for a smooth transition.

"Not a problem," said Gabe.

"Where will Raman and I go? Aren't all the teams fully staffed?"

"Actually no, they aren't. We have a team in South America with only four. The other two were killed in an ambush. Apparently, they had been mistaken for rebels and never saw it coming. You and Raman would fill the other slots." Laughing, Gabe added, "I'd love to see the looks on their faces when they wake up to find two more people they didn't see or know when they went under."

Raman said nothing. He had gotten worse and hardly listened to anything being said.

With this settled, the great Princess Charm-E-Ine made a speech from her office that was broadcasted all over Africa and the rest of the world. She announced to a stunned, and in some cases heartbroken, audience that she would be abdicating the throne as the Princess Charm-E-Ine of the Union of African Nations, effective six months in the future on August 1, 2147. "During those six months, I will select a successor from a slate of candidates presented by each member nation." Charmy promised to select a successor who would maintain the ideals of a benevolent dictator for a smooth transition. To ensure that was to be the case, she would also select a council of advisors who could, by unanimous vote, remove the Princess or Prince for due cause.

On August 1, 2147, Princess Charmy abdicated. After the coronation ceremony, Gabe-Re-El, Raman-I-El, and Charm-E-Ine donned their antigravity packs under the cover of darkness and headed for South America. More than a few people noted what appeared to be winged beings flying through the night sky, surrounded by a glow. Some fell to their knees and prayed that this was a positive sign for the future.

Chapter 49
Trade

If not to the UNSC on Earth, it certainly was obvious to the humans at High Point and the Tall Ones that trade could be mutually beneficial. The Tall Ones knew their planet was running out of useful carbon, the same stuff Earth wanted to get rid of. TCe apparently had deposits of rare earths and other minerals not yet identified by the human scientists, but they seemed to have some interesting and potentially useful characteristics. Kristie noted, "So one planet's trash can be another planet's treasure." *I wonder,* she thought, *if this could be the final solution to Earth's need to correct the damage done by too many carbon emissions?*

If the Tall Ones, or Mobile Ones for that matter, didn't write it down, the humans would have had no idea what they might be thinking. They weren't exactly jumping up and down, which would have been interesting to see, but they did write that they were excited with the possibility of trade. Non-destructive exploration by the humans, with the help of the Mobile Ones, was expanded to other unoccupied parts of the planet to see what might be possible. It turns out that there was a lot of potential, but it wasn't going to be free. Trade meant exchanging one thing for another, and the "thing" the Tall Ones wanted was carbon, preferably in the form of carbon monoxide and carbon dioxide.

Even after all these years, Earth still had a problem with global warming due to earlier carbon emissions. Current carbon emissions were not the major issue. It was past transgressions that were the problem. When the ecosystem had reached a tipping point, getting things back into balance had proved to be more difficult than could be imagined. Even when a balance of sorts had been obtained, it would take centuries to repair the damage that had been done to the ecosystem. A major first step could be the removal of the remaining carbon pollution on Earth and sending it TCe, where it would be welcomed. How to accomplish it on a scale that would make a difference would be the issue, and it was more than just a little detail.

As with any great enterprise, a trade agreement was laid out. The Tall Ones weren't quite sure what an agreement would be, as they always agreed with each other. When they got the concept, they became tough negotiators. They still weren't thrilled with the heavy machines tearing up the landscape, but they would allow it to happen one location at a time, with restoration to be completed as well before any new location was allowed. If they could've smile, they would've been smiling over the emissions from the earthmovers. Good stuff!

Getting carbon dioxide and carbon monoxide to TCe in large quantities would be tricky. When the Star Ships were built, carbon had been extracted from the ocean and was used in making the hulls of the ships. The politicians had touted this technology as a way to clean up the oceans. It did make for a very good product, but the effort that went into making this happen was expensive, and the amount of carbon concentrated was insignificant overall.

Using that technology to produce what the Tall Ones wanted was going to be a huge problem. Also not forgotten was the promise made to the Stranglers. If that wasn't honored, they would be back on land with the likelihood of having an advanced defense against the human machines.

Adding to the problem of production was a belief from some, including some in the UNSC, that mankind should just take what it wanted from TCe. "Why do we care about a bunch of trees, even if they are supposedly intelligent?" was the prevailing thought. Fortunately, their noise was drowned out by more rational voices.

Almost lost in all the discussions was the actual cost of doing business. The Gates required a huge amount of power whenever they were activated, and they needed a support staff. While the bean-counters were having a field day showing why this wasn't going to work, their noise was also drowned out, this time by the Earth's ecologists, who had been looking for the miracle cure for Earth's ecosystem for more than 100 years.

The UNSC squandered a great opportunity when it was finally settled that trade would start. Instead of embracing a trade

260

deal and enhancing their image with the world, they allowed a private pact to be established. The UNSC and its Directors were reportedly too involved with their new "very wonderful, very beautiful, secret mission."

To get a trade deal like this moving, it required individuals with experience and foresight. That part was actually easy, and the newly formed enterprise called Star Struck Trading Company was born. Barrels of liquid carbon dioxide and carbon monoxide were sent to High Point. From there, the Mobile Ones distributed the contents among the Tall Ones and the Stranglers and brought empty barrels to an active mining site. These were then filled with refined rare minerals, and they were returned to High Point and then back to Earth. The Mobile Ones had to do all the heavy lifting, quite literally, but they didn't seem to mind. It wasn't very efficient, and the amount of material traded initially was small, but it got things started and all concerned were pleased with the start.

The Star Struck Trading Company President, Neil Dodson, saw this as a great retirement job. His two Vice Presidents were Kristie Marshal and Sharon Hooding. In time, Astron Hooding would take charge. The company made sure everyone that had been part of the mission had an opportunity to own stock. Those that bought in weren't disappointed.

Would Earth and TCe eventually have their ideal carbon neutrality? If so, the discovery mission launched from Epsilon Eridani in 2107, nearly forty years ago, would have been worth it.

Chapter 50
Carbon Neutrality

The idea of carbon neutrality on Earth was somewhat dependent on the way it was viewed. With the reduced human population, carbon emissions from that source had been reduced. Many had argued that climate change had nothing to do with human activity, while the rational people of Earth—the ones that didn't believe the Earth was flat, for example—noted that while climate changes were nothing new, it was hard to believe that ten billion people wouldn't have an effect on the planet.

With the human population on Earth reduced by ninety percent after the 2071 pandemic, some thought the problem was solved and that the annual climate cycles would revert back to cooler temperatures. But that wasn't the case, once the tipping point had been reached in the early twenty-first century, climate change wouldn't reverse automatically. With glacial melting caused by the warmer temperatures, there was less reflective areas for the sun's rays further warming the atmosphere. This, in turn, caused even more glaciers to melt. That was one part of the so-called tipping point.

In the future, the Earth's temperature might get warm enough that CO_2 would be actively removed by chemical weathering, where the CO_2 combines with rocks at the Earth's surface. Combined with the many other factors that created Earth's atmosphere in the first place, the Earth would eventually heal. Perhaps this might take thousands of years, so humans needed to help the healing if they were to survive as a species. It was thrilling when TCe was discovered, and it was learned that the species of that planet craved carbon dioxide. This was the serendipitous panacea humans might have hoped for.

The euphoric thought that a "magic pill" had been found with TCe soon disappeared, however, when inconvenient realty set in. If CO_2 in any form were shipped to High Point on TCe, it would have to be in massive quantities to make any difference on Earth.

Such massive quantities would be completely impractical to liquefy and were beyond what the Gates could handle.

Still, in spite of the many issues facing all concerned, trade was proving to be beneficial. After a very difficult start with the Tall Ones and Mobile Ones, Admiral Dodson had made a breakthrough that fostered an eventual relationship between the humans and the Tall Ones. However, the Tall Ones were becoming keenly aware that Earth was getting the better part of the trade. They wanted more in the form of help for their ecosystem.

To potentially ease the inequity, the humans did promise to search for a possible fossil-fuel source that could be used on TCe. With no practical historic memory of the planet, there was the remote possibility that with enough "digging" some history of the planet might be determined leading to a solution. This made the Tall Ones feel a little better, as it was one more idea to keep hope alive.

Feedback from the Tall Ones' colony on Earth provided an amazing description of the bio-diversity on Earth. This was not only in the form of plants and animals, but also at the microscopic level. Humans, and the Second People from EEb for that matter, were equally amazed at the limited diversity on TCe. Obviously, the two planets had evolved very differently, but perhaps an introduction of more things not indigenous to each planet could help.

It took some time for oxygen to appear on Earth. When it did appear, it took a very long time to stabilize at about twenty-one percent. Eras like the Great Oxidation Event brought levels much higher, causing other reactions to bring it down. Animals came that used oxygen came into the picture and gave off carbon dioxide. It was these negative and positive feedbacks stabilizing the concentrations of oxygen in the atmosphere that provided the ecosystem all life on Earth enjoys.

How TCe developed the way that it did would take many decades of research to understand. The Tall Ones, while demonstrating a high level of intelligence, hadn't really considered history that far back. After learning about Earth and EEb, they were now curious, but for now they wanted to balance their carbon level.

Even though carbon neutrality might not be something that could be gained right now on Earth, there were more things that could be done on TCe if some of the events that occurred on Earth were artificially introduced to TCe.

Fire, a consumer of oxygen producing CO_2, was not an option. There was no tectonic plate movement, so there were no active volcanoes spewing CO_2 into the atmosphere. There were no enzymes giving off CO_2. There were just three major species of life that were like plants but weren't. It wasn't clear what they were, but unlike plant life, where respiration uses nearly as much oxygen during the night as it produces during the day, these creatures used whatever carbon source might be available to live and then gave off oxygen. There was no respiration. On a smaller scale, there were some microbes and bacteria on TCe, but it was nothing like what had developed on Earth.

After a great deal of concentrated study by the humans, the Second People, and the Tall Ones, a multi-faceted approach was approved. It wasn't ignored that the humans on TCe were adding CO_2 to the biosphere just by being there, and CO_2 was also being added with the mining operations.

A larger, more proactive and dedicated approach to increasing CO_2 levels included some dramatic effects. Explosives were strategically placed in some of the inactive volcanoes to get them to erupt. This worked in about one out of three attempts.

At some point in TCe's past, CO_2 concentrations were very high, which is likely why life on TCe developed as it did. In any case, it was discovered that high concentrations of CO_2 were locked into a layer of the massive glaciers emanating from the planet's poles. Large sections of these glaciers were broken off, forming icebergs that would eventually find their way to warmer water, where they would melt and give off CO_2.

Lastly, with some reluctance, the Tall Ones agreed that some microbes and enzymes like Rubisco, which produce carbon dioxide, should be studied and perhaps introduced at a very small scale in a controlled experiment.

It didn't take long before favorable results were enjoyed, though TCe was a long way from reaching the carbon levels they needed in the biosphere to be considered healthy. The Stranglers, in particular, were finding the melting icebergs to be quite refreshing and true to their word, they stayed in the sea.

When the Star Ships had left EEb bound for Tau Ceti, the goal was discovery. When TCe was studied up close, there was the hope that their discovery would lead to carbon neutrality on Earth. It didn't. But it did help an indigenous species on TCe to find its path to carbon neutrality.

The end...or is it?

Epilogue

The people of Earth still didn't have the ecosystem stability they craved, but it was getting better; they were adapting to the colder north and south latitudes as well as the very warm central latitudes caused by shifting ocean currents. The climate was still changing, but it now seemed to be changing for the better. Forests were coming back and flourishing in areas where there had been none, and glaciers were no longer shrinking. While much of this was due to the decrease in the world's population, either rightfully or unrightfully some credit was given to the carbon exchange with TCe.

Worldwide this caused people to wonder what other benefits could be gained if space exploration was to continue. Inspired by what Africa had done, the rest of the world was gradually moving from a lethargic state to one seeking bolder action. The status quo was giving way to curiosity and an adventuresome spirit was becoming more widespread.

Admiral Neil Dodson and his Vice Admiral Kristie Marshal returned to Earth and resided for a while in New Zealand. They found some contentment in retirement. Fishing in the lakes and streams and this held Neil's interest for a bit, while Kristie found gardening intriguing.

However, when the UNSC decided that trade with TCe should be done through a private firm, Neil and Kristie determined they were the best ones to make sure this enterprise didn't get out of control. Thus, the Star Struck Trading Company was formed. They also saw this as an opportunity for the crews of the Star Ships to receive compensation for the many years they had been in space. Rich ore of many kinds coming to Earth in exchange for carbon and technology to produce carbon on TCe made Star Struck Trading Company extremely rich and influential. This would lead to something in the future that would go way beyond just trade.

The settlers of New Polyarnaya on TCf became more and more docile as time went on. Life was actually quite good for them.

The abandoned spaceship they found was likely what led to the population of the sheep-sized animals on the planet. The first child conceived on TCf had hair that was more featherlike than hair. As she grew, her parents would often find her chewing grass. She was five years old before standing up.

Star Ship Russia was left alone, but it was not forgotten. The UNSC was too busy with their "truly wonderful plan" to worry about it.

Admiral Katherine Hickey found herself with a fleet of Star Ships in a holding pattern while the UNSC continued to develop their plan. However, it remained a secret. Katherine was quite certain the UNSC had no idea of any plan and that she might have to take Admiral Dodson's advice and lead rather than follow, or simply just get out of the way.

With the fleet parked, Katherine went back to Earth with her husband, Dakota, and daughter, Celeste, while Dakota established a facility to build the components for more Gates. Apparently the UNSC in their "plan" development forget there were no more Gates. When this deficiency was pointed out to them, they asked Dakota "to do something." He did. Vice Admiral Yue was more than happy to be left in charge while the Admiral was away.

Zanck and his fellow Second People space travelers went back to EEb. They had many fascinating stories to tell. Some of the most interesting were at the expense of their fellow travelers.

The colony of Tall Ones and Mobile Ones on Coats Island prospered. For the Tall Ones, possessions other than knowledge meant little, though the adornments provided by the birds were increasing their sense of individuality. The Mobile Ones liked "things," and being very clever they were able to use some human technology to make their mobility even greater.

Sharon and Raman's child, Astron grew into a handsome, very large, well-built man with a ferocious appetite. Once firmly established, Star Struck Trading Company operations were eventually turned over to Astron to manage. His people were all very loyal, which might have been because of some very special abilities he had that were perhaps not quite human. Astron remained in charge until one day… well, that's another story, isn't it?